everything after

ALSO BY JILL SANTOPOLO

More Than Words

The Light We Lost

everything after

JILL SANTOPOLO

G. P. PUTNAM'S SONS

NEW YORK

PUTNAM
— EST. 1838 —

G. P. PUTNAM'S SONS
Publishers Since 1838
An imprint of Penguin Random House LLC
penguinrandomhouse.com

Library of Congress Cataloging-in-Publication Data

Names: Santopolo, Jill, author.
Title: Everything after / Jill Santopolo.
Identifiers: LCCN 2020042811 (print) | LCCN 2020042812 (ebook) |
ISBN 9780593086964 (hardcover) | ISBN 9780593086988 (ebook)
Subjects: LCSH: Psychological fiction.
Classification: LCC PS3619.A586 E94 2021 (print) |
LCC PS3619.A586 (ebook) | DDC 813/.6—dc23
LC record available at https://lccn.loc.gov/2020042811
LC ebook record available at https://lccn.loc.gov/2020042812
p.   cm.

International edition ISBN: 9780593332672

Printed in the United States of America
1   3   5   7   9   10   8   6   4   2

BOOK DESIGN BY KATY RIEGEL

For Andrew.

For always.

everything after

i

MAYBE THIS WILL *help.*
Maybe I won't think about you anymore.
Dream about you.
Maybe I won't have to keep wondering.
Always wondering:
Were you even real?

1

AS SHE WALKED down Astor Place toward her office, Emily Gold rested her hand on her abdomen, trying to figure out if it felt different. If there was something new in there, a constellation of cells that would grow as she did, would end up as a tiny person with deep brown eyes like Ezra or wavy auburn hair like her.

Emily hadn't known she wanted a baby until she met Ezra. Then the idea of creating a child with him, of having another person living in this world who had his intelligence, his compassion running through their veins—it seemed like something she would have to do, the way she had to breathe, to blink, to swallow. And once she wanted it, once she knew it had to happen, she became immediately afraid that it wouldn't. That she couldn't. The fact that they'd put it off for a couple of years didn't help—Ezra had wanted to get a promotion first, a raise, an apartment, to make sure they'd be able to give this child everything they possibly could. Now the time was right. They'd been trying for seven months—months of hope and anticipation and disappointment. And now she was late. Only by a day, but still.

Every hour made it feel more real, more possible.

"Dr. Gold."

Emily had been walking up the steps to NYU's School of Global Public Health, and turned her head as she swiped her card key through the lock on the front of the building.

"Tessa," she said to the student looking up at her. "It's good to see you. I hadn't realized you were back."

Tessa smiled. Her eyes looked tired, but the grin was genuine. "I've been meaning to come by, but there was a lot to get settled."

"How's the baby?" Emily asked her.

"Zoe," Tessa said. "She's good. Mostly sleeps through the night now, which is awesome. My mom helped out a lot over the summer—Zoe and I went to Ohio while Chris was starting his new job here. But now we're back and it's just me and him and Zo. We've made it through our first week. I found a couple of freshmen who are up for babysitting while I'm at class. So far, so good."

Emily stepped aside so her friend Priya, another psychologist at the mental health center, could walk through the door. "I'm so glad, Tessa," she said. "If you need to talk, you know I'm here. I'm glad things are going well with you and Chris."

Emily didn't trust Chris, not after the way he'd initially reacted, not after the hours Tessa had spent in her office in tears. He'd seemed self-absorbed, not understanding what a pregnancy would mean for Tessa, not fully accepting his part in it. If Emily were Tessa's friend, she would've had some choice words to say about Chris. But as her therapist, she kept her mouth shut and helped Tessa with her side of the relationship, figuring out what she needed and how to communicate that. Something had worked, because Chris had come through in the end.

Tessa smiled again. "I'm glad, too." She laughed. "And happy I ran into you. But now it's time for Statistics for Social Research."

"Oof," Emily said. "You didn't give yourself a break with that one."

Tessa shrugged. "I figure it'll help with law school."

Tessa's dream was to be a human rights lawyer. She wore socks with Ruth Bader Ginsburg's face on them and had spent half a session once telling Emily about Amal Clooney's life story. Emily had enjoyed hearing it.

Two students walked into the building and Emily recognized one of them as her nine a.m.

"I should go," Emily said. "But I'm so glad to see you. Bring Zoe by some time."

Tessa hiked up her backpack. "I will," she said before she turned away.

Emily really hoped Tessa would be okay. When she'd come to the center last year, she'd been so petrified—of being pregnant, of telling her boyfriend, of telling her parents, of what this would mean for her life and her dreams and her future. Emily had helped her through all of it. She'd even gotten permission from the clinic's director to see Tessa as a long-term case. It was why she'd taken this job. She wanted to be there for these kids, the way she wished someone had been there for her, back when she was in college—someone more than her sister, Arielle. Luckily, later she'd found Dr. West, who changed her life and changed her path. She wondered, sometimes, if Dr. West found the job as difficult as she did.

2

BEFORE HEADING INTO her office, Emily filled her mug with herbal tea instead of coffee, something Arielle had said was better for fertility. Though the truth was, it was irrelevant. By this point, either she was already pregnant or she wasn't. She and Ezra had been tracking her cycle since their second wedding anniversary, when they moved into their new place and he was finally ready to start trying. Tracking her cycles together with Ezra was one of the benefits of marrying a doctor—everything about the human body was up for discussion. That was his area of expertise, after all. Hers was the human mind.

She wasn't sure how much longer her mind could take the crushing loss of hope each time her period started again, each time a month passed and the only thing growing inside her was disappointment. Seven months felt like forever. She'd been imagining this child for so long. For two years and seven months, to be exact, since she'd been ready to try right away. Which made each month that she wasn't pregnant even more excruciating. But perhaps this month would be different.

Emily sat down in her office and quickly reviewed her notes for her first patient, her fingers running along the pages as if they were playing scales on a piano. So many years later, she still couldn't shake the habit. She closed her notebook and let her hand stray to her abdomen again. If there was a baby in there, its brain was only starting to develop, not actually a real brain yet. Forty to forty-three days—that was when brain activity first sparked.

Kai walked into her office and sat down on the couch, holding one of the granola bars they always put out in the reception area. Free food, both to lure college students in and to help take care of them when they weren't caring for themselves. He looked over at the aquarium.

Emily had discovered years ago that watching fish swim seemed to relax people, or maybe it was the quiet burbling of the filter. Either way, her patients seemed to like it. And it gave them something to talk about when they were working up to what was really troubling them. It gave her something to look at, too, when she wasn't sure if she'd be able to hold it together, wasn't sure if she could be the anchor they needed her to be.

She quickly glanced at the framed quote on her desk. John Wesley: "Do all the good you can, by all the means you can, in all the ways you can, in all the places you can, at all the times you can, to all the people you can, as long as ever you can."

Then she cleared everything else from her mind as she focused on her patient. She wasn't going to let him down.

ii

WHEN I MET *your father, the first thing I noticed about him was his smile.*

It appeared, slow and easy, across his face when he saw me walking toward him.

We were in a folk music club in the basement of an old church, the spring of my sophomore year. He offered me his chair and a beer. I offered to share the cup of popcorn I'd snagged on my way in.

We listened to a woman with a smoky voice sing about a crystal castle she'd build in the sky.

He called me his crystal queen.

3

AFTER KAI LEFT, Emily heard a knock on her office door while she was writing up notes. Three staccato raps. She knew those raps; they meant "I. Love. You." Ezra had been knocking on her door like that for the last four and a half years; it began soon after they started dating, soon after she got her job at NYU, a few months before her twenty-ninth birthday. Originally, he'd said it meant "Em-il-y," but that changed three months in. It became "I. Love. You." A love that had only grown from there.

He knocked again.

Emily opened the door, and her worries about her patients, about whether she was pregnant, disappeared when she saw his face.

"Hey, love," he said, as he stepped into her office and took her into his arms. She lifted her face up for a kiss, and he brought his lips to hers.

"You feel so good," she told him, once they stopped kissing, when she leaned her head against his shoulder.

He smelled faintly of soap and cologne. She brought her finger up to his name, embroidered on the left side of his button-down, right above his heart, the letters that spelled *Dr. Ezra Gold*. A gift from his doctor parents when he completed residency, and a favorite of his.

"What happened?" she asked.

He taught one class a week in bioethics during NYU's spring semester, and otherwise practiced medicine at NYU's children's hospital, a mile and a half away, specializing in pediatric blood cancers. He and Emily had started working at NYU the same year, even though Ezra was four years older. His job needed more training than hers did. But he never quite got trained in how to handle when he was feeling overwhelmed by what he was facing, what his patients were facing. He had to figure out how to deal with that on his own. Sometimes he needed to leave the hospital, to jump in a cab for the nine-minute ride to Emily's office. Sometimes he needed a kiss to get through the rest of the day. Sometimes he needed to tell her what happened. Other times she had to be a detective, trying to figure out why he was so silent at home, what had hurt him so deeply.

"It hasn't been the best morning," he said, holding her tighter. "But better now that I'm here with you."

"Good," she told him, wondering if today was a day she'd have to dig, if he would let her in or push her away.

WHEN THEY SPOKE for the very first time, in the elevator in the Global Public Health building, Emily had been surprised that Ezra noticed her. She'd seen him around—in the hallways, walking from the subway—and he always seemed absorbed in thought, as if the only world that existed was the one in his head. He wore round tortoiseshell glasses, which added to the sense that he was somehow separated from the world, looking at it through a window. And he kept to himself. Only a handful of people on the faculty knew anything about him other than his name.

Once they got together, Emily realized that Ezra's studious appearance, his quiet reserve, masked the heart of a doctor who felt deeply for his patients and their families, and who was always thinking about what he could do to make their lives easier, how he could practice medicine more ethically, not just to make their health outcomes better but their quality of life, too. He tried, tirelessly, to find trials his patients could be part of to improve their outcomes.

"Your husband is an angel," his patients' parents would tell her when she went to the hospital to pick him up at the end of a long day. She thought so, too—though those parents never saw the toll the job took on him. The nights he stayed awake staring at the ceiling afraid of the dreams that might come, the hours he spent inside his own head, unable to find the words to express how he felt. The worst was when one of his patients died, and he spiraled into self-doubt and silence. Sometimes for days.

"Don't dwell on failure," Emily had heard Ezra's father tell him when he felt that way. "Just learn from it." A sentiment that Ezra seemed to have internalized, like he did so many of his parents' beliefs.

What she told him, though, was that a death wasn't his failure. It was the world acting out its plans. He wasn't a god. He couldn't fend off the inevitable forever. But Ezra didn't see it that way. Emily wondered if it was easier to believe it was all in his power. It made failure harder, but it made everything else more meaningful.

"WANT TO TALK about it?" she asked him, lifting her cheek off his shoulder.

Ezra shook his head, his wavy brown hair falling in front of his glasses. It somehow always seemed like it needed a trim. "I'd rather not," he said.

"You don't have to," she told him, brushing his hair out of his eyes, knowing he'd tell eventually, when he was ready.

It might take hours, days, sometimes even weeks, but she knew how to give him his space when he needed it. And she could usually comfort him when he was finally ready to talk. She could read people like she could read music, feeling the emotion between the notes, the way to tease the meaning from the melody with her fingers. She wondered, sometimes, if Ezra'd had to marry a therapist, if someone who hadn't been trained in psychology could've made a relationship work with him.

"Thank you," he said, and kissed her again.

"How about I come get you at the end of the day?" she asked. "Maybe we can walk home? Stop for dinner on the way?"

"Lady's choice," he told her. "I love you."

"I love you, too." She wove her fingers through his. "You have to head back now?"

"Now that I'm fortified, I'll be able to handle it all."

"Good." She knew this wouldn't be the end of it, but it was what he needed now, and she was happy to give it to him.

They kissed one last time, and Ezra left Emily's office. She stood at her second-floor window to watch him appear below her on Broadway, hailing a yellow cab amid the traffic and jumping inside. Sometimes she still couldn't believe that she and Ezra were married—that this beautiful, brilliant, broken man brought her more happiness than she'd felt in more than a decade. It made her strive to be better, to make sure she was a woman worthy of a man like that.

———

ARIELLE HAD ARGUED with Emily when she told her, three years ago, that she was going to take Ezra's last name.

"But you've got a doctorate," Ari said. "You're one of the authors on a clinical study." Arielle had been particularly proud of her sister's byline on that paper.

"You took Jack's name," Emily said. "Mom took Dad's. I don't see the problem."

"But I'm staying home with my kids," Ari said. "You're different."

"I'm not," Emily protested. But that wasn't the real reason she wanted to take his name. She didn't feel like Emily Solomon anymore; she wasn't who she used to be. Without music, with Ezra—she was someone new. And changing her name to Emily Gold—it felt right. It felt like she was taking ownership of the person she'd become.

ANOTHER STUDENT APPEARED in Emily's door frame. Emily looked up at her. Someone new.

"Come in," she said.

The girl sat down and looked at the fish tank.

"Is that a betta?" she asked.

"It is," Emily answered. "I'm Dr. Gold."

"I know," the girl said. "I'm Callie."

And they talked about fish until it was time for more serious matters.

iii

YOUR FATHER TAUGHT *me to play guitar.*

"You know Dire Straits?" he asked. We were in my room. It was summer, and we'd both stayed in the city, a plan we hadn't made together but were both glad we'd chosen. He'd gotten a job working at a recording studio, I was folding and refolding shirts at a boutique that sold clothing neither one of us could afford. Our relationship had started slow, like a ballad, but then picked up speed the more we got to know each other. Weekly trips to the Postcrypt to listen to music together in March turned into drinks and dessert in April and walks through the city in May, where we talked about our families, our favorite books, our dreams, and our nightmares.

Soon we were hanging out in each other's dorms, studying for finals sprawled across each other's beds.

And then it was June, and we saw each other almost every day. One night, we were in his room, the window was open, the fan was on, but we still felt the warmth—sticky on our skin.

He didn't wait for my response about Dire Straits before he started playing.

But it was a song I knew, about Romeo on the streets serenading Juliet.

"Indigo Girls." I told him. "They cover this."

He stopped playing and laughed. "Of course," he said.

"What's that supposed to mean?" I asked him.

But he was playing again.

I watched his fingers. I heard the chords, felt the notes vibrating inside me. And before long, I was singing with him. Our voices wove into each other. The whole world fell away. The heat and the humidity were gone. It was just me and him and the music. I was awash in it. We finished the song staring into the blacks of each other's eyes.

"Wow," he said.

Soon he was behind me on the bed, his guitar on my lap, his legs on either side of mine, his fingers showing mine how to coax a chord out of the instrument, how to strum.

"You're a natural." He kissed my neck as he said it.

And maybe I was. Or maybe it was just that everything with him felt natural.

4

ON TUESDAYS, EMILY, Priya, and another psychologist in their office, Reuben, had a consultation group. There they talked about how their patients affected them, worried about whether they were actually helping in the right way or saying the right thing, and sometimes asked for advice. They discussed their pasts, the way their own experiences and preconceptions might stop them from being as effective as they could be.

"I saw T today," Emily told them. Calling their patients by their initials gave the patients enough anonymity while also making it easy for everyone to remember who they were talking about.

Emily had talked about Tessa a lot during the last school year. Emily worried to Priya and Reuben that she identified too closely with Tessa, that there were events in her own past that made her less objective than she might be otherwise, that made it hard for her to separate her personal feelings from Tessa's story the way she tried to with all of her patients.

"How is she doing?" Reuben asked. They were sitting in his office, which he'd decorated with tapestries on the walls and a big ficus in the corner. He had a couch on one side of the room, where Priya and Emily were sitting, and an armchair opposite it, where he was sitting with his feet up on a coffee table. He'd just gotten a haircut, and his short twists were gone, replaced by a buzz cut. He clearly hadn't gotten used to it yet, because he kept running his hand over the top of his head.

"She seemed good," Emily said.

"I'm glad," Priya answered, leaning forward on the couch, her elbows on her knees. "She had a rough go of it."

Emily nodded. "I still worry about her."

Priya smiled. "Of course you do. You worry about all of them."

Emily laughed. "You know me well."

"How was it for you?" Priya asked. "Seeing her again."

Emily thought about it. "I was just relieved she was okay."

"Because you weren't," Priya said, a fact more than a question. "When you were in college."

"Right," Emily answered. "I wasn't."

Then Reuben started talking about a patient he was worried about, J, who went silent when Reuben asked him about how it felt seeing his brother in rehab.

"I shouldn't have asked it that way," Reuben said. "Maybe if I'd phrased it differently, eased into it . . . I know he freezes people out, freezes me out, when things get too hard. I screwed up."

"You've got him talking before," Priya said. "He trusts you. You'll have another chance."

Reuben shook his head. "I'm always afraid that kids like J won't come back. That this is the week they'll decide I'm useless. That they're wasting time sitting here with me when they could be playing video games or hanging out with their friends or whatever."

The white noise machine hummed quietly in the background.

"I don't think they come because they feel like time with us is useful or useless," Emily said, turning to Reuben. "I think sometimes they just need to know there's someone who cares.

Someone who will wait for them to be ready. Someone who will listen when they finally do talk." She was thinking about her patients, but she was also thinking about her husband. He wasn't too different from some of these kids. From Reuben's J. She wondered whether, if she actually was pregnant, her child would be the same way.

"Speaking of people who finally decide to talk," Priya said, "I saw a new patient today. I asked her what brought her to the counseling center and she told me that she can't stop thinking about the night this summer that she had too much to drink and passed out, and when she woke up, a guy she'd thought was her friend was standing over her, about to ejaculate on her stomach. I had the hardest time not jumping out of my chair in outrage. She told me she can't sleep unless her bedroom door is locked and bolted, and she hasn't touched alcohol since. When I hear stories like that, I just . . . I can feel the rage rising inside me. It's like . . . it starts to boil until I become a vessel containing only that. I wanted to tell her to report it to the police, to make that asshole squirm. Even if he's not charged in the end, it's worth it to show him he's not entitled to masturbate wherever he pleases, on whomever he pleases." Priya's voice was getting louder. "I was practically shaking with indignation when she finished her story." Then she took a couple of deep breaths. "I have to figure out how to stay in the room."

"Sometimes I feel like we're sin eaters," Emily said, quietly. It was something she'd been thinking for a while.

"We're what?" Reuben asked.

"Sin eaters," she repeated. "When my mother died, I learned everything I could about death. And back in the Middle Ages there were these people whose job it was, after someone died, to eat their sins. Not literally, but they'd have to eat a meal that was believed to have absorbed the sins of the dead person. It made it so that the person who died was pure enough to go to heaven. Their soul had been cleansed by the sin eater. Sometimes I feel like we're sin eaters, consuming stories instead of food."

Reuben and Priya were quiet for a moment. Then Priya spoke. "I want to be a sin transformer," she said. "I want to take the shit that happens to people and help them use it to become someone stronger."

Emily sighed. "Sometimes that happens," she said. "But sometimes shit doesn't make you stronger. Sometimes it's just shit."

"Fact," Reuben agreed.

Emily wondered, as she had been more and more often lately, if this was a job she could do forever. She happened to be good at it, or so people said, but she wondered how long she could eat people's sins, help people sort through shit, before it would overwhelm her. She was worried it already was.

5

EMILY WAS PACKING up at the end of the day, opening and closing her hand to see if she could stop it from aching, when her cell phone vibrated. It was Ezra: Not sure when I'll be able to leave. You okay hanging out with me for a little? I told Malcolm's dad I'd stay until he got back.

Emily replied: Of course. Her fingers really ached, which meant it would rain soon. Even though there wasn't scientific backing for it, Emily knew it was true. The fingers on her right hand always ached before it rained, ever since her accident in college. And every time they did, she blocked thoughts of the beautiful music she used to play, the way it moved her soul. She'd chosen a different path.

Thank you, Ezra wrote back. I love you so.

Malcolm had been three the first time he was under Ezra's care—he and his family came from Philadelphia to be treated in New York because his parents had heard that Dr. Gold was the best they could do for their child; he had the most up-to-date research, used the newest methods. Malcolm had been in remission for three and a half years, and now he was seven and not doing well. His mother had gone to Philadelphia to be with his brothers and sister for a few days and was coming back tonight.

Through her position at NYU, Emily had worked with Malcolm's family a few times when he was in treatment years ago—

she spoke to his siblings about how they felt about Malcolm's illness. Those kinds of discussions overwhelmed her, though, and she hardly ever saw patients at the hospital now. But it was nice to still be able to walk the hospital halls to find her husband with whatever patient he happened to be spending time with at that moment.

Instead of taking a yellow cab, Emily walked the thirty minutes to the hem-onc wing of the children's hospital, through Stuyvesant Square Park, past Peter Cooper Village, and up through NoMad, where the buildings seemed to be growing taller each day, rivaling the skyscrapers she could see peeking up from Midtown and Murray Hill. When she arrived, she found her husband sitting by Malcolm's bedside, holding the little boy's hand. Ezra's lips were moving, but it was only when Emily got closer that she could hear what he was saying—what he was singing, actually, his voice a pure tenor. It was one of his favorite Beatles songs, about blackbirds and broken wings flying once more.

Emily didn't say a word. She stood in the doorway listening to her husband sing to a little boy who was sedated, who was intubated, whose life he was trying to save. Emily closed her eyes and thought of Malcolm's siblings, the ones she'd spoken to; they'd felt so helpless, so angry. Ezra's voice was clear and perfectly on pitch, fine-tuned in college a cappella groups and playroom jam sessions with his patients. He hardly ever sang at home, but Emily wished he would. She could listen to him sing forever. Then his voice caught, and Emily opened her eyes. He was crying—and her heart felt so full that she wasn't sure she'd ever love him more than she did in that moment.

She took up the end of the song, finishing it for him, softly singing the lines about waiting for the moment to arise. That imagery always spoke to her the most.

Ezra looked at her in the doorway; she could see the tears in his eyes. And she realized. "Malcolm's the patient you didn't want to talk about earlier."

Ezra nodded and wiped his eyes. "He is. There's nothing left that I can do."

Emily pulled a chair up next to him and sat down, wrapping one arm around his back, steeling herself for him, making herself his anchor. "You don't need me to tell you that science can't always cure everyone. That all you can ever do is your best, but sometimes it won't be enough."

"I know," Ezra said, leaning his head against her. "That's why Einstein believed in God."

"That's right," she said. "That's why Einstein believed in God."

"It still feels like a failure," he whispered.

"Oh, Ez," Emily said, pulling herself close to him, wrapping her arm around him tighter.

Ezra looked back at Malcolm. "I said I'd stay until his dad came back—he went to get Malcolm's mom from the station. Her train just got in."

"We can stay as long as you want," Emily said.

Ezra nodded.

After a moment of silence, Emily began singing quietly, fingering the piano chords on the chair handle for "Let It Be." When she got to the part about broken-hearted people living in the world agreeing, Ezra joined her just as quietly giving the song's answer. *Let it be. Let it be.*

And the two of them sang Beatles songs to Malcolm until his parents returned to sit vigil.

iv

AFTER OUR IMPROMPTU *guitar lesson, I told your father that I could play piano. But that I hadn't touched a keyboard in three years—since my mom died. We were drinking beer in his dorm room, relaxing together on his bed.*

"So there's music in your soul," he said.

"I used to think it was in my fingers," I told him. "When I was a kid, I would hear a song on TV or on the radio, and then I'd walk over to my mom's baby grand and play the melody by ear. When my dad asked me how I knew which notes to play, I told him my fingers knew."

Your dad laughed. "I used to do that, too. We didn't have a baby grand, though, just a janky old upright with chipped keys." He took a sip from his Guinness. "I want to hear you play," he said.

I drained the rest of my beer. He was one ahead of me, and I was trying to catch up. I'd only tried to play once after your grandmother died, eight days after she was gone, when shiva had ended and the house was silent again. I'd ended up sobbing underneath the piano, overwhelmed by thoughts about her, about her teaching me "Hot Cross Buns" and "Mary Had a Little Lamb" when I was tiny, her presence strong and warm beside me, about later, when she couldn't play any longer and would sit with her eyes closed while I played her favorite songs. About how I'd never play them for her again.

After that, any time I felt the urge to play, I would remember that rush of emotions, the pain of my memories, and I would stop. But for the first time I thought that maybe, with your dad next to me, that wouldn't happen. Playing guitar with him had been almost magical, absent of that pain. And I missed it. I missed the songs. I missed the piano. I missed how I felt when I played. But it didn't matter anyway.

"I'd play for you," I told him. "But I don't have anything to play on."

"There are some pianos in the music building," he said. "And luckily you are dating a music major. So I have access to the practice rooms."

I picked up his beer and drank the rest of it in three big gulps. I was going to do this. I wasn't going to think about it, I wasn't going to second-guess. I was going to play the piano again. Hopefully, I wasn't going to fall apart.

"Okay," I said. "Let's go."

With his university ID in hand and his guitar case on his back, he unlocked the door to the music building and we found a practice room with a piano inside.

Your dad closed the door and I sat down on the piano bench, running my fingers along the keys. The instrument brought me so much joy and such pain. I still can't hear Beethoven's Moonlight Sonata or Grieg's "In the Hall of the Mountain King" without thinking of your grandma.

That's what I played for your father that night. "In the Hall of the Mountain King." When I finished, he was looking at me like he had just gotten a gift, one he'd been waiting for his whole life.

"Queenie," he said, shaking his head. "You don't just play the piano, you play the piano. You're . . . you're amazing."

I shrugged, my eyes wet with tears. "I'd be better if I hadn't stopped lessons when my mom got so sick. But it's something I've always had a knack for. My mom loved listening to me play."

We'd talked about my mom before, on our walks through the city, at night, in whispers in the dark, when I couldn't get her out of my head before I went to sleep, when I missed her so much it felt like it was taking over my whole body.

Your dad sat next to me on the piano bench then and held me. "I got you," he said, like he always did. And those words, his arms, his voice made the feeling of loss ebb enough that there was room inside me for other feelings, too.

A FEW WEEKS later he told me to close my eyes before we entered his dorm room. He led me by the hand through the maze of books and clothes and shoes on his floor. Then he stopped.

"Okay," he said. "Open them."

I was standing in front of a keyboard, all set up on a stand with an amp and headphones and a damper pedal.

"It's for you," he said. "Happy two months before your birthday."

I was blown away. "For me?" I said. "Really?"

He nodded. "Someone with your talent needs her own instrument. I've been checking Craigslist and finally found a keyboard that's worthy—some Upper East Side parents bought it for their kid who gave up on lessons after a few months. They just wanted it out of their house. It was practically free, but it's top of the line."

I turned it on and started playing. The music was in my fingers, just like it had always been.

6

AFTER THEY LEFT the hospital, Ezra and Emily turned away from the East River, away from the rushing traffic on FDR Drive, and Ezra said, "I know you wanted dinner out tonight . . . but I'm afraid I won't be the best company."

Emily took his hand. "How about pizza and *Law and Order*?" she asked, as they headed west to Lexington Avenue, the hospital buildings giving way to tall towers of condos. *"Special Victims Unit."* It was one of their go-tos. An easy way to spend time with each other but still be in their own minds. Together but apart.

"Throw in a bottle of wine, and you have yourself a date."

Emily paused.

Ezra noticed. "Wait," he said. "It's . . . did your period . . . ?"

"Not yet," she said. "But I'm not going to get too excited. It still might."

Ezra pulled Emily to him and kissed her in the middle of the sidewalk, people swirling around them. His hands wrapped around her waist and held her body against his. She could feel the hardness of his muscles against the softness of her breasts. She loved how her body yielded to his.

"Get a room!" a cabbie shouted out the window of his taxi as he sped by, but they didn't care. They barely even noticed.

7

FOUR DAYS LATER, Emily and Ezra both had the day off.

"Anything?" Ezra asked, as Emily got back into bed after an early-morning trip to the bathroom.

She shook her head and smiled.

"Can we get excited yet?" he asked.

She slid closer to him, not wanting to get her hopes up, but also wanting to know, wanting it to be true.

"I hope our baby has your hazel eyes," he said, looking into hers. "And your pouty lips." He kissed hers.

She kissed him back and said, "Nuh-uh, I hope our baby looks just like you."

She loved his Roman nose, his prominent cheekbones, his deep black eyelashes.

Ezra slid his hands under the T-shirt Emily had worn to bed, running his fingers in circles around the warm skin of her breasts. They felt heavier to her than usual. Then her focus was back on her husband, whose hand was now sliding down her stomach.

"Totally recreational," he whispered.

Emily laughed. They tried not to make sex seem like a chore, but sometimes, when Ezra came home from an overnight call and woke her up because she'd texted him that she was ovulating, it seemed more an item on their to-do list than the sweet, romantic joining together it had been before sex was about fertility and the best position to ejaculate in so gravity could help them conceive.

Emily reached for him, not thinking of any of that. Just thinking about how much she loved her husband. How beautiful she found his body. How complete she felt when he was inside her.

"I love you," he whispered, as she wrapped her legs around him, pulling him closer.

"I love *you*," she answered, rocking into him, matching his rhythm.

Then the pitch of his breathing changed, and he thrust harder. Her breathing changed, too.

His body stilled as he let out an "Oh" that was as much breath as it was sound.

Emily kept rocking against him until she came, too.

And then they both lay back on their pillows, Emily not worrying about tilting her pelvis up, elevating herself on a pillow, something her sister said absolutely helped with conception.

"Good thing the baby can't see yet," she said.

He laughed. "So you think it's real?"

"I'm cautiously optimistic," she told him, then took a breath. "We can take a test today."

"I'll get one right now!" he said, practically jumping out of bed, one leg in a pair of jeans before she could even respond. "I'll be right back."

"We can get one later," she said, laughing.

Ezra smiled and kissed her again while buttoning his jeans. "Why put off until this afternoon what you can do this morning?"

Still laughing, she watched him grab his keys and wallet on his way out the door. When they first started dating, when they first were married, Ezra and Emily talked a lot about children, about the risks you took when you had them: What secrets would be hidden in their genetic code? What pathogens might they come in contact with? What accidents could befall them? Ezra said he thought about that every day—how kids could get sick, get hurt, die. But that it didn't stop him from wanting to take the risk, once he was sure he could provide for a family, once he could care for one the best way he knew how.

"If you look at the statistics, it's actually not that bad," he'd said. "When I get too freaked out, I just read the statistics."

"But when the statistic is your child, the percentage doesn't really matter," she'd told him. It was only a small percentage of women who died from multiple sclerosis in their late forties, but that wasn't much comfort when her mother was included in that percentage. It freaked Arielle out so badly that when she was twenty-two, two years after their mother died, she'd started searching for a husband and vowed to have a child by twenty-six so that if she ended up with MS, too, if she died at the same age their mom did, she'd have a chance to see at least one child graduate from college, something their mother never had.

"That's true," Ezra had acquiesced, "but I've gotta find some way not to make myself crazy."

She'd squeezed his hand then. "Having good coping skills is pretty sexy," she'd said.

And they'd both started laughing. "I can cope with so many things," he'd told her.

Emily wondered now, years later, if that was really true. He could get by with a kiss sometimes, he could talk to her sometimes, but often he needed to retreat inside himself and work things through alone, awash in his own frustration and anger. He managed. He went back each day ready to fight for a child's life, to teach medical students how to fight. Over and over and over again. But she wondered at what cost—to him, to her, to their marriage. She felt the difficulties of her own profession, but his were so much worse—especially when he believed he was in control of it all, when he took each death personally. Emily wished she knew how to better help him—but she discovered that all she really could do was love him and try to understand him and hope that would be enough.

WHILE EZRA WENT to the drugstore, Emily got out of bed, made coffee for both of them in her bathrobe. One cup of caffeine, she knew, was okay. Though maybe she'd just have half, to play it safe. Maybe a quarter. She took the prenatal vitamin she'd been taking for the last eight months, but now it felt more like a promise, less like a wish and a prayer.

Behind the kitchen was a door to a small second bedroom that would be perfect for a baby. They'd just have to find a new place for their boxes of textbooks and extra paper towels and whatever else they'd been storing in there since they moved in. Much to Emily's chagrin, the room had basically become a glorified storage unit. She kept promising herself she'd sort through it the next time Ezra was on call. Now she really would have to. No more procrastinating.

Emily looked down at her body. She'd been so afraid for the last few days that this was a false alarm. That stress or exercise or worry about getting pregnant had just made her period late. But she felt it—that fullness in her breasts, the intensity of her sense of smell—she knew something was different.

V

AFTER A FEW *weeks back at the keys, I felt comfortable there again. Your father would start something on the guitar, I'd pick it up, and we'd speak through our music, telling each other how we felt, what we wanted.*

"Everything just disappeared," I told him one day, after we'd been playing for hours. "Everything but you."

"I always feel that way," he said, putting his hand on my arm, "when I play with you."

The pressure of his fingers was all I could think about. I moved closer to him. He floated his finger down to my wrist, and then bent to put his guitar on the carpet.

"We don't need instruments to make music," he said. And we didn't. Every day with him felt like a new song, a new melody.

He touched my cheek and looked into my eyes. The rhythm of our playing filled me. I leaned toward him. Our lips touched, and the music inside me crescendoed. We kissed and kissed.

We lay together on his bed, like we had been for the last months, touching each other, exploring each other's bodies with our fingers and lips.

Then he pulled off my tank top, I tugged down his jeans. We both slid off our shoes. And the world was gone again. It was just me and him and the harmony of our breathing. It was skin against skin and breath against breath.

I felt his fingers and his tongue, and then he was back kissing my mouth and he whispered, "Do you want to?"

We hadn't yet. I wanted to be sure of him, sure of us. He'd given me the time I needed to be certain, understanding that this wasn't a choice I could take back or undo. And now I was. So I answered with a kiss of my own and a soft "yes."

He reached over and fumbled in the pocket of his guitar case for a condom. I felt lost without him against me. And then he was kissing me and I was wrapping myself around him, pulling him closer. We rocked into the heat and the warmth and the music.

"Are you really sure?" he asked.

"Never surer," I said.

I felt the fan blowing warm air across my skin.

And then I felt him, inside me.

And I was part of someone else for the first time.

8

EMILY AND EZRA smiled that whole day.

"We need to do things!" Ezra said. "We need to prepare!"

Emily laughed, swinging their clasped hands as they ambled down 2nd Avenue together, past restaurants and shops, dry cleaners and convenience stores, the city traffic humming beside them. "We have months to prepare. Plus I'm sure Ari has a list of what we need, filed away in her folder of spreadsheets." Ari was always organized, the librarian of the family, keeping track of everyone's schedules and making shopping lists and putting photographs in albums, labeled with the proper date. "We can just enjoy it now. Enjoy being happy." Emily's photos were in a jumbled shoebox somewhere under her bed.

"Let's take our embryo on its first trip to a jazz club. I think there's an open mic thing going on this afternoon. I want to make sure our child loves jazz."

Emily lifted up Ezra's hand and kissed it. On one of their very first dates—the first one after they had lunch together at a deli near the School of Global Public Health—they went uptown to Cleopatra's Needle and listened to a jazz bassist play while they drank cocktails at the bar. Emily loved that Ezra loved music. And while jazz wasn't her top choice, she loved how relaxed he looked when he listened, how the music seemed to take over his body, change his mood. And his love of jazz made her love it when she was with him—she hoped their baby would, too.

"Let's go, then," Emily said.

It was September, and there was a soft breath of fall in the air.

"I love September in Manhattan," Ezra replied.

They took the subway up to 86th Street and walked along the west side of Central Park. The trees were just starting to turn golden, and it seemed like the whole city was out enjoying the day. Even taxicabs seemed to honk with good humor instead of anger. The sky felt bluer, the sun brighter than before. Soon they could hear guitar music floating through the trees.

"It's Saturday!" Emily said. "That Guitar Man is playing!"

Ezra looked at her. "Forget the jazz club?" he asked.

"Forget the jazz club," she echoed. She loved listening to That Guitar Man, even though it sometimes made her melancholy, sometimes made her think about the life she could have led, the shows she could have played, the people she could have touched with her music. But it also reminded her of falling in love with Ezra. On one of their early dates, the two of them had been walking through Central Park when they discovered a hill full of people listening to a man playing the guitar, singing and dancing with him. They'd joined the group, and Ezra had asked a man leaning against a tree what was going on.

"He's That Guitar Man from Central Park," the man said. "Comes every Saturday from May until around October, as long as it's not raining. *The New York Times* wrote him up and everything. They called him 'the most famous person in New York that nobody knows.'"

Then the guitar man started playing a song called "Tom Cruise Scares Me," and Ezra and Emily were hooked. They spent the rest of the afternoon with the people on the hill, listening and dancing and eating soft pretzels and ice cream from a vendor who was parked close by.

"This is delicious," Emily had said, dipping a piece of her pretzel in mustard.

"You're delicious," Ezra had countered.

"This day is delicious," Emily added.

They were happy and falling in love—with each other, with the music, and with the world. And they carried that feeling of happiness with them through the years that followed, protecting it, nurturing it, and letting it blossom, trying to blot out the darkness.

vi

UNTIL I MET *your father, the last time I'd played music for an audience was in a piano recital the year I was fourteen. I played Joplin's "Maple Leaf Rag." I flubbed the fingering once, and cringed internally, but no one seemed to notice but me. All the parents and other kids were transfixed, and then broke into cheers and applause when the last note rang out. My parents handed me a bouquet of flowers and took me out for dessert afterward. I remember how filled with happiness I felt—music did that to me, playing the piano did that to me, the audience's reaction to my song did that to me. I would've kept working with my teacher, but my mom—your grandmother— got sicker. And any after-school activities that weren't school-sponsored weren't allowed anymore. It was just too difficult for her and my dad. So I stopped my lessons, even though my teacher told me it broke her heart. I kept singing—in the school choir—and I still played at home for my mom, but it wasn't the same. And then she died the summer before my senior year of high school. After that, I stopped playing completely.*

Your father gave music back to me, and it was like it had been waiting, dormant inside me, for something—or someone—to bring it to life. Like a garden, seemingly dead all winter only to bloom, like magic, in the spring. After we'd dated for half a year, after we'd made music together all summer, he asked me to perform with him. It was at a bar downtown, playing some rock-'n'-roll covers. He was on guitar. His roommate was going to play drums. A friend of theirs was on bass. But he needed someone to play keys. Even if I hadn't wanted to, I would've done it for him, but I did want to. The music that he'd awakened inside me made me feel more alive, more real, more grounded than anything else had since your grandmother died. My feelings came out through my fingers—and with your dad, I was able to channel those feelings, not let them take over. When I played I felt like more than me, like I was part of something larger. And so I spent the first two weeks of the fall semester practicing whenever I wasn't in class.

THERE WEREN'T A *ton of people in the bar that night, but we had the best time—your dad and Tony and James and me. We were ravenous afterward—especially your dad, who could never eat before a show—so we spent everything we made on pizza and cheap wine. With the taste of Chianti on his lips, your father told me he loved me for the very first time. The guys went home and we went out dancing until the sun came up, letting our bodies come together and apart as the music ebbed and flowed.*

"Isn't the world beautiful?" he whispered to me, as we walked home in the glowing morning light.

And even though I still missed my mother more than I could express, even though she was the one person I most wanted to talk to about making music and my new keyboard, my new love—with my heart still high on performing, my body still buzzing with music and with wine and with him, I had to agree that it was.

9

"WE SHOULD GO pregnancy grocery shopping," Ezra said, as he and Emily walked home from the subway, past the supermarket on their corner. "More protein and calcium, no cold cuts . . . I'm trying to remember what else I learned during my ob/gyn rotation. I'll look for my notes tonight."

Emily laughed. She'd had enough friends who'd been pregnant recently that she knew the rules by heart. "No alcohol, no unpasteurized cheese, no raw fish—no raw animal protein at all, really—limited caffeine, make sure you wash all your vegetables thoroughly."

Ezra looked at her, puzzled. "Wash all your vegetables thoroughly?" he echoed.

"Toxoplasmosis," Emily answered. "From the dirt they're grown in."

Now it was Ezra's turn to laugh. "Good point," he said. "We'll wash all our vegetables thoroughly. And I'll eat what you eat. No fair that you have to give up alcohol and sushi and deli meat if I don't. No more alcohol for us."

Emily kissed Ezra's cheek. "You really don't have to do that," she said.

He turned and kissed her on the lips. "But I want to," he answered.

———

IN THE GROCERY store, Ezra and Emily decided to buy the ingredients for homemade spaghetti and meatballs. One of the things they'd registered for when they got married was a pasta machine, which Ari and Jack got them, along with a series of classes on how to actually make pasta. "It didn't make sense," Ari said, "to get you something you wouldn't know how to use."

They'd made pasta maybe ten times in the last two and a half years. Emily had to admit that without those classes, they probably wouldn't have made it at all. They used the bread maker and the waffle iron even less.

EMILY LOVED WATCHING Ezra doing things around the house. He was remarkably domestic but did everything with a doctor's concentration, with medical precision. He sewed torn seams in their clothing as carefully as if he were suturing a child, using the same zigzag stitch he'd learned in medical school. He excised rotten spots in apples as if he were cutting out a tumor, making sure it had clean margins on all sides. And he followed recipes only if they made sense, questioning any step that seemed like it might cause a culinary problem down the line. They even adjusted recipes that had been passed down from his great-grandmother. *A glass of flour*, one read.

"Well, that's ridiculous," Ezra had said, the first time he tried to make his nana's chocolate squares. "Does she mean a tall glass or a short glass? A mug? A tumbler?"

"Maybe she means about a cup?" Emily offered. "It's probably an old recipe. One that wasn't written in the U.S."

Ezra looked at her, then at the recipe, then at the oven. "Huh. Well, we're going to find out how much we should really use," he said.

That day, they made three trays of chocolate squares. One with a cup of flour, another with ten ounces, and another with twelve—the amounts that their two glasses held. They'd decided that the juice glasses, which held only about four ounces, probably would be much too small. All three options tasted good—but the consistency of the ones with ten ounces of flour seemed the best. So Ezra fixed the recipe.

EMILY WAS MAKING those same chocolate squares for dessert, while Ezra made the meatballs for dinner, because the smell of the raw meat made her gag.

"It's like someone turned up the volume on my nose," Emily said. "Do you have cinnamon gum in your pocket?"

Ezra reached into the front pocket of his jeans and pulled out a pack of cinnamon Trident. "I had no idea pregnancy would give you a superpower. Maybe we should test it out. How far away do you have to be from this cinnamon gum not to smell it?"

"You're bananas," Emily told him. "For now, though, would you mind sticking it back in your pocket? It's accosting me."

Ezra did as she asked, and lined the meatballs up in a frying pan while she slid the brownies into the oven. Then they worked together to make pasta. Fettuccini was the easiest, so that was what they made.

"Are you okay telling our families before the twelve-week mark?" Ezra asked.

She nodded. "We'd tell them if something went wrong anyway, so . . ." She shrugged, hoping, praying that nothing would.
"Might as well tell them now."

Emily thought of her dad, living with his second wife in New
Mexico. A woman who was nice enough but who Emily could
never think of as a stepmom or any other version of a mom. He'd
be happy. Send a gift. Fly east to meet the baby. He came about
once a year to see Ari's kids, Hunter and Tyler, and Ari flew their
family to Santa Fe once a year to see him. The sisters often talked
about the fact that their mother would never have been a twice-a-
year grandmother, but he seemed fine being a twice-a-year grandfather. She'd call him later. She'd tell Ari first.

After dinner, as Ezra was dialing his parents, who Emily was
pretty sure would drive in from New Jersey tomorrow just to take
them out for dinner to celebrate, she pulled out her own phone
and sent a text to her sister. She used the exact same words she'd
sent last time: Can you talk? I'm pregnant.

vii

YOUR DAD AND *I were so careful.*
We were always so careful.
Until one day we weren't.

10

THE NEXT WEEK, Emily was walking down Broadway to get a sandwich for lunch from Crust, which called itself a Brooklyn deli, even though it was located in Manhattan. Ari had been so exhausted the first few months of both of her pregnancies that she'd fall asleep no more than twenty-five minutes into any movie that Emily brought up to Connecticut to watch with her, but Emily didn't feel that way—not now, and not the other time either. She felt, somehow, powerful. Though also more likely to cry at a credit card commercial or TV movie or a story Ezra told her about one of his patients. It was all she could do these last few days to make sure she didn't cry at her own patients' stories—the happy ones and the sad ones.

As Emily turned the corner, she saw Tessa, wearing her backpack, carrying a diaper bag in one arm and a whimpering baby in the other.

"Hey," Emily said, hurrying over to her. "Can I help you carry something? Where are you headed?"

Tessa looked at her with tears threatening to overflow her eyes. "My babysitter canceled. And Chris couldn't stay home from work. And now I'm late for class and I have to bring Zoe and she's been fussy all morning and ＂

Emily looked at the baby, who had a thick thatch of hair, chocolate-brown like Tessa's. "I'll take her," she said, impulsively.

"It's lunchtime for me now anyway. Just pick her up from my office after class." The minute she said it, she knew she shouldn't have. She knew this wasn't something a therapist was supposed to do for a patient. She knew that when she walked back into the center with Zoe, Priya would have something to say about it— and she wouldn't be wrong. But Emily didn't rescind her offer. She wondered if Dr. West would've done the same thing for her.

"I can't—" Tessa was shaking her head.

"It's fine," Emily said. "You won't be able to pay as much attention to your professor if you have to handle her, too."

Tessa sighed. She looked like she was going to object again but then seemed to change her mind. "Thank you," she said, handing over Zoe and her diaper bag. "There's a bottle in here for her. She'll probably want it pretty soon. And diapers and a change of clothes and a pacifier and everything."

Emily adjusted the diaper bag on one shoulder and settled Zoe on her hip. "We'll see you soon," she said. "And here—I'll give you my cell number. If you're nervous, text me and I'll send you back a photo. Prove to you that this kiddo and I are doing just fine."

"I don't think that'll be necessary." Tessa laughed but typed Emily's cell number into her phone anyway and then waved one last time and hurried toward the arts and sciences building.

Zoe started whimpering louder, but Emily rocked her back and forth, swaying like she'd done when her nephews were tiny, and Zoe quieted down.

"I'm Emily," Emily told the baby, even though she knew that at six months old, developmentally the baby had no idea what she was saying. Words didn't have meanings yet. But she kept talking, knowing the sound of her voice could be soothing. "Some kids I know call me Auntie Em. You can, too, if you want."

Zoe leaned over and started sucking on Emily's shoulder.

"You're hungry, aren't you?" she said. "Well, I'll get you that bottle as soon as we make it to the deli. I'll order my sandwich—I think it'll be an egg salad on rye with tomato—and while we wait for my lunch, I'll give you yours. How does that sound?"

Zoe continued sucking on Emily's shirt, and Emily could feel it getting saturated with baby drool. She laughed.

This is what it'll be like, she thought. *I'll be covered in drool, and I won't mind a bit.*

AS EMILY SAT in the deli feeding Zoe, waiting for her sandwich, a ballad she'd never heard before came on the radio, but the melody somehow felt familiar. So did the voice. She listened to the lyrics.

I build you a castle in my dreams
With towers
With turrets
With everything always how it seems
I thought my love for you would die
Would wither
Would fade
But it beats strong inside me still
So I build you that castle on a hill
A crystal castle on a hill

The artist sang, his baritone strong and full, with a rasp that gave it added warmth. It felt familiar but at the same time, new. With a jolt, Emily thought she recognized the singer, but then she wasn't sure. So much time had passed. She hadn't heard his voice in years.

There was so much emotion in the performance that Emily found herself blinking back tears. She felt ridiculous, crying in a deli because of a song on the radio, and quickly wiped her eyes with Zoe's burp cloth.

"It's just pregnancy hormones," she told Zoe. "That's all. That's all it is."

After burping Zoe, Emily slipped the sandwich into the diaper bag and walked back to her office. But she couldn't get the song out of her head. *It beats strong inside me still. So I build you that castle on a hill. A crystal castle on a hill.* The melody was familiar. And that voice. With those lyrics. Could it really be him?

11

THE NEXT WEEK, while Ezra was on call, Ari came over to help Emily go through the piles of stuff in the second bedroom. She walked into Emily and Ezra's apartment with a hiking backpack, the one she'd carried on a family trip to the Grand Canyon the year before.

"Are you staying the night?" Emily asked when her sister came through the door.

"I wish," Ari said. "I brought you all my maternity clothes."

The women were just about the same size, Ari a little softer around the edges, not quite as muscular as her younger sister.

Emily unzipped the bag. At just shy of seven weeks pregnant, she wasn't showing. Even Ezra couldn't see the difference in her body. She could feel it, though.

"Did you vacuum-pack these or something?" Emily asked, pulling out what looked liked a compressed plastic-wrapped cube of clothing.

Ari nodded. "It saves so much space in the attic."

Emily started laughing and Ari looked at her quizzically until she started laughing, too, realizing belatedly why someone might find vacuum-packed clothing funny. It was often like that with Ari. It took her a moment to get out of her own brain, to switch her point of view, but when she did, she could laugh at herself. Or understand why something she said might have been hurtful.

Emily often wished Ari were able to do that before she said the hurtful thing, but at least she understood afterward.

Arielle sat down on the couch and started un-vacuum-packing the clothes so Emily could see what was there.

"Here," Emily said, as she went into the kitchen. "I made parmesan monkey bread and tomato sauce."

Her sister smiled at the dish. It was something their mom used to make, though as she got sicker, she needed their help to open the jars and eventually to roll the balls of dough in grated parmesan cheese. Now that she was pregnant, Emily found herself thinking about her mom even more often.

"She would've been so excited," Ari said, pulling off a section of the bread to dip in sauce. Emily didn't have to ask who she meant.

"I know," she said. "There's so much I wish I could ask her."

Ari sighed. "I know it's not the same, but you can always ask me."

Emily nodded. Her sister wasn't a replacement, but for the past sixteen years she'd been the next best thing.

"How are you feeling?" Ari asked her.

"Pretty good, actually," Emily said. "Just really emotional."

"Does it make you think . . . ?" Ari didn't finish the sentence. The two of them hardly ever had to.

"Yeah," Emily said, answering what her sister hadn't needed to ask. "All the time."

viii

YOUR FATHER WAS *playing music everywhere he could, some-times by himself, and sometimes with James or Tony or me or all of us together. It was his goal, his plan after graduation: to get a record deal, to perform all over the world, to share his music with everyone he could. We didn't talk much about "after"—after he graduated, when I would have one more year to go. In the meantime, he'd be-come a favorite at a local coffee shop and had started writing his own songs. Songs about the dreams he had, the love he felt—for me, for music, for family, for life. In the song he wrote about me called "Queen of All the Keys" he sang about how he loved to watch me play piano. Honestly, even then I thought it was a little silly. His lyrics were me-diocre at best. But the melody was beautiful. And whenever I walked into the coffee shop, everyone there called me the queen. To play along, I started braiding my hair into a crown around my head when we performed together. The coffee shop fans loved it.*

Then one afternoon he got a call from a talent buyer at Webster Hall who had been to our coffee shop concerts. The opening act for Rilo Kiley had gotten stuck in a snowstorm in Michigan, and the club needed someone to replace them. Could he perform that night, the guy wanted to know. The show started in five hours. He could bring his band, or go it alone, if they weren't available. They'd tried every-one else, but it was a rough night. The club just needed someone to warm up the crowd, fill some time before the band went on.

When your father hung up the phone, it was the happiest I'd ever seen him. Though he tried to play it cool, he couldn't stop grinning. His beautiful dimpled smile had taken over his face. It was like he'd been blessed by the rock gods. Like the most perfect gift imaginable had fallen into his lap.

"You and me, Queenie," he said, not even bothering to ask the guys to change their plans. "Let's do this together."

I couldn't say no to that grin, to that happiness. Plus, I loved being on stage with him. The two of us together in Webster Hall was the best way to spend a Saturday night I could imagine.

We put together a set list, some songs he'd written, some covers that had a similar vibe, and I put on a pair of faux-leather pants with a tight black tank top and heels—high enough to look sexy but low enough that I could stand in them while I played. My hair was full and wavy, cascading down past my shoulders. I braided the top half in a crown and left the rest loose.

"God," he said when he saw me. "How did I get so lucky?"

I kissed him hard, raking my fingers down his back as I told him I loved him.

I haven't been on a stage in a while, but there's nothing like it. When it's working, when the audience is into you, the air feels electric. It's like everyone's consciousness has somehow connected in that room, like we're all riding one big wave of emotion that rises and falls and crashes with the music.

That's what it was like that night. It was perfection. It was your father's dream become a reality. His energy fueled the whole room.

We ended the night with a duet inspired by Moulin Rouge's "Elephant Love Medley," and when your dad sang about how he was made for loving me, I could see how true he believed it was. And that *was how I felt, too. We were made for this. We were made for each other. We were made to be together, up on stage, sharing a dream, sharing a future. In that moment, his dream became my dream, became our dream. The medley ended with a kiss, and the crowd's cheers were so loud they made my ears ring.*

Afterward, we were surfing on the high of it. We drank free cocktails and champagne, we shared a joint someone offered us, we accepted compliments from fans who wanted to know when our album was coming out.

"Soon," your dad said. "Soon."

"Really?" I whispered, when we had a short second to ourselves. If we could spend our lives like this, performing, being adored, creating music, loving each other—I didn't even want to think about it because it seemed so wonderful, so perfect, so ideal.

"Really," he answered, kissing me hard.

We were college sweethearts who could bring down the house. We were young and happy and talented as all get-out. He was more talented than I was, more charismatic, too. I couldn't command the stage like he did, but I could keep up. And because we knew each other so well, we jelled up there. The connection between us did something special to the crowd.

There was a green room that we eventually made our way to when it was so late it was early. The minute we got there, the minute we closed the doors, his hands were on my hips and mine were on his. Soon we were fumbling with buttons and zippers, my shoes kicked off into a corner, leather pants peeled off my legs, exposing lace underneath.

I don't remember all that much, to be honest. The drinks, the drugs, the experience, the adoration, the love—it had all gone to my head. Even now, the night comes back to me in pieces, like a shattered mirror, a dream. I was straddling him on the couch, I was on my back on the floor, on a table, against the wall. I was abandoning myself to him. I felt like starlight, like moonbeams, like a crystal queen.

12

"I HEARD HIM on the radio last week," Emily said to Arielle as they sat on the couch dipping monkey bread into sauce.

"*Him* him?" Ari asked.

Emily nodded. "He's going by a different name, but I'm sure it's him."

She'd looked up the lyrics to the song she heard in the deli, and the artist was named Austin Roberts. He'd grown up in Austin. And Roberts . . . they'd talked about stage names once, about flipping his first and making it his last. And with the sound, with the lyrics, with that voice, with a melody that sounded so similar to "Queen of All the Keys"—it had to be him. She hadn't looked for a website, though, or any social media profiles. She was worried about what it would feel like to see his face again, after so long.

"Can I hear?" Ari asked.

Emily pulled the song up on iTunes. There was a whole album, she knew. She'd found it that afternoon. But she'd only bought the one song. She hit play and watched her sister listen to the lyrics, listen to him sing. Without even thinking about it, Emily started playing along, her right hand tapping the melody on the back of the couch, her left playing chords on her thigh. She knew it would be nearly three more months until the embryo inside her would be able to hear music—or anything at all—but she wondered if her child would like this song, would love music the way she did.

When the song was over, Arielle sat for a moment. Emily could see her processing, biting her lip as she considered her words. "Is that about . . ." she finally said.

"I think so?" Emily said, her eyebrows crinkling. "I think it's about me."

On their first date, he'd called her a crystal queen. It seemed impossible that the song would be about someone else.

Ari was quiet for a moment. "What are you going to do?"

Emily shrugged. "Nothing, I guess? I don't know."

"You're not tempted to email him?" Ari said as she picked up her glass of water. "I would be."

"Of course I'm tempted," Emily said. "But that feels like opening up a lot. Like that Greek myth storybook Mom used to read us—I don't want to be Pandora."

Ari laughed, a sound that quickly turned rueful. "At least someone gave you a box."

Emily looked closely at her sister. "Are you okay?" she asked.

Ari took a sip of water. "I turn thirty-six in two months."

It took about three seconds for the significance to hit Emily. "When Mom got diagnosed," she said. "Are you having any . . . ?"

Ari shook her head. "I don't think so, but any time I trip over a crack in a sidewalk or drop my keys, I worry that this is it. It's coming for me. And then I think about the choices I've made, giving up being a math teacher to raise my kids, getting married so young, and I wonder if I'm ever going to get to visit the Great Pyramids in Egypt."

Ari was all over the place. Emily could barely parse what she was trying to say. She was afraid of getting sick, of regretting her life choices, of never living to see her dreams come true.

"You know," Emily said, "Dad is sixty-four and totally healthy. If you want to look to a parent to predict your fate, your health could be like Dad's just as much as like Mom's."

Ari ran her hand though her wavy hair, twisting it into a bun and then releasing it. "I feel like I need to plan for the worst-case scenario. Then it won't be as hard if that ends up as my reality."

That was one of the differences between the two sisters. Ari always planned for the worst, always had an umbrella in the car and canned food in the kitchen cabinet. Emily, through whatever quirk of personality, always planned for the best. But that meant things hit her even harder when they didn't go as she hoped they would.

Emily slid over on the couch to hug her sister. "You can go back to teaching," she said. "And plan a trip to Egypt. If Jack doesn't want to go, I'll go with you. No matter when you got married, you found a great guy who loves you and who you love, and same with your kids. They're awesome. But no matter whether you've got thirteen years left or sixty-five, you should make sure you're living your life the way you want to live it. And that can change, too. If you decide that you're done staying home, you can work. The boys are older now anyway. Their lives changed, and yours can, too, if you want it to."

Ari bit her lip. "Do you think someone would hire me?" she asked. "I've been out of the classroom for so long."

"You won't find out unless you try," Emily replied.

Ari leaned her head against her sister's. "Does it feel nice," she asked, "to be someone's muse? To be the subject of his song?"

The corner of Emily's mouth lifted. "A little," she admitted.

The sisters kept talking until midnight, when Ezra came home and was surprised to find them on the couch together under an afghan, the cold remnants of a plate of monkey bread still on the coffee table.

"I should go," Ari said, when she realized what time it was.

"But come back, soon," Emily responded, realizing how rare it had become for the two of them to get time alone to talk, uninterrupted, for hours.

"Yes," Ari said. "Soon. Because we still have to clean out the second bedroom."

Emily laughed. "I'd forgotten we were supposed to do that."

"Next time," Ari said. "Next time."

ix

AFTER OUR NIGHT *at Webster Hall, for the next two weeks all
your dad wanted to do was play. It was nearing the end of the fall
semester, and he half-assed his papers and exams, spending more
and more time writing songs, recording, trying to parlay our evening
performance into something bigger, something more. I paid attention
to my schoolwork, but I was with him whenever I could be. Harmonizing, tweaking his song lyrics, adding depth to the musical arrange-
ments. He kept encouraging me to write my own, but I preferred to
tinker with his. And it was working! People were booking us. In New
York City, in New Jersey, in Texas, where we planned to go for Christmas to visit his family. We had professional photos taken, my hair in
its half crown, your dad with the five o'clock shadow that made me
shiver when he kissed me.*

*"We're gonna be stars, Queenie," he'd say, when he fell, exhausted,
into bed at night.*

*I kept dreaming about it—the two of us, on the road together.
Cuddling up at night in a tour bus. Wowing sold-out crowds in all
fifty states. And Europe, too. Maybe Asia. And Africa. And Austra-
lia. Latin America. Feeling that adrenaline rush. High on him, on
me, on us. Webster Hall really changed us—changed me. Made me
think that music was a real possibility—for both of us. Maybe I didn't
have to finish college. We didn't talk about that part—the exact logistics. But we talked about the future all the time.*

"We could be huge," he kept saying. "We could be the Sonny and Cher of our generation. The Johnny and June Carter Cash." It seemed crazy but not out of the question. I thought about that crowd. The response we got. The applause. The bookings in our calendar.

WE WOKE UP the morning after we had our photo shoot wrapped around each other, my breast cupped in his hand, our legs twined together.

When I shifted my position, he did, too.

"We're gonna be so big, Queenie," he said, his beautiful voice hoarse from sleep. "I was just dreaming about it. You and me, we're gonna make history."

"I'd love that," I whispered back. "Rob and Emily, reaching the top of the charts."

"Maybe I should change my name," he mused.

I knew he didn't like his name: Rob Barnes—he thought it sounded like a sentence with a verb you could conjugate: I rob barns. We rob barns. They rob barns. Go, rob barns!

"Tanner Barnes?" I asked, using his middle name instead.

"Bluer barns," he countered. "Redder barns. My first name's a verb, my middle name's an adjective, and my last name's a noun. What were my parents thinking?"

I laughed, more awake than I had been. "You could always use Robert," I said. "Or move it to the end. Pick a new first name."

"I wish I had a name like yours, Emily Solomon."

While we were talking, he'd been running his hand lightly over my breasts under the covers, his fingertips playing against my skin the way they would dance on the frets of his guitar.

His touch made me shiver, and I rolled toward him, kissing away whatever the rest of the conversation held.

"I love you, no matter what your name is," I said, before I slipped under the quilt, kissing down his chest, taking him into my mouth.

"Get back up here, Queenie," he said, his voice halfway between a growl and a moan.

I kissed my way back up, until he bent and caught my mouth with his.

"You, you, you," he said between kisses, as he slipped a condom on underneath the covers.

"Me, me, me," I answered, as I wrapped my legs around him.

Our lovemaking was exuberant. We laughed as we kissed each other, twisting the bedsheets as we flipped and turned.

"Let's try this," he breathed, rolling us over.

"How about this?" I propelled myself forward, wrapping my legs tight around his waist.

It was always like this with us, experimenting, learning, unafraid to try new things, to figure out what worked for us. He was the first person I'd ever slept with; I was the second person he had. We loved exploring what we could do, how we could bend, finding our limits individually and as a couple.

That day we ended with me on my back, my feet against his chest as he stood next to the bed, rocking inside me. We orgasmed at just about the same time, calling out to each other in unintentional harmony.

When he pulled out to slide off the condom, for some reason I'll never know, my mind flashed back to that night in the green room. "We didn't use one," I said, stopping him as he started walking to the wastepaper basket. "At Webster Hall. We didn't use one."

I could tell he was searching his mind, too, trying to put together the pieces of the night. "It's probably fine," he said finally.

I was trying to remember the last time I'd gotten my period. I was terrible at tracking it. There were so many other things going on— school and music and him and just dealing with life as a twenty-year-old whose mom had died three years before and who still hadn't completely dealt with the loss.

"When did we play with the guys at Prohibition?" I asked him, as he sat down on the bed next to me. I remembered adding a panty liner before that show, just in case the set went long.

He picked up his phone and looked at the calendar. "I think it was about a month ago. It was a Friday night."

"Can you count the days?" I asked him, already feeling my heart flutter.

"Twenty-six," he answered, after staring at the screen on his phone for a moment.

I breathed a sigh of relief. "I haven't missed my period yet," I said.

But it didn't come the next day, or the day after, or the day after that, either.

I started to panic.

13

A FEW DAYS later, Emily slept in.

"I'm surprised the smell of the coffee didn't wake you," Ezra teased, when he kissed her awake after leaving a partially filled mug on her nightstand.

"What coffee?" she asked, sleepily, trying to stretch out her back. It'd been aching all night. Probably just the ligaments of her uterus stretching, Ezra had said, when she'd mentioned it at dinner. He didn't seem too worried about the spot of blood she'd seen in her underwear either. "It happens in a lot of pregnancies," he said, though it had really freaked her out, sent her heart racing.

Still, Emily had let his reassurances wash over her. Convince her she was fine. Forget about what had happened last time. At just about this far along, too.

"Did you lose your superpower?" he asked. His voice was light, but Emily could hear an undercurrent of worry.

"I guess so," she said carefully. "Maybe it was just a first-six-weeks-of-pregnancy thing."

"Maybe it was," he conceded. He ran his hand down her body from shoulder to toes, on top of the blanket. "I have grand rounds today," he said, "so I should go, but you'll call me if you need me?"

Emily sat up, her back still aching. "You're worried about me," she said.

"It's probably nothing," he answered. "I'm not a gynecologist."

Then he kissed her one last time and headed out the door.

Emily got out of bed and took a shower. "Just be okay," she whispered to the cells she hoped were still dividing inside her. Even though they couldn't hear her, maybe they were somehow able to know what she was trying to say, somehow able to intuit the urgency with which she was saying it. "Keep growing. I want to hear your heart beat."

In five days they were going to the doctor for an eight-week check-up. In five days, she would get her first glimpse, her first listen. She'd been imagining what that heartbeat would sound like—soft, legato, like a muted drum. She really wanted to make it to that appointment.

Emily and Ezra hadn't talked about a name yet, what they were going to call this not-yet-a-baby, and all of a sudden it seemed important. She sent a text to Ezra. I want to name the baby after my mom, she wrote. Eden if it's a girl, and Edward for a boy. Her mother's name was Edie.

Okay, Ezra wrote back quickly. I love you.

As Emily got dressed, she kept up a steady one-sided conversation, the way she had with Zoe. "I love you already," she said. "So does your dad. We want you to grow big and strong, with round cheeks and dimpled fingers. We'll take such good care of you. I promise."

Emily knew her words wouldn't matter, but it was still a promise that felt important to make, whether anyone could hear her or not.

X

YOUR DAD CAME *into the bathroom with me and sat on the edge of my dorm's bathtub while I peed on a pregnancy test I hadn't wanted to buy. We had to wait for three minutes.*

"'Here Comes the Sun' is three-oh-five," he said.

So we sang together, quietly in the bathroom, and after the first few bars, I forgot to freak out, I forgot to be worried, I just listened to your dad's voice and tried to match it with my own.

But when the song ended and we looked at the plus sign on the test, I don't think either of us felt like the sun had come.

I'm so sorry we didn't feel differently.

But I want to tell you the truth.

14

EMILY LOOKED AT the calendar in her phone. She counted to be sure. Seven weeks and two days. That was how long she'd been pregnant so far. She looked at the appointment in her calendar and counted the five days with her finger, touching each one. Somehow, it felt like if she could make it to eight weeks, if she could listen to her baby's heartbeat, everything would be okay. She knew that wasn't true. But in her heart it felt real.

She willed it to be real.

xi

MAYBE IT WAS *the power of suggestion, or the shock or stress of it, but for the next couple of days, my breasts felt painfully heavy and I cried practically whenever anyone looked at me. I'd talked to Ari but wished for nothing more than to be able to talk to my mom, tell her what happened, listen to her advice. Ari said I should tell our dad, but I didn't. He'd been depressed since our mom died and I left home to go to school. Ari and I were both gone now, and I didn't want to put this on him, too. At least not yet. Not until I had to.*

Your dad slept in my dorm room with me every night. He kept saying it would be okay but never said how.

Three days later, as we were going to bed, I whispered to him: "Should we get married? Should we be a family?"

He stared at the ceiling for a while before he answered slowly. "I think it would be a mistake," *he said.* "I've been turning it over in my mind for the last few days and . . . I don't think we should get married because of this. We should get married because we want to get married, because we're ready to commit ourselves to each other. If this hadn't happened and I proposed to you tonight, what would you have said?"

I already felt tears pooling in my eyes, but I knew the answer: "I'd have said you were crazy," *I told him, honestly.* "That we're too young. That there's so much more we have to learn and to figure out. That I love you like mad, but we've only known each other for ten months."

He slid closer to me, and I rested my head on his shoulder. "Yeah,"
he said. "So if we get married now, I think we'd be making a mistake.
But that doesn't mean we can't have this baby, raise this baby, if you
want to. And maybe get married later." He paused. "Do you?" he
asked. I didn't answer, realizing in that moment that he was telling
me he didn't. Trying to think about whether I did. Thinking about
what it would mean for me, for him, for both of us, for our lives, for a
child's life, for our music. He clarified, "Do you want to be a mom?"

And I rolled over so my face was hidden in the crook of his neck
and sobbed. Because I didn't. And I felt horrible that I didn't—like I
was betraying biology, like I was betraying society, like I was betray-
ing you, growing inside me.

He held me, and he kissed my forehead and stroked my hair and
said it would be okay. But I really had no idea how it would.

15

EMILY WENT TO work. She listened as students told her about their anxiety, about their fights with their roommates, about how they missed home. They told her about the racist comments someone made to them in the cafeteria, about how an econ professor called on the men in the class more often than the women. They told her about how they were worried about their friends who drank too much or smoked too much. About being attracted to their TA, about their eating disorders and their depression. She listened, she asked pointed questions, she posed her advice as a "what if?" She tried not to think about what might or might not be happening in her body. She wondered if she was even helping these students. If any of what she said made sense. Or even mattered. She tried not to cry.

Between patients, she would whisper "I love you" and "please be okay" to the cells inside her.

She kept mentally scanning her body for pain or problems. Her back still ached, but other than that, she felt okay.

It's going to be okay, she kept telling herself. *It's going to be okay.* Even though, deep inside, she was pretty sure it wouldn't.

xii

YOUR DAD SAID *that I needed to get a blood test, to make sure I really was pregnant, which I thought was ridiculous—I was, the test we took in the bathroom said so, plus I could feel it—but I agreed to go for one. Not on campus, I told him, and not with my regular doctor. So we agreed to go to a clinic.*

That weekend Hanukkah was starting, and my dad wanted us to come over for a family Hanukkah dinner—me, Rob, him, and Ari. I knew it wouldn't be like the Hanukkah parties we had when my mom was alive, but he was trying. And Ari and I were trying, too.

"We can go before dinner at my dad's," I said.

So we rented a car, and we drove up the Hudson River to a clinic we'd found on Google.

When we got there, three people with signs were protesting the clinic, which also performed abortions. They were shouting at the women who walked in.

I watched the women cringe, rush past. "I can't," I said to him. "I can't walk in with them shouting at me. Even if that's not why we're here, I can't do it."

"Not even with me next to you?" he asked. "Not even if I cover your ears? If I sing at the top of my voice?"

I smiled for a brief moment but then shook my head. "Not even then," I told him. I felt shame enough at being young and accidentally pregnant. I wouldn't face that anger, even with your dad by my side.

He looked at me and sighed. He was so patient, trying so hard. "I understand," he said, finally. "I wouldn't want to walk through that either."

"I really am pregnant," I said. "I told you—I can feel it. And the test we took confirmed it. We don't need a blood test."

The windows were up on the car—it was winter and cold out—but we could still hear the voices chanting, though we couldn't make out the words.

"Okay," he said, even though I could tell he wasn't quite convinced. "But if that's the case, then you do need a doctor. And we really need a plan."

"I know," I told him. "But let's celebrate Hanukkah at my dad's tonight. We can talk later, when we drive back to the city." Back then your grandpa still lived in the house your aunt Ari and I grew up in.

Your dad nodded and turned the key in the ignition. "Of course," he said.

I knew we had to face the future, face what was happening inside me and what that meant for us. But I wanted to spend an afternoon wrapped in my dad's love, and then talk to my sister. I grew up looking to her for advice, for guidance. And with your grandma gone, she was the only one I felt like I could talk to.

16

IN THE LATE afternoon, Tessa showed up in Emily's office, the last patient of the day, and the first time she'd made an appointment with Emily since she came back to the city.

"How's it going?" Emily asked her, after the door was closed, after Tessa sat in her usual spot on the couch, leaning against the left armrest. Emily tried to get comfortable in her chair, discreetly massaging her back as Tessa spoke.

"Not the best," Tessa said. "I'll be honest. Not the best."

"What do you mean by that?" Emily asked, trying to focus all her attention on her patient, but it was difficult.

Tessa sighed. "Chris is always working—he wants to make a good impression on his new bosses, and I totally get it. But he doesn't come home until late and I barely get to see him. Zoe hardly ever sees him at all except for on weekends, when he wants to go out for brunch and for drinks with his friends. And I have so much reading to do for class, plus papers, and exams to study for, that I feel like I have to choose between school and them all the time."

Emily nodded sympathetically while her old thoughts on Chris resurfaced: totally self-absorbed. But she couldn't change Chris. Tessa couldn't, either. So they had to figure out what Tessa could do to change her situation, change her response. "Have you thought about taking fewer courses this semester? I know you have a few more weeks to drop without it being recorded on your transcript."

Tessa wiped her eyes. "I have. But I want to get through this as quickly as I can. I want to be a lawyer, and there's so much more ahead of me."

"I hear you," Emily said, "but what would it mean if you took a little more time?"

"It's more money I'd have to borrow, for one," Tessa said. "And I just . . . I want to be like Ruth Bader Ginsburg." Emily looked down to see if Tessa was wearing her RBG socks. She wasn't. Her socks were plain white, which somehow made Emily feel sad, though she made sure not to show it. "She went to law school with a baby. And her husband had cancer. And she was still the top of her class. If she could do that, I should be able to do this. She probably didn't have any trouble introducing solids to her baby, either. Zoe spits everything out."

"A lot of babies do, at first," Emily told her, wanting to say something reassuring. Her heart really went out to Tessa. She saw so much of herself in this young mom—or so much of who she might have been. She admired how Tessa went after things— boldly, bravely, not compromising her plans unless she absolutely had to—but that aspect of her personality, so different from Emily's own, also worried her. If you don't bend, sometimes you break. Not every woman can be Ruth Bader Ginsburg. And it's better to figure that out when you're young, before you disappoint yourself too deeply when the realization does hit. At least then you have other options, at least then you don't feel stuck in a life that doesn't quite feel like it's yours—like Ari seemed to. Like Emily did sometimes, too.

xiii

WHEN WE GOT *to your grandfather's house, he greeted us both with hugs.*

"My musicians!" he said. He'd come to hear us play a few times, and Ari told us that it was all he could talk about to her for days after. "Do I get my own personal concert?"

I looked at your dad and he shrugged.

"Sure," I said. Playing music was an easy way to make your grandpa happy. I had memories of cuddling with him on the couch, listening to my mom play when I was really small. And I played for him later. When my mom was at the hospital I would play the Eagles or Queen or the Rolling Stones for him. In those last couple of years, anything I could do to make him smile seemed worth it.

I sat at the baby grand in the living room, and your dad picked up the guitar that always rested next to it. Ari had taken lessons as a kid, but they never really stuck. Still, the guitar stayed, almost as if it had been waiting for your dad to come into our lives.

"What do you want to hear, Mr. Solomon?" your father asked, tuning the strings.

"How about some Kansas?"

Your dad raised an eyebrow at me. "Queenie?" he asked.

I flexed my fingers. "I think I could do 'Dust in the Wind' or 'Carry On Wayward Son,'" I answered. It had been a while, but I was sure I could still get some of the progressions pretty easily, especially if your dad was leading with his guitar and vocals.

"I think I know all the words to 'Dust in the Wind,'" he answered. "Let's do it."

I closed my eyes and listened to your dad play the opening guitar riff, then started fingering the second guitar's riff with my right hand, my left playing chords. After we got through that bit, your dad started to sing.

I loved the earthiness of his voice, loved hearing it without a microphone distorting its raspy quality. I didn't want to join in, to mar his beautiful sound with my own. But then your grandpa started singing along, deeper than your dad, and not as beautiful, but on key. I joined in then, balancing their lower register with my higher tone.

The electric feeling that shot through the music at Webster Hall had made its way to your grandfather's living room. Only he was part of it now, too. Music is transformational like that, when you're part of its creation.

When the song ended, I looked up, and wasn't surprised to see that all three of us had tears in our eyes.

Your grandfather cleared his throat, all of a sudden embarrassed by his singing or his emotion or something else I wasn't sure of.

"Now I know where you get it from," your dad said, winking at me and then smiling at your grandfather. Though I knew my musical ability was my mom's.

Ari had walked in while we were playing, and she hadn't taken her coat off. She was just standing in the entryway, watching.

"Well," your grandfather said, "I was going to go into town to pick up some of those dura logs for the fireplace. Anyone want to keep an old man company?"

Your dad looked at me. I was looking at Ari. "I'll come," he said.

Your grandfather seemed chuffed by the offer, and the two of them took off into town.

Once they left, Ari wrapped me in a hug. "How are you holding up?" she asked me.

I shrugged. "Okay, I guess." Then I paused. "Actually, not really okay at all."

She nodded and rubbed my back. "Of course you're not."

"I don't know what to do," I told her, sitting down on the couch.

She sat beside me. "What happened, exactly?" she asked.

So I told her the whole story—about the show and the green room and not getting married and how I knew your dad didn't really want to raise a baby, even though he'd never come straight out and said it.

"What would Mom say?" I asked her.

She thought for a moment. "Well," she said, "Mom always said that whatever happened to us was God's doing and any choice we made was the one we were supposed to make. Which probably doesn't help much."

I thought about that. It was the way our mom was able to accept her illness, her death. Everything happens the way it's supposed to happen.

"Does that mean that if I agonize over this, I'm supposed to be agonizing over this?" I asked Ari, half joking.

She smiled. "I guess so."

We sat for a moment.

"Do you believe that?" I asked, quietly.

Ari looked at me seriously. "I try to," she said.

She walked across the room and picked up a photo of the three of us—Ari, me, and your grandma. "What if it's her spirit?" she asked me. "You know how there are those stories about past lives and recycled souls? What if that baby has Mom's soul?"

I looked at her in shock. "How could you say that to me?" I asked her, my eyes brimming with tears. "Now if I decide to do anything other than raise this baby myself, I'll be thinking about that."

I got up and grabbed my coat.

"Wait," Ari said. "Em, I'm sorry. I shouldn't have said that out loud. I'm sorry. I didn't mean—it was a thought. A fleeting thought."

"Just forget it," I said; my tears were full of anger and disappointment and guilt. I opened the door.

"Where are you going?" she asked.

I scanned the yard. I didn't really have a plan. And then my eyes landed on the oak tree on the other side of the yard. "My old tree house," I said. "Don't follow me." It was somewhere I went often as a kid when I needed to be alone. I'd tell her not to follow me then, too.

I could see my breath making mist in the cold air as I walked quickly across the lawn and climbed up the broken ladder to the house my father built when I was eight years old. I did my homework in there, ate my after-school snacks, had my first kiss at twelve with one of our neighbors, Jared Stewart.

Once I got inside, I saw what a mess it had become. Dead leaves, dead bugs, dirt. I used my gloved hands to sweep what I could out the windows and entry, and then leaned back against the wall where I'd carved ES loves JS, after Jared's and my first kiss. We kissed a lot more after that—for two years, until I didn't want to kiss him anymore. Or anyone. I wanted to focus on my mom and on school and on choir and that was it. Letting too many people in made everything seem worse, seeing their pity, their sympathy. I couldn't handle it.

I looked for something sharp in the tree house and found the bottom point of an acorn that must've blown in from higher up in the tree. With it, I scratched ES loves RB into the soft wood next to the first inscription.

Soon after, I heard someone climbing up the ladder of the tree house. "I said leave me alone, Ari," I yelled.

"It's me!" your dad answered.

"Oh," I said. "You can come in."

He laughed as his head popped into view. "Thank you for the audience, my queen."

I smiled, too.

"What happened with Ari?" he asked. "She feels really bad."

"She said something dumb," I told him, leaning back against the wall. "She said that maybe my mom's soul has been reincarnated and that's why I'm pregnant."

He sat down next to me, his back against the same wall.

"You don't want to raise this baby," he said, looking out the window.

"No," I said. "You don't, either."

"No," he said. "I don't. We've got this amazing thing going with our music, and I don't want to risk it. If we slow down, if we get off the train we're on now, I don't know if we'll ever be able to jump back on."

We were both quiet for a minute as the words settled around us. As their meaning did.

"Do you want to carry this baby?" he asked softly, sliding his gloved hand into mine. "Do you want to have it at all?"

I followed his gaze out the window and watched some pine needles swirl in the winter wind.

"I don't know," I told him, honestly.

"That's what I thought you'd say," he said.

He let go of my hand, pulling a little plastic bag out of his pocket and rolling a joint. "Just a little," he said, as he lit it and inhaled.

When he breathed out, it smelled so good.

"One hit," I said, and then filled my lungs. I felt myself starting to relax. It was working already. Or maybe it was psychosomatic. But whatever it was, it felt good. Then I took another hit. And another. And one more after that. Deep drags that I held in my lungs until it felt like they'd burst.

"Hey there," your dad said, taking back the joint. "Now that we know, you probably should chill with stuff like this."

I thought about my mom's theory: all things happen the way they're supposed to. I was supposed to smoke. He was supposed to take the joint away.

"Why do you keep saying everything's going to be okay?" I asked him. "How do you know?"

He shrugged. "After my parents got divorced, my mom always used to tell me and my sisters that everything is always okay in the end, and if it's not okay, it just means it isn't the end."

"So whatever happens, it'll be okay." I leaned my head against his shoulder, feeling relaxed and kind of blurry around the edges.

"Yeah, whatever happens, it'll be okay."

I looked up at him, his eyes looking extra vivid, extra green. "Do you want me not to have this baby?"

He looked at me carefully, like he'd been having this conversation in his head for days. "I want you to make whatever decision feels right to you. It's your body. I don't want you to make a decision because you think it's the one I want you to make, and then regret it. I'll be here no matter what."

I leaned over and kissed him. Even though I felt unlucky for so *many reasons, in that moment, I felt so lucky that he was the man I was going through this with.*

We kissed until your grandfather's voice pierced the quiet winter sky calling us in for dinner.

And that was when everything went wrong.

17

WHEN EMILY STOOD up to get her coat to head home for the day, she made it only two steps before the intensity of the cramp in her stomach made her pause. She put her hand on the bookshelf to steady herself, her back hunched forward in an effort to stave off more pain.

She looked up and saw Priya in the door frame of her office, her coat on, her bag in hand, ready to head home.

"Are you okay?" Priya asked. The two women shared a wall between their offices. And sometimes shared lunch or a walk to the subway, too. Priya had come to ask if Emily was ready to leave for the day.

Emily shook her head. "I think I'm having a miscarriage," she said.

xiv

YOUR DAD CLIMBED *down the tree house first.*

"Be careful," he said. "Some of this wood feels rotted through."

I knew I didn't have to use the ladder.

"Want to see how I used to get down?" I called out the door.

"What are you talking about?" he called back.

I climbed out the window and lowered myself onto the branch below.

"Queenie?" he said. "What are you doing?"

"This branch was my elevator," I told him. "Once I get close to the end, my weight bends it low enough to the ground that I can hop right off."

"Are you sure you want to do that?" he asked as I started walking, my arms out for balance.

"I did this all the time," I said, as I walked farther from the trunk. But the branch didn't feel as supple as it used to. It wasn't bending the way I remembered. I took another step.

And then the branch gave way. My body swung as I grabbed for the tree, but my fingers couldn't find purchase. I was falling.

"Rob!!!" I screamed.

"Shit!" I heard him yell.

He must've tried to break my fall, because the next thing I knew, I landed half on him, half on the ground, my wrist snapped back, my fingers underneath, his knee pushing straight into my stomach, knocking the wind out of me.

I couldn't breathe.

The pain in my hand was excruciating.

My dad came running.

I was crying.

Then we were in my dad's car and every bounce made me wince.

At the hospital they set my broken wrist and three broken fingers.

I didn't tell them I was pregnant. Your dad didn't, either.

"She's lucky," they said.

"You saved her from a lot worse by breaking her fall," they said.

They sent me home with painkillers I wasn't sure I should take.

I wouldn't be able to play piano for eight weeks, maybe longer.

I wouldn't be able to play the shows we'd booked in Texas for Christmas.

I wouldn't be able to record the CD we were planning next month.

I wouldn't be able to do what I loved with the man I loved.

I was devastated.

XV

TWO DAYS LATER *my stomach started cramping. I started bleeding.*

"I guess you weren't pregnant after all," your dad said to me.

"I guess," I said.

But I knew that wasn't true.

I knew you had been there.

I knew I had lost you.

But I pretended I hadn't.

I pretended the pregnancy test was wrong.

I pretended it didn't matter to me at all.

I pretended for months.

18

EMILY AND EZRA spent the night in each other's arms.

"I wanted this baby so badly," Emily murmured as they held each other.

"I know," Ezra said, "me too."

He wrapped his arm around her and pulled her closer.

"We did everything right," she said. "We would've been such good parents."

"And we will be," he said. "We will be."

Emily couldn't believe this had happened to her. Again. After waiting so long, after dreaming for so long. After taking months to get pregnant this time. Was it punishment? Was she getting what she deserved?

She cried until she fell asleep.

EZRA WATCHED HIS wife sleep, wondering how much pain a human being could absorb, how many times his heart could break, at home, at work, day after day, before it would be broken for good.

xvi

I DIDN'T GO *with your dad to Austin for Christmas. My wrist hurt, my fingers hurt, and what I was calling my period was heavier and longer than usual. There was so much blood. Plus I couldn't play piano. I was too miserable to meet his family, too sad to be on stage, too busy blaming myself to enjoy being with anyone. Instead, I curled up in my childhood bed and reread all ninety-seven of the Baby-Sitters Club books that were still in my bedroom, along with three super specials and six Baby-Sitters Club mysteries. Then I read* The Red Tent, *which is the book I was reading to your grandmother when she died. I read it through twice.*

Your dad got a friend from high school to sub in on keys for all of our gigs in Texas. They didn't perform our "Elephant Love Medley"-inspired closing. He said that was just for us.

Ari stayed home, too, even though she was living in Connecticut, getting her master's degree. She brought me my favorite foods, set up screenings of our favorite movies in the rec room in the basement, bought me new sweaters with arms baggy enough to fit my cast, and kept telling me that everything that happened was the way it was supposed to happen. I was grateful she was there, but I longed for my mother. Not that she was able to really take care of us in the end, but being able to talk to her, being able to hear her words, feel her next to me, was always comforting.

Jack came over sometimes—he and Ari had just started dating the month before—bringing an arsenal of board games with him. He, Ari, and I would play Settlers of Catan and Balderdash and Scattergories until way after dark. And then I would say I was tired so that Ari and Jack could spend some time alone. I felt bad that she was spending her whole winter break in the house with me, but she said she didn't mind. And Jack honestly didn't seem to mind hanging out at our house, either. As long as he was with Ari, he was happy.

When Ari tried to bring you up, to ask if she could take me to the gynecologist, to be sure everything was okay, I stopped her. "The pregnancy test must've been wrong." I said. She looked at me like she didn't believe me; she was my sister, she knew what my period was usually like, how this time I'd bled through my pajama pants, through the overnight maxi pads she'd gotten for me. But she closed her mouth and never asked again. I wonder, now, if your grandma had still been alive, if she'd have made me talk more. Asked more questions. If I would've felt comfortable telling her in a way I didn't with your grandpa. Regardless, my body did what it was supposed to in that situation. After ten days, I'd stopped cramping, stopped bleeding. I didn't talk about you for six months. Until I had to. Until I thought I'd crumble to pieces if I didn't.

While Ari and I were inside the house, cocooning ourselves in blankets, our father put on his winter coat, took his chain saw and his goggles, and cut down the oak, tree house and all.

He didn't buy any more dura logs all winter.

19

THE NEXT DAY Emily decided to call in sick.

"Are you sure?" Ezra asked. "Do you really want to sit here all day? You can do some good at work, at least. Your kids need you."

Emily shook her head. "I wouldn't be able to focus," she said, pulling the blanket up to her chin. She was still physically shaken from the day before—there was so much blood, so much cramping—and she was emotionally shaken, too. All she could think about was the fact that mixed in with that blood was the beginning of a baby. At some point she had wrapped those cells up in toilet paper or flushed them down the toilet. Or maybe she hadn't yet. What if she hadn't yet? She wanted to do that here, at home, not in the office.

Ezra was quiet for a moment. "I'm going in," he said. "I need to distract myself. I need to do something. Fix something. Someone."

Emily had assumed he'd want to stay home, too. That they'd be together. That they'd mourn this lost pregnancy the way she never did the last one. That together they'd heal and grow even stronger than they had been. She wanted him with her, to take care of her like he always did when she wasn't feeling well, but she didn't want to ask—if this was what he needed to do to make himself feel better, she wasn't going to stop him. She didn't want to be alone all day either, though. "I'll call Ari," she said. Just like last time. Ari was her rock. Ari had always been her rock.

The night before, Ezra had sent an email to everyone in their family telling them what happened. And then they all had called, and Ezra had spoken to them for her. Repeated the story over and over. Explained where and when and how. All the details that people want to know because they don't know what else to say. He'd done what she needed him to do. Now she would do what he needed her to do, even though it hurt to do it. *He does this*, she reminded herself, *this is how he copes with things he can't handle*. For the first time in their relationship, she wished he were different.

After Ezra left for work, Emily asked Ari to come over, and then pulled her dog-eared copy of *The Red Tent* from the drawer in her nightstand. It had been traveling with her for years, from nightstand to nightstand. As the book she had read to her mother in the months before she died, it felt like the last thread attaching her to her mom. Emily'd ended up finishing the last chapters on her own, the week after her mother's funeral. But somehow there was still comfort in the book, comfort in how it connected her to her mother, in how it connected her to a time when her mother was alive, when the pressure of her hand on Emily's arm meant so much.

Emily read, lost in another world, not thinking about her own, until Ari arrived and let herself in.

"Em?" she called.

"In here," Emily said. She folded down the page she was on and put the book on the bed next to her as Ari walked into the room. When the two sisters saw each other, their eyes filled with tears.

Ari slipped off her jacket and shoes and climbed into the bed next to Emily, both of them on their backs, looking up at the ceiling. Ari slid her fingers into Emily's, and the sisters held hands, the way they had each night for a week after their mom had died, not letting go until they'd both fallen asleep and their hands unclasped in their dreams.

"You're okay," Ari said. Not a question, a statement.

"I feel like this is my punishment," Emily whispered, the thought that kept circling round and round in her mind. "For what happened in college."

Ari squeezed her hand. "Do you really believe that?"

Emily thought for a moment. "Intellectually, no," she said. "But I still feel that way. Otherwise why would this happen to me now? What if . . . what if it really was Mom's soul and then I was an idiot and it was my fault that . . ."

Ari turned toward her sister. "Em, you've gotta forget I ever said that. I wasn't thinking. I didn't even really believe it then. I don't know why I thought it, why I said it. It was dumb."

"But maybe it was true. And that's why—"

"It's not true," Ari said, interrupting her sister. "And even if it were, it wouldn't have anything to do with what happened now. I looked it up last night. Twenty-five percent of all recognized pregnancies end in miscarriage. And the WHO website said two hundred thirteen million women get pregnant each year. So think about it, that's more than fifty-three million miscarriages." She paused. "In one year."

Emily let out a small laugh. "That sounds like something Ezra would say." She wanted to tell her sister that she wasn't a number, she wasn't a statistic, she was a person. But she knew that Ari took comfort in numbers the way Ezra did. Even if it didn't help, she knew Ari was trying.

Ari laughed, too. "I'll get you a shirt: *I love people who love statistics.*"

Emily stopped laughing and was quiet for a moment, processing her fears, knowing she could share them all with her sister. "Maybe there's something wrong with me, Ari. Maybe I'll never be able to stay pregnant for more than seven weeks."

Ari sighed. "It's possible," she said. "But it's also possible that what happened in college is completely unrelated to what's happening now. You fell out of a tree. You were taking painkillers. You were getting high. It's not entirely surprising that you miscarried then. And that was at, what, six weeks? So a different time marker."

It was five weeks and six days.

"What about now, though?" Emily asked, her voice small. "I did everything right. I feel like I studied and studied for a test that I somehow failed." That was the part that scared her the most. She could do everything right and still miscarry.

"Maybe you just weren't meant to have this particular baby at this particular point in time," Ari said. "Maybe it's like Mom said—everything that happens is exactly what's supposed to happen."

"But I want to be a mom," Emily said, tears overflowing her eyes. "I want to be a mom now. I waited until Ezra was ready, and . . . I want to be a mom."

"I know," Ari said, gathering her sister in her arms. "I know you do."

And while it didn't change what had happened, just being in

her sister's embrace made Emily feel better. It made her feel like at some point she would learn how to live with this loss the way she had learned to live with so many others. And that, no matter what, she could count on her sister to be there, helping her along the way.

xvii

I WENT BACK to school after winter break, but nothing felt the same. I was grieving a loss I refused to acknowledge, and one I did— the loss of my ability to play piano, at least for a while.

Your dad found a guy who could play the keyboard, but I still went on stage to sing. The bars that booked us had booked us because of the demo that had us performing together. They'd booked both of us. So I sang. I sang backup, I sang harmonies your dad wrote for me. I sang in our duet finale, which was a hit every night. I was performing, but I felt weird without an instrument, wrong. When I told your dad, he gave me a tambourine. I felt even weirder with the tambourine.

Also, the keyboardist was a jerk. I'm not just saying that. He really was. He showed up late for call, he took smoke breaks instead of hanging out with the rest of the guys. No one liked him, even if he was a great musician. Your dad and I were both counting down the days until my cast came off. I kept thinking that once it did, everything would go back to normal. I would be happier, your dad would chill out a little, things would be the way they were before. Of course, we hadn't figured out what came next, what the next year would look like, whether I would stay in school, but we were so focused on my hand getting better that we couldn't see that far.

———

"YOU'LL NEED SOME *physical therapy*," the doctor told me when he took the cast off.

Underneath the fiberglass, my arm and hand had atrophied. It looked small and pale and weak next to my other hand.

"I'm ready to work," I told him.

"That's my queen," your dad said.

And I did work. I worked so hard.

But a body can only heal so much, so fast.

20

TWO DAYS LATER, Emily could tell that Ezra was irritated that she still hadn't gone back to work. It wasn't what she expected from him. And she wasn't quite sure how to respond.

"This isn't good for you," he said. "You can't wallow. Your patients need you. Once you're there, you'll forget. It'll be so much easier. Seriously, I know what I'm talking about."

"Next week," Emily said. She was beginning her third reread of *The Red Tent*. She knew what she was talking about, too. And while she respected intellectually that Ezra dealt with loss and grief differently than she did, she couldn't help but feel hurt that he wasn't more upset, that he said she was wallowing. Their baby had died. Inside her. She needed time to mourn. And he was acting like it was just a blip on the radar. To her, it felt like a jet fighter had just dropped a bomb on their city.

"Don't forget my parents are coming," Ezra said. "For the hospital fund-raiser."

Emily had forgotten. Both about her in-laws coming and also about the fund-raiser. It was a yearly gala that benefitted the children's hospital, and Ezra had been going for as long as he had worked there. His parents, looking for reasons to come visit their only child now that they were retired, had been coming for the past couple of years.

Emily wanted to say, *I'm not going*, but she could tell that Ezra wouldn't take that well. Especially after he'd basically just told her to get over herself so things could get back to normal already. There was nothing that bothered him more than self-indulgence, and she could tell he was thinking her behavior was bordering on that and would give her a lecture if she told him she wanted to stay home. So she didn't.

"Right," she said. "Are they staying at the Gregory Hotel again?"

Ezra nodded. "So are we. Remember? They liked the convenience so much last year, heading right up to bed once the event was over, that they booked us a room, too. I'll throw some stuff in a duffel later. Don't forget to pack your bag. I think it'll be good for you to get out of here tonight."

Emily's heart plummeted. When they'd talked about it months before, it seemed like it would be a fun night out at a fancy hotel complete with plush bathrobes and a gourmet breakfast with his parents. But now Emily didn't even want to go to the event to begin with, much less sleep over in a hotel when her own bed was only a fifteen-minute cab ride away. There was no way she'd be able to muster up excitement for breakfast in the Garden Room. She wasn't even sure she'd be able to muster up an appetite.

The hotel really was beautiful, though. And Emily had met the hotel's owner, Nina, a few times because Ari's husband worked at the brokerage firm where she invested her money. She'd stopped by Jack's fortieth birthday party last year and had been especially kind to Hunter and Tyler.

Ezra grabbed his phone and keys. "Okay," he said. "I'll be back later."

Emily got out of bed to hug him good-bye, knowing it wasn't worth telling him she'd rather sleep at home that night. "Love you," she said.

"You too," he answered.

But Emily could tell the response was automatic. His mind was already on his patients. Hers was still stuck on the child they'd lost. The maternity clothes she wouldn't wear. The birth that wouldn't happen next summer. The jogging stroller she wouldn't be pushing through the park.

She wished she could take comfort in statistics. But even when you know you're one of fifty-three million, it's hard not to feel like the only one.

21

LATE THAT AFTERNOON, Emily put down her book, packed her own duffel bag, and looked into her closet. She had to get dressed. She had to get dressed up. She had to put on enough of a show that no one would know how crushed she felt inside.

"Alexa," she spoke to the white circle on the living room floor. "Please play rock music."

"Accessing your Pandora rock music station." The circle blinked at her.

"Thank you," Emily said.

Emily and Ezra always laughed at how excessively polite they both were to this machine, an anniversary gift from Ari and Jack.

"It just feels wrong not to say please and thank you," Emily always said.

"I know," Ezra answered. "It shouldn't, but it does."

Alexa or Pandora or whoever started playing music, and Emily pulled out the three dresses in her closet that were appropriate for tonight's event. One she remembered wearing last year, so she put it back. That left a strapless black sheath dress that she'd worn to the wedding of one of Ezra's fancy doctor friends a few months before, and a royal blue chiffon gown that Ari had given her because she couldn't wear it with a bra. The back was cut too low; Ari had worn it once and felt uncomfortable in it all night.

Emily didn't mind going braless for a night, and decided to wear the blue. Then it would feel a little like Ari was with her at the gala.

SHE LEFT THE music on while she showered, even though she could barely hear it over the rushing water. She looked down at her body. In the last few weeks—the last months really, ever since they'd started trying—she'd imagined the day she would look down and wouldn't be able to see her feet. She'd imagined rubbing cocoa butter into the skin on her stomach and feeling a baby kick back at her. She'd imagined this so frequently that it seemed like it would be a reality, and now . . . it was gone.

Emily let her tears mingle with the spray from the shower head, rinsing soap from her face as she wept. How could Ezra go back to work? How could he be okay? How could he make her go to this stupid fund-raiser tonight and pretend that nothing was wrong?

WHEN SHE GOT out of the shower, Alexa was playing the Kiss song "I Was Made for Lovin' You" and Emily felt like she was transported back to the stage at Webster Hall, when she and Rob were riding the music, before she got pregnant the first time, before she fell, and before everything after.

"Alexa," she said, as she toweled off her hair. "Please play 'Crystal Castle' by Austin Roberts."

This time, instead of his music bringing her to tears, it stopped them. It reminded her that she was strong, that she had survived so much, and that she could do it again.

She asked Alexa to play the song on repeat.

xviii

WE HAD A *gig planned for a month after my cast came off. It was a huge one. One I'm still not sure how your dad made happen. We were playing the Bitter End—one of your dad's goals before graduation, and one of our favorite places to hang out even when we weren't playing. It was epic. And I really wanted to be in perfect shape for the show.*

But in the week leading up to the gig, I was worried. When I played too long, my hand hurt. It throbbed like nothing I'd ever experienced before. And my fingers didn't move as quickly as I wanted them to, didn't press down as hard on the keys.

"I don't know if I can do this," I whispered one night, in the dark, while I was icing my hand in bed.

"Of course you can," your dad told me. "You've put in the time, you've let yourself heal. You're ready for your comeback."

I laughed, but I knew that my hand didn't know I was ready for my comeback. My hand could only do what it could do.

THE NIGHT OF *the show, I dressed in what had become my usual performance attire—black pleather pants, a tight black tank top, and heels. Your dad gave me a good-luck necklace to wear, with a four-leaf clover charm on it that fell right between my breasts. I braided my hair into its half crown, the rest of it long and wavy.*

"You ready?" he said.

"So ready," I told him. I flexed my fingers. They ached. But it would be okay. I kept telling myself that it would be okay. I popped two extra-strength Tylenol before I left the room.

THE GUYS AND *I all downed a good-luck shot before the show, and then we started playing. For the first forty-five minutes, everything was great. Then my hand started to throb. By an hour and ten minutes in, I couldn't stand the pain anymore and started playing one-handed. Your dad noticed the difference in the music and looked over at me, raising an eyebrow as he kept singing. I lifted my hand and shook my head. Sympathy radiated from him to me, but we both knew we had to keep going. The set went on for another twenty minutes, and we'd make it to the end.*

When that song finished, your dad looked at all of us and nodded twice. That meant he was adding something to the set list.

"I've got a new song I want to try out for you all tonight," he said into the mic. "My band doesn't even know it yet, so I'll give them a short break."

He looked at me and winked.

I love you, I mouthed back.

Your dad was always working on something new, and this song was fun, with a great upbeat rhythm and an earworm-y melody. The lyrics needed some work, but he had the audience dancing and clapping along by the second verse.

I wanted so badly to ice my hand—the only thing that seemed to provide any relief once the pain started—but didn't think that would look too great. Nor would walking off the stage while he was performing. So I stayed and listened and danced and felt my hand throb.

The one song break wasn't enough, but I knew it was all he would be able to give me. I played through the pain for the next two songs, and then it was time for our duet to close the show.

"ONLY LOVE CAN *break your heart," your dad said, walking toward me. "But you know I love you." And then he bent and kissed me—way before it was choreographed. "I'll have to say I love you in a song."*

I turned away from him, the way I was supposed to. "Come on, Rob, not this again."

The audience cheered. We had real fans now, and they loved this part.

"Go, Queenie!" someone yelled from the crowd. "Glad you're back on keys!"

"Love me do," your dad sang.

We got through the medley. We got to the final kiss. Everyone clapped and hollered and whistled, and then we left the stage and, out of sight of the audience, I collapsed into a mess of tears.

"It hurts so much," was all I could say from my spot on the floor. "It hurts so much."

Your dad got a bowl of ice for my hand, and two shots of vodka for me.

"Here," he said, crouching down next to me and handing me one. "Medicine. I promise it'll make you feel better."

I did the second shot he brought over. And then a third that Tony was carrying. Between that and the ice, the pain dulled.

"Maybe some weed, too?" your dad suggested.

"I just want to go home," I told him.

I could tell he wanted to stay, to celebrate our gigs the way we usually did, but he came home with me. We were silent as we rode the subway with our instruments. My hand still ached—just an echo of the pain that had been there, but enough to make me remember. I couldn't do that again.

"I think I need a break from the band," I told your dad.

"You can just sing more, play less. Give your hand a few more weeks. We can get the douchebag keyboardist back."

I laughed.

"I'm serious," your dad said. "We need you." Then he looked me straight in the eyes. "I need you. I hate being up there without you. You make it all magic."

I laid my head on his shoulder. "We'll see," I told him.

I didn't feel like I made anything magic. I felt like our world was unraveling and it was all my fault.

22

EMILY WAS CURLING her hair, the music switched to jazz, when Ezra got home. The front door slammed and it made her jump.

"Ezra?" she called out. He didn't usually enter the apartment that way. She wondered if it was the miscarriage that was upsetting him—or something else. Living with him often meant picking up on the tiny cues.

"Hey, Em," he called. "Want a glass of wine?"

Reflexively she was about to say no, but then answered, "Sure. But aren't we about to go to a fund-raiser with lots of drinks?"

Ezra came to the bathroom with a glass of cold white wine in each hand. "You look great," he said, handing her one.

She looked at his face. It looked tired. His eyes were puffy. Was he that much more upset about the miscarriage than he let on at home? Was he crying at work, where she couldn't see him?

"How are you feeling?" she asked.

"Rough day," he said, leaning against the doorjamb.

"What happened?" She took a sip of the wine and then put it down on the bathroom counter so she could finish her hair. She wondered if one of his patients had taken a bad turn, or if he'd gotten into an argument with the hospital administration again about getting his patients into clinical trials. She hoped it wasn't Malcolm.

"Don't worry about it," he said.

She looked at him, her eyebrows drawing together. Something was wrong. Something other than what they'd experienced together.

"Ez—" she started.

"Don't," he said. "Don't try to shrink me." He took a big gulp of wine. "I'm gonna jump in the shower. I'll be ready in fifteen."

Emily was taken aback. He'd never said that to her. Never implied that he saw her questions as intrusive. She didn't say anything. Just nodded and looked back at the mirror, watching herself raise the curling iron to her hair, wishing she could walk through like Alice and spend some time in a world on the other side. It felt like the white knight was talking backward. Was the red queen off with her head?

Maybe there would be a mirror Ezra in there who would sit with her and hold her and tell her she could mourn as long as she wanted. Someone who would let his pain mingle with hers, bringing them closer. Maybe they could walk through the looking glass together.

23

EZRA AND EMILY met up with Ezra's parents in the bar at the Gregory on the Park.

"Oh, honey," Ezra's mom whispered, when she hugged her. "How are you doing? You know, it happened to me, too, a few years after Ezra was born."

"I'm okay," Emily answered, in a way that made her mother-in-law hug her harder.

"I'm always here for you," she whispered, her voice teary. "Please. Call whenever you want to talk."

"Thank you," Emily said, knowing that saying any more might bring her to tears, too, and she didn't want to risk it. But she did want to talk to her mother-in-law, ask her how long it took her until she stopped crying, if it was different if you already had a healthy child, different if you were older when it happened, knowing you didn't have much time left. Those would be questions for another time, though, if she ever had the courage to ask them.

Ezra's dad gave her a tight hug but didn't say anything. He didn't have to. Emily could tell what he wanted to say through the strength of his arms. This was a loss for them, too.

Both of Ezra's parents were doctors. The first time the four of them went out to dinner after Emily and Ezra's wedding, a woman came over to the table and said, "Dr. Gold!" And all four of them looked up. The woman had meant Ezra's mom, who, before she retired, was the chief of breast imaging at Princeton Medical Center. The woman was ten years cancer-free, after Ezra's mom diagnosed a malignancy. Dr. Gold had gotten up from the table and hugged the woman.

"It makes all the training, all the long hours worth it when something like that happens," she said, when she sat back down.

Ezra's father was an ophthalmologist. He'd said his favorite part of the profession was when he got to fit someone for glasses the first time, and all of a sudden the world sharpened for them and they could see everything differently.

In Ezra's parents, Emily could see the seeds of his passion, his empathy, his need to make the world better, even if it was for just one person, one family, one child. But she could also see the high standards he held himself to, the self-sacrifice, the need to appear fine, even when he wasn't.

Emily remembered the second or third time she'd gone with Ezra to visit his parents in New Jersey. He'd knocked over a wineglass that had shattered on their terra-cotta floor. He'd apologized over and over until his father said, "We don't dwell on failures, Ez. We acknowledge, we vow to do better, and we move on."

After looking at the expression on Ezra's face, one that contained the understanding that his father saw his accident as a failure, Emily realized that it hadn't been easy for him to grow up in that house, the sole focus of two hypersuccessful parents. She was glad they hadn't seen this miscarriage as a failure, even though that was how it felt to Emily.

———

THE FOUR GOLDS walked into the fund-raiser together and started circulating, chatting with the people they knew, getting drinks, visiting the food stations for pasta or freshly sliced pastrami or charcuterie or cheese. Emily wandered over to the silent auction area and bid on a week at a vacation home in East Hampton that she knew Ezra would like, donated by a man named Darren Maxwell, and a dinner at the chef's table at Daniel, donated by the chef himself, which, if Ezra didn't want to go to, Ari certainly would.

"Hey, Emily," a woman said. Emily turned around. It was Hala, one of the doctors who worked with Ezra.

"How's Ezra doing tonight?" she asked.

"Fine?" Emily replied, her answer more a question than she meant it to be, as she remembered their conversation before he got into the shower, his puffy eyes.

"I'm so glad," Hala said. "I was afraid he would take it personally."

"Yeah," Emily answered, not wanting to ask what Hala was talking about. It couldn't be the miscarriage. It must be something else entirely. Something work-related. Clearly something she should have known about. It was easy to fall back on her therapy training: "How are *you* doing?" she asked.

Hala shrugged. "Well, it wasn't my patient, but I think we're all a little shaken."

Emily nodded. "Understandable," she said, running her finger around the rim of her wineglass, hoping again nothing had happened to Malcolm.

Hala looked over at the silent auction. "I heard there's a ski weekend in Vermont in the offerings. Did you see it?"

"I did," Emily said, finishing the last of her wine and handing the glass to a server who was coming by to collect the empties. "Over in the right corner, I think."

"Thanks." Hala walked over, leaving Emily to wonder what in the world happened to Ezra today at work. What could have left all the doctors shaken?

As she was wondering, the pianist who had been playing jazz all evening started the "Maple Leaf Rag." Emily was drawn toward the piano. She stopped a polite distance away and watched the musician's fingers fly over the keys. Soon Emily's fingers were playing an imaginary piano, mimicking what the pianist was doing exactly. The music was still inside her; it had always been inside her, she just hadn't let it out for years.

xix

YOUR DAD AND *I fought for the next two months, while I sang more and played less and left frustrated after every gig, mad at myself and mad at the world. We fought about how much my hand hurt. ("It's excruciating," I said. "It can't be that bad," he said.) We fought about the stupid tambourine. ("I hate it," I said. "Singers play them all the time," he said.) We fought about whether I was a singer at all. ("I'm a keyboard player," I said. "Who can't play the keys." "You have a beautiful voice," he said. "Just sing with me.")*

We fought about other things, too. About the fact that he was graduating that May, and I wasn't. ("Just quit school," he said. "Come with me on the road." "You have a degree," I said. "I want one, too.")

And then one night, at the end of finals week, we fought about you. ("You know, I really was pregnant," I said. "I could feel it." "That's bullshit," he said. "No one can feel that so early." But I could. I did. I knew it was you in there.) We were both high. We'd been fighting about other things first. We were frustrated with each other. With the world. With the hand we'd been dealt and were trying to play out, but we both thought we should throw different cards on the table. I hadn't planned for you, I hadn't wanted you, but as I found myself upset with your dad about so many things, I discovered that part of what I'd been upset with him about all these months was the way he'd denied your existence. Created a world in which I couldn't talk about you, think about you, come to terms with my own guilt, not just for my stupid actions but for what was in my heart—what was in his heart, too. And perhaps, though I didn't realize it until just now, I was angry at him for us getting pregnant at all.

I wouldn't look at him.

"Maybe this isn't going to work," he said, finally. His voice was flat. It felt like we had reached the end. There was a cliff, and we had to either hold hands and jump and trust that together we could make it to the other side, or each find our own way down alone.

For the first night in a really long time, we slept in separate beds, in separate rooms, in separate dorms. The next morning I played the keyboard until my hand was burning. An hour and a half. That was all I could do, and even then, I was pushing myself to endure a pain so intense, I wasn't sure if I'd be able to handle it again. I wasn't strong enough. My hand wasn't strong enough. And I know that if I couldn't play, we wouldn't be able to work anything else out. That was the crux of it. That was what bound us together. Our music was our love, and our love was our music. I couldn't quit the band and still be with him. And I didn't want to stay in the band if I couldn't play the keys. I felt like a novelist who had lost the ability to type, an actress who had lost the ability to speak.

I went over to your father's dorm with a garbage bag filled with the things he'd left in my room. "I think you were right," I said, when he opened the door.

He took the bag I was holding out to him. "Queenie," he said, "I didn't—"

"Don't," I told him. "This isn't going to work, and we're only hurting each other now." Tears were gathering in my eyes. I wiped my nose on the back of my hand.

He was quiet, the garbage bag clutched in his hand. I could tell he was trying to figure out what to do, what to say, whether to say any-thing at all.

"I'll always love you," I told him, my voice choked in my throat. "I'll always love what we had—and what we created."

"We're gonna be stars," he said, his voice trembling. "You're my Cher, my June Carter Cash. You're my queen."

"I can't be anymore," I told him. I was trying to keep my voice in check, but I couldn't. It was wobbling worse than his was. "I'm bro-ken. I'm . . ." I searched for an analogy he would understand. I reached for the Astros, his favorite team. "I'm a pitcher who's lost her ability to throw."

"But you can still catch," he said.

I shook my head. "I'm not a catcher. If Roger Clemens couldn't pitch anymore, they wouldn't make him a catcher. They wouldn't ask him to play outfield. You're asking me to play outfield. You can get a better outfielder, someone who loves it."

We stood together in silence, tears quietly flowing down our cheeks.

"I tried," I said. "I really tried."

He wiped his nose on the bottom of his T-shirt. "You can keep try-ing," he said.

I flexed my fingers. "I can't," I said. "It's too much. I can't. I wish I could. And it's not just that. There's school, too. It's too fast. It's too soon. There's too much pressure. I messed up too much."

I wrapped my arms around my torso, trying to hold myself to-gether, trying to keep myself upright.

"I wish it were different," he said.

"Me too," I said. "I wish it were like before."

We were both sobbing now. I wanted to hug him, I wanted to com-fort him. And I could tell he wanted to do the same for me. His hands were pressed awkwardly against his sides, the garbage bag at his feet.

"I'll always love you, too," he choked out.

We stared at each other, neither one of us wanting to be the one who turned away. I knew it had to be me, though. So I did.

He didn't stop me. He didn't fight it anymore. It seemed like, as hard as this was for both of us, he knew it was the right thing, too. For a while, the two of us being together was perfect. And then it wasn't.

In ending my relationship with your dad, I ended my career as a musician, and I threw away the future we had been imagining together. But after a long while, I found another part of myself.

I wonder sometimes if there's a way to have both. But if there is, I haven't found it.

24

AS THE FUND-RAISER continued, Emily kept drifting closer and closer to the pianist. She watched his fingers from behind. She watched how his body moved to the rhythm of the music. She'd played like that, too. In "Queen of All the Keys," the song Rob had written about her, there was a line about how she danced while she played, her hips swaying, her whole body moving to the music.

Not far from the piano was a high-top table with one chair next to it. Someone must've taken the other one to add to a group nearby. After a while, Emily got herself another glass of wine, slid onto that chair, and enjoyed the songs. She saw Ezra across the room, chatting with some other doctors, and wondered what it was that he hadn't told her about his day, but then she lost herself in John Coltrane and Duke Ellington, Dizzy Gillespie and Jimmy Heath. All of Ezra's favorites.

After the pianist played "Gingerbread Boy" and nailed the piano solo in the middle, Emily unclasped her purse and walked over to drop a $20 bill in the brandy glass he was using as a tip jar.

The man, who looked like he was maybe ten or so years older than Emily, smiled at her as he finished the tune, his fingers moving without him paying attention to them anymore. "You're my best audience tonight," he said. "I saw you fingering along with me. You play?"

Emily looked down at the Steinway. "I used to," she told him.

The pianist transitioned from "Gingerbread Boy" into "Blue Skies." "You're looking at this piano the way I looked at a bottle of vodka before I got sober," he said to her. "Good news for you is that a piano won't rot your liver."

Emily laughed.

"You wanna play?" he asked. "I'm due for a break anyway. They were going to pipe some music in for fifteen minutes, but I'd be happy to let you take over instead."

"I couldn't," Emily said, even though she wanted to sit down on that piano bench so badly she could feel the desire pulsing through her body, traveling from her heart to her wrists to her fingertips.

"I saw how your fingers move," the pianist said. "I'm pretty sure you could. How 'bout I slide over and you give one song a go? If I'm wrong and you can't really play, I'll just take over again and finish up with one more song before my break."

Emily looked down at the piano and then flexed her fingers. She hadn't touched a piano in nearly thirteen years. But she found her fingers playing imaginary keys all the time—scales on her knees while riding the subway, chords along with the radio while waiting for takeout, whole theme songs while she was watching TV. Was it like riding a bike? Like swimming? Or would she sit down on that bench and fail spectacularly?

"I'll try a song," she said, her heart speeding up in anticipation or fear or another emotion she wasn't quite able to name.

The pianist finished "Blue Skies" and slid to his left on the piano bench. Emily gathered up the skirt of her gown and sat next to him.

"Do you need music?" he asked.

Emily shook her head. She took a deep breath and laid her hands lightly on the keys. The piano was beautiful. The keys were smooth and gleaming. It felt familiar, like putting on a favorite sweatshirt on the first cool night of summer.

"Does it have to be jazz?" Emily asked the pianist, putting her hands in position to start the "Maple Leaf Rag," though not sure if she'd be able to remember enough to get through the whole song.

"Play whatever you want," he said.

With his permission to play anything, Emily moved her hands into a different position. She'd listened to the song so many times at this point that she knew it in her heart, in her bones, in her fingers. Plus it was so similar to the song she once played with him. The one he sang about her. His queen.

She closed her eyes and began to play—"Crystal Castle." Her hands felt a little stiff, a little weak. The power she used to have in them, the strength, had lessened. Her fingers weren't moving quickly, either. She slowed down the song's pace, slid her foot onto the damper pedal, and then added harmony, the way she used to when she sang with him. Her right hand was playing both their vocal parts, or what she imagined her part would be in this new song. Her left was taking care of the guitar chords he strummed while he played.

With her eyes closed, Emily felt like she was inhabiting a world where music was all that existed. She became the music in a way she couldn't explain. The sound was her and she was the sound, the rhythm, the vibrations. Everything she'd been feeling over the past few days came out through her fingers: the love, the despair, the guilt, the sorrow, the hope, the frustration, the pain. She got to the end of the song before she opened her eyes again, feeling as if the raging storm inside her had calmed.

When the world came back into focus, the pianist was standing next to the bench, a smile dancing across his lips, and there was a crowd around the piano—Ezra was there, and so were his parents, and a handful of his friends.

"I knew you could play," the pianist said to her. "But I didn't know you could play like *that*. Brava."

As Emily smiled at him and thanked him for convincing her to give it a try, she heard Hala ask Ezra, "How long has Emily been playing?" And Popper Hopkins, the chief pediatric surgeon, was saying, "I thought she was a therapist—does your wife play professionally?" And then Ezra's father was turning to him and saying, "Why have you been keeping Emily's talent from us? She's fantastic. Why haven't you bought her a piano?"

Emily looked up and saw Ezra's face turning red. "I'm going to take the woman of the hour to the bar for a drink," he said to them all, not answering anyone's questions.

"Do you want to keep playing?" the pianist asked.

Ezra was coming toward her; Emily shook her head.

"Emily?" he asked, when he got to the piano bench. He was looking at her as if he wasn't sure who she was. "Why didn't I know you could play piano?" His voice was light, but she could tell it was an effort for him to make it sound that way.

Emily cocked her head at him, the music still tingling through her body, pulsing calmness with every beat of her heart. "Of course you did," she said. "When we first met and you talked about your college a cappella group, you asked me if I was into music, I told you I used to sing and play piano, and then broke my hand and stopped. That's why my fingers hurt right before it rains."

He took a drink from the highball in his hand, not saying anything.

"I fell out of a tree house, remember?" Emily said, standing up.

He stayed silent for a moment longer, and took another drink.

"How old were you," he asked slowly, after he swallowed, "when you fell out of that tree house?"

"Twenty," Emily said. She turned to the piano player and said, "Thank you. I needed that."

"Truly my pleasure," he told her. "I hope you take it up again."

Ezra put his hand on the small of Emily's back and steered her into the corner of the room near the bar.

"You were twenty when you fell out of a tree house? I always thought you were, like, ten."

"I wasn't," Emily said, realizing that Ezra seemed upset. "I guess you didn't ask how old I was before tonight, and I never mentioned it. Is that what's upsetting you?"

"No, that's not what's upsetting me," Ezra said, his voice soft but steely. "What's upsetting me is that my wife is some kind of piano virtuoso and I had no idea. We've been together for more than four years. How didn't I ever know that? Do you know how . . . stupid I felt just now, with my colleagues asking me questions about you? And my dad? I didn't know any of the answers."

"I'm not a piano virtuoso," Emily said, trying to calm him down. "Seriously. I took lessons when I was a kid, I was pretty good, I was in a band for a while in college, that's all. I'm sorry you felt embarrassed back there, but it's really not a big deal."

"Wait," Ezra said, looking up from his drink. "You were in a band? In college? Why didn't I know that, either?"

Emily looked around. They hadn't attracted any attention yet, but she was worried that they would. "Why don't we go up to our room to talk about this," she said. She didn't want them to be the postparty hospital gossip. Besides, their bags were already upstairs, and she wouldn't mind getting out of her heels. Getting out of this whole party that she hadn't wanted to attend to begin with. To their left, Ezra's parents were chatting with the head of cardiology and her wife. Emily wondered if it was about her piano playing or about something else entirely. She caught her mother-in-law's eye and pointed toward the door. Dr. Gold nodded.

"Fine," Ezra said, putting his hand on Emily's back to steer her out of the ballroom, Emily grabbing a handful of her dress so she wouldn't trip.

When they got into the empty elevator, he started up the conversation again. "You were in a band?"

Emily nodded. "Yes," she said. "I was in a band for a few months. I played piano and sang. Then I fell out of a tree house, broke my hand, and eventually stopped doing both."

The elevator opened onto their floor. They were silent again, walking down the hallway, until Ezra opened their hotel room door. Neither one of them noticed the elegant decor or the chocolate truffles left next to each side of the bed.

"What were you doing in a tree house when you were twenty?"

Emily closed her eyes. She'd never told anyone this story after she told it to Dr. West thirteen years ago. It was still painful. All of it. She did her best to work through it, get past it, and then lock it away. She knew it was part of what made her the person she was, but it felt private—and, if she was honest with herself, she still felt ashamed of how she'd acted then. She blamed herself for so much.

"What were you doing in that tree house?" Ezra asked, sitting down on the side of the bed.

"What happened at work today?" Emily asked him, stalling—

and also wondering if dealing with that first might defuse whatever was going on with him now. "Hala mentioned something . . . and it actually made me feel pretty bad not to know what she was talking about. I had to pretend."

Ezra took off his glasses and rubbed his eyes. Then he put them back on and said, "You first."

Emily sat down across from him on a little settee covered in plush velvet. The idea of telling him this story, of sharing it, made her panic. He was such a good person, so straight-edged. He never drank before he turned twenty-one, never smoked or took any medication that didn't come with a prescription. She hated how this story made her look. It didn't feel like her anymore. It felt like a story she'd read about a person she'd once known. And there was no rule that said married couples had to share everything. There were stories in her past that Ezra didn't know—and stories in his past she was sure she didn't know. His first kiss, for example; she had no idea who it was with. Or why he chose to do his residency in California, so far away from his parents. He got to keep those stories; she got to keep hers. "My story is my story, Ezra. It's mine to share when I want."

He looked like she'd slapped him. She hadn't realized what she said would sound that way, would make him react like that. She was usually better at reading him than this, but she felt like ever since the miscarriage, her sensors were off. Maybe she was too focused on herself, on how she felt.

"You don't want to share your story with me? You haven't wanted to share your story with me before?" He loosened his tie, looking like it might be choking him.

Emily's head felt fuzzy from the wine, but not fuzzy enough that she couldn't think straight. Still, she opened up a bottle of water sitting on the table next to her and took a sip. "You didn't want to share what happened at work today with me," she pointed out as she recapped the bottle. Logic usually worked with him. "There are some things you don't tell me, either."

"It's not the same," he said.

"Isn't it?" she asked.

He shook his head, leaning forward, his elbows on his knees. "What happened when you were twenty, Emily? Why won't you talk about it?" Then his face looked stricken. "Did someone—Oh, Em, did someone—"

"No," Emily said quickly. "Not that. Thank God, not that."

"Then what?" Ezra's eyes were filled with emotion; his concern for her was there, even through his anger, his hurt.

Emily took a deep breath. When he looked at her like that, like she was someone so precious, someone he cared for more than anyone, her heart always grew a little; it swelled with her love for him. And that swelling of love made her feel strong enough, sure enough of him, to overcome her worry. Besides, he'd asked. She'd never kept anything from him when he'd asked.

"I was dating a musician," she said. "We were in a band together. And we were young and stupid and got pregnant. And I got into a fight with Ari about it and climbed up into an old tree house at my dad's house in Westchester. And then my boyfriend came up, and we got high, and I climbed out of the window instead of the door—it was dumb, but I thought I had a smart reason—and then I fell. And he caught me, but I broke my wrist and three fingers."

Ezra's face was white. "Where's . . . the baby?" he asked, his knuckles gripping his knees.

"I lost it," Emily said, "after I fell." And she started crying, thinking not about that baby but about the other one. The one who would have been hers and Ezra's.

Ezra stood and then sat down next to her. "You had this whole life, this whole . . . ordeal . . . that happened to you and you never told me."

"I never told anyone, except Ari and Dr. West."

Ezra was looking down at his hands.

Emily saw them in his lap. His hands were usually so calm, but now they were twisting around each other.

"You didn't trust me?" he asked. "You didn't trust me enough to tell me this?"

"It's not about trust," Emily said, trying to find the right words to make him understand. "It's about . . . it's about not wanting to be that person anymore. Not wanting to associate myself with the way I acted then, the decisions I made, the pain I was in."

"But this is such a huge part of you. I feel like I married someone I don't really know."

"You know me," Emily said, trying to look him in the eye, but he was still looking down, still focused on his hands.

"I don't feel like I do," he said, lifting his head. "I feel like you've been lying to me for years."

She looked him straight in the eyes. "Ez," she said. "I didn't lie to you about anything. I'm still me. I'm still the same person." Emily thought to apologize for not telling him, but she didn't. She was sorry he was hurt, but she didn't think she'd done anything wrong. It was her story.

"It doesn't feel like you are," he said, leaning against the back of the chair. "When have you been practicing piano?"

"I haven't," she said, simply.

"You can play like that without touching an instrument for more than a decade?" He looked at her incredulously. He'd never looked at her like that before.

"Believe what you want to believe. I'm telling you the truth." The therapist part of Emily recognized that the trust in their relationship was now broken and needed to be repaired, but she responded before thinking about whether it was the right thing to say.

"I hate that I don't believe you," Ezra said. "I hate that you made it so I don't believe you."

There was a pause. A moment where they both looked at each other, sized each other up.

"I hate that you don't believe me, either," she said, finally. She didn't want to explain, didn't want to tell him how many times she'd listened to that song and why. How she'd known how to play it years ago, and that she'd been playing it in her mind all afternoon, imagining her hands on the keys again. She knew she should. Still, she'd answered so many of his questions. It was time for him to answer hers.

"What happened to you at work today?" she asked again.

This time Ezra responded. "Malcolm died," he said, flatly. "And his mother blamed me. She was hysterical. Her husband had to hold her back. She—she tried to hit me. She said that I killed him, that if I were a better doctor he would still be alive. It was . . . awful."

"Oh, Ez, I'm so sorry," Emily said. She thought of Malcolm's siblings. She thought of the pain they must be in, that his mother must have been in to act that way. And she thought about Ezra, too, how those words had likely confirmed his own feelings, his own failure. Probably made him feel exposed in front of his colleagues. She wondered when he'd cried. Where he'd been. She wanted to hug him, but he'd wrapped his arms around himself, leaving no room for hers. "I wish you'd told me," she said. "Not just so I would've known what to say to Hala, but so I could help you."

"I didn't want to upset you even more," he said. "You've been so sad."

"Are you saying it's my fault that you didn't tell me?" That was what it sounded like to her. It was her fault when she kept something from him, and now it was her fault when he kept something from her. Emily tried to get him to look at her, but he was still turned toward the window, at the lights shining bright around the edges of Central Park.

"I don't know," Ezra said. "Maybe."

"I can always take on more for you," she said. "And I can't help you if I don't know what's wrong. I can't be there for you."

He turned to her. "I can't either, Emily. We could've talked about what happened in your past, and how it's affecting you now. We could've walked through that together, instead of you reading in bed alone."

Emily felt the heat rising in her cheeks. "I wanted to stay home with you, Ez. I wanted us to walk through this together, but you left. You went to work and you left me alone."

"Em," he said, "I love you, but other people need me, too. Other people like Malcolm. Children who are dying. How can you stop me from helping them?"

Emily took a deep breath. She realized how differently they felt about this, how differently they looked at it. She had to make him understand. "Our baby was dying, too. It died inside me. And then you disappeared. To me, those cells were a child—one who I imagined learning to walk, learning to talk, going to the playground with, taking trick-or-treating on Halloween. That baby was real to me. There isn't a hierarchy of loss, Ezra. You can hurt or not hurt, but don't dismiss my pain."

Ezra stared at her, as if he didn't know where to go from there. As if he were about to dismiss her pain again, and now that she'd told him not to, he had nothing else to say.

She thought about her sister, about her mom, about how their love for her seemed unconditional. She wanted to feel that from Ezra, too.

"Do you really want to know all my secrets?" she asked, part of her aware of what she was doing, that she was saying something she knew would upset him in the hope that he would prove his love was unshakable, that their love was bigger than this.

He stared at her for a moment. "Now that I know there are more, how could I say no?" he asked.

It was Emily's turn to stare out the window into the dark of the night. She pushed forward, not looking her husband in the eye. "My ex-boyfriend, the musician—he wrote a song and it's on the radio. It's called 'Crystal Castle.' It's the one I played tonight."

"I've heard that song before . . . it's about some guy who still loves this woman who . . . wait . . . is it about you?"

Emily shrugged. "I don't know."

"You don't know?" His voice cracked on the last word.

She shook her head. But then she said, "I think it probably is." She hoped he would rise above whatever pain those words caused, would stay through the pain, get through it together.

Ezra stared at her for a long moment and then got up and went into the bathroom. Emily stayed seated on the settee next to the bed. She felt somehow like the air in the room had changed, like it had gotten colder. There was a feeling in the atmosphere she'd never felt when she was with Ezra. She sat, still in her heels, not changing out of her gown, waiting for him to come back, to say something to her.

Ezra came out of the bathroom with his face washed, drops of water still sparkling on his hairline. "I think I need a night to my-self," he said. "I'll just go home."

"What does that mean?" Emily asked. Had she gone too far? Shared too much? Was his love for her completely conditional?

"Just what I said it means. I need some time alone. I just . . . I need to process what happened tonight. It's been a really long day. On top of a really long week. I just . . . need space."

Emily looked at Ezra. He seemed so beaten down. So tired. She'd seen him like this before, when he'd gotten into an argu-ment with his father, when funding he applied for didn't come through, when he made a choice for a patient that didn't work out the way he'd thought it would. She'd learned to let him be. But it had never been about her before. They'd never gotten into an ar-gument that made him look like this in all the time they'd been together. And while she'd been fine giving him space to process when the problem wasn't about her, it didn't feel fine now. She'd just told him how alone she'd felt, how lonely. "You can't keep running away," she said. "When things get hard, you can't just leave."

"I'm not leaving," Ezra said. "I'm just . . . breathing. I can't breathe with you here. I can't think."

Emily took a few deep breaths of her own, slowing her heart rate. No matter how disappointed she was in him, she knew he needed to come to conclusions himself. To figure himself out.

And she needed to let him. "Then you stay," she said, standing and picking up her duffel bag. "I'll go home."

"Are you sure?" he asked.

"Positive," she told him, slinging the bag over her shoulder. "Should I expect you home in the morning?"

"I think I should probably still grab breakfast with my parents," Ezra said. "I'll go straight to work after that."

"Okay," Emily said again, realizing she had just been disinvited to breakfast. She walked to the door. "I'll see you after work, then."

"I'll call," he said, as he walked with her.

After she left, she heard him slide the dead bolt.

And she turned and went home by herself.

XX

YOUR DAD STARTED *touring with a band that summer. Not ours but a new one he joined. I heard they were playing all over the country, but I never saw them.*

He invited me to one of the shows. Sent me passes to go backstage. But I couldn't. I didn't. I was too depressed. Spinning too quickly into a whirlwind of regret and despair that I couldn't pull myself out of.

I haven't seen him since he graduated.

I changed my email address so he couldn't find me again.

But I think about him all the time.

25

EMILY GOT OUT of the cab and walked into their empty apartment. It was warm and smelled faintly of Ezra's cologne. She kicked off her heels and opened up the window, letting the breeze cool the room; when it did, it swept the cologne out into the night.

Emily slid down onto the living room couch. She felt raw, like she'd tumbled off a bicycle, scraped the skin from her knees and hands, except it was her heart that had been scraped bloody. Dr. West had once told her that when you let yourself love someone, you give them the power to hurt you. It was why she hadn't let herself love anyone for so long. But now she loved Ezra, she loved him deeply, and he'd hurt her deeply. But she'd hurt him, too. She knew that. She both was and wasn't looking forward to him being home tomorrow night. They needed to talk, they needed to work through this, but she knew it wouldn't be easy for either one of them.

With a sigh, Emily picked up her phone to text him good night but thought better of it. She'd give him the night to himself. She'd text him tomorrow. Instead, she decided she should probably try to sleep. It was late, and she needed to function the next day.

But she hated sleeping in their queen-sized bed without Ezra. She felt his absence every time she rolled into the space where he should've been, every time her hand slid onto the cool sheets that should've been warmed by his body. Whenever he was on call, it was only when he crawled into bed at three or four or five in the morning that she relaxed enough to really sleep.

Maybe she'd sleep on the couch tonight.

"Alexa," she said to the circle. "Please play 'Crystal Castle' by Austin Roberts." She needed to hear it again. Was it really about her? Could he possibly still be thinking about her so many years later? She'd imagined he'd moved on quickly, met someone else, met six someone elses. Groupies who followed bands around, who would see him play and then follow *him* around.

Emily listened to the first few bars and then said, "Alexa, where does Austin Roberts live?"

"Los Angeles," the machine said to her.

She was glad it wasn't still New York City.

xxi

EVEN THOUGH IT *was my choice, even though I was the one who finally said we should end things, I missed your father desperately. The idea of never having him in my life again, never having his music in my life again, was so overwhelming that some days I couldn't get out of bed. Some days I couldn't bring myself to eat. Or when I did, the food seemed to turn rancid in my throat, making me gag.*

I couldn't listen to music. I couldn't play. I kept thinking about how lonely I was. How I felt like a puzzle with a whole chunk of pieces missing. About how I'd screwed up his life, too. We were going to be Johnny and June Carter Cash. Sonny and Cher. Except then I fucked the whole thing up. A few months after he'd reached out to me, I was tempted to call him, to find him, to tell him I was wrong. But the pain in my hand stopped me. The pain in my heart stopped me, too. As distraught as I was, I knew it would never work.

I didn't bother looking for a summer job, even though I kept my dorm room in the city. I'd saved up enough from the gigs we'd done to float until September, when my dad would help me out again.

Instead, I reread all of the books I'd only had time to skim during the semester: Candide, Pride and Prejudice, Sense and Sensibility, Emma, Wuthering Heights, Don Quixote. *And then the one that always comforted me:* The Red Tent.

Ari was taking classes over the summer in Connecticut, living with Jack, but one Sunday she was in the city for a matinee with some of her friends and came by to surprise me afterward. It was a bad day—actually, a bad week. I hadn't washed my hair in too long, and I was nested in a pile of blankets reading Emma. I'd also probably lost about ten pounds since the last time she saw me. And I didn't have ten pounds to lose.

"Whoa," she said, when I opened the door. "What's going on?"

So I told her, through tears, how sad I was, how much I missed Rob, how much I missed playing music, how much my hand hurt, how I worried that I'd messed up Rob's life by breaking up the band, and how guilty I felt about you. How Rob didn't even believe you existed, but I knew. I knew you did. And I knew it was my fault that you were gone. Everything was my fault.

"I love you so much," my sister said to me, as she wrapped me in her arms, "and I wish I could fix all of this."

"But you can't," I said.

She shook her head. "But I can find you someone who can help."

That's what my sister—your aunt—is like. She always wants to help and is one of the few people who is smart enough to know when she can't, and instead finds you someone who can.

The person Ari found me was Dr. West. And I truly do think Dr. West saved my life. Or at least helped me build it into something new, something meaningful, something I could be proud of.

She helped me become a person I could be proud of.

26

THAT NIGHT, BEFORE Emily went to bed, she decided she was going to go back to work tomorrow, Friday. So she made herself a list. It was something Dr. West had taught her. Something she did with her own patients now. It made things less overwhelming to break them down into small chunks, to be able to cross things off a list. And she wanted to be okay tomorrow. She wanted to go to work, like Ezra had suggested, to help someone. And then she'd see him afterward, for dinner, when his day was over, and they'd talk. They'd fix things, the way they always did for other people, only now it would be for each other. It would be hard, but they'd do it. And then when she reached over at night, she'd find him next to her in bed and be comforted. They'd be Emily and Ezra, for better or for worse, for now and forever.

1. *Shower*
2. *Get dressed*
3. *Eat breakfast*
4. *Go to work*
5. *Eat lunch*
6. *Go home*

7. *Make dinner for Ezra*
8. *Talk to Ezra over dinner*
9. *Go to bed*

Nine things. All she'd have to do tomorrow was nine things. She could handle that.

27

WHEN EMILY GOT to work the next day, Priya was waiting in her office with a yogurt and granola parfait and a cinnamon latte, Emily's breakfast of choice when she was being indulgent.

"How are you doing?" Priya asked as she handed them over.

Emily took a shaky breath, surprised by the gesture. "I'm doing better," she said, her voice wobbling, and then added: "Even if it doesn't sound that way."

Priya put her hand around Emily's shoulders. "I'm sorry," she said. "It sucks."

Emily started to laugh, which stopped the tears that were threatening to fall. "Says the psychologist."

"Says the psychologist," Priya agreed. "You know, I used to try to reason things away. I'd tell myself, well, it's not as bad as being tortured as a prisoner of war, or starving to death, or dying painfully of a completely preventable disease in a remote village without modern medicine. And that's true. But also, it doesn't take away from the fact that some things just suck. What was it you said a couple of weeks ago in our consultation group? 'Sometimes shit is just shit'?"

Emily smiled at her. "This is one of those times."

Priya turned so she was facing Emily. "I know you don't love the idea of something shitty making you stronger, so I'll just say: Don't forget that not everything is shitty."

Dr. West had said that, too, when Emily was twenty. She acknowledged that sometimes you get dealt a crappy hand. And there was no reason for it. And accepting that is important. But then she told Emily that sometimes it helps to look at the parts of life that don't suck. Because even if your hand is crappy, you always have at least a few good cards.

"Like what?" Emily had asked her back then, the first time they met.

"You tell me," Dr. West had said. "What in your life isn't terrible right now? What's one of your good cards?"

It hadn't taken Emily long. "My sister loves me and is really supportive."

"Great," Dr. West had said. "What else?"

"Except for my hand hurting, I'm healthy," Emily had said.

"And?" Dr. West prompted her.

"And my dad has enough money to help me pay for school. And I managed to get a 3.6 this past semester. And I really liked reading the books for the literature classes I was in. And I have somewhere nice to stay for the summer. And I have enough money from gigs to pay for it. And . . ."

Dr. West had let her continue. She'd gone on, eventually listing things like: "Chocolate exists in the world and I get to eat it" and "New York has four seasons and they're all beautiful in different ways."

"How are you feeling?" Dr. West had said, when Emily had exhausted all the things that were good in her life.

"A little better," Emily had admitted.

That didn't fix anything, of course, and she still had to wade her way through her emotions, detangling them and unwrapping them, before letting them coil back up, neater than they were before. But it was a life preserver, that list, something to hang on to when she felt like she was about to go under.

"You know," Priya said, "I had a miscarriage four years ago, just before I started working here. The year before we had Anika."

"I'm so sorry," Emily said, moving closer to her.

"It was scary," Priya said, twisting the bracelets on her wrist. "I took misoprostol, that pill that's supposed to make it happen faster. The cramping was so bad. And the blood. Neel wanted to take me to the emergency room."

"No one talks about it," Emily said. "Or if they do, it's in whispers. And they leave out the details."

Priya slid her bracelets off her wrist and then back on again. "It's hard. To talk about. To go through."

"Is it still hard?" Emily asked, hoping her friend would give her a road map, a course to follow so she would know how she'd feel next.

"It is," Priya said slowly. "But then sometimes I look at Anika and I think—if I'd had that baby, I wouldn't have had her. And . . ." Her voice drifted off.

"Does that make it easier, or harder?" Emily asked.

Priya looked up at her. "Both," she said. "But truly, once I had Anika, once she got older, I stopped thinking about it as much."

She picked up her coffee cup from the table in front of the couch and took a sip.

"Thank you for telling me," Emily said.

"I do still think, sometimes, about how old that child would be now and whether—" There was a commotion outside in the waiting area, students coming in, saying hello, taking granola bars. Priya looked at her watch. "Maybe a conversation for another time?" she said. "We both have patients soon, and I should go, but please come talk to me whenever you need to. I think one of the hardest things was how taboo the subject seemed to be. How it seemed shameful to share my pain. So . . . come talk if you need to. You're not alone."

"Thank you," Emily said, her eyes tearing up again.

She and Priya hugged, and then Emily locked her emotions away so she could talk to her first patient of the morning. Shower, Get Dressed, Eat Breakfast, Go to Work. Four down, five to go. And she'd see Ezra, and they'd talk and fix things and everything would be better. She could handle it. She could handle it all.

xxii

THAT FALL, I *went back to school with a renewed purpose. I wanted to be a therapist. I wanted to help people the way Dr. West was helping me. I thought maybe if I did, everything that happened would make sense. It would be like my mom said—things happen the way they're supposed to, and I was supposed to help people. It felt good to think that way.*

28

TESSA CAME INTO Emily's office that afternoon.

"How's it going?" Emily asked her.

Tessa closed her eyes briefly before opening them again. "How often do you think is too often to leave your kid with a babysitter?"

"Do you think you're leaving Zoe with a babysitter too often?" Emily asked back.

Tessa shrugged. "Chris and I hadn't been going out at all, as a couple, you know. And I thought maybe if I went out with him more on the weekends, it might be good for us. But the stuff he's doing—day drinking at a ball game, going out with his coworkers to a rooftop bar—it's not stuff we can bring Zoe to, or we could, but it would change the vibe and we'd probably have to leave early and Chris would hate that, or he'd tell me to leave with her and he'd stay, and I didn't want that, either. So now she's with a babysitter for at least some part of every day. And I feel like I'm . . . I'm choosing Chris over her. Is that terrible? Am I terrible?"

Emily felt a surge of envy and reminded herself to take a deep breath. "I think Chris is pressuring you to make a choice that puts you in a terrible position." She tried to keep her own feelings neutral. She wanted to help Tessa, she felt for Tessa. But she was also, she realized, jealous of Tessa, whose body had produced a beautiful baby girl without even trying. "Have you talked to Chris about any of this?"

Tessa nodded. "Sort of. I tried hinting once that maybe he could come home earlier and be with her while I'm studying—I wouldn't feel quite so bad that way—and his suggestion was that we ask one of our moms to keep Tessa until I finished school."

"How did that make you feel?" Emily asked, keeping her face unreadable, even though it felt like a vise was squeezing her heart. Having this conversation with Tessa right now seemed almost cruel.

Tessa pulled the tips of her hair in front of her eyes, examining her split ends. "Like he doesn't really care if she's around. Or maybe worse, doesn't actually want her around. He said it's not true, just that he wants things to be easier for me, but I don't know. It's not like she's a box of sweaters we can leave in my mom's basement. She's an actual person, our *baby*, and it would change her relationship with us if we asked one of our moms to take care of her until May. But I don't want to dismiss his ideas, either." She looked up at Emily. "What do you think?"

Emily smiled slightly, sadly, but didn't say anything. There was a brief silence in the room until: "You want me to figure out what I think," Tessa said.

"You got me," Emily answered. She was glad she'd been able to keep her voice steady when saying that, because all she could think about was the unfairness of it all. That she and Ezra had everything they needed to take care of a baby and they didn't have one, and then here was Tessa whose boyfriend was making it clear that they weren't ready for a baby, and perhaps didn't even really want one but had one regardless.

While Tessa kept talking, Emily wondered if this job made

her take herself out of the equation too often, tamp down her own thoughts and feelings and opinions too much. She was always waiting for other people to decide how they felt, giving them space and helping them figure out their own minds, and ignoring her own. She'd been trained to be objective, to be patient, which were good traits in general, but she wondered if sometimes it put her in a strange role in her marriage. The way she'd been trained to interact bled into her relationship with her husband. It created a situation in which Ezra expected her to be a wife who comforted him, and usually she could be. But sometimes, when she was the one who was hurting, she didn't have the emotional strength to comfort him. She couldn't be anything more than a wounded woman who needed comforting herself.

29

THAT NIGHT, EMILY got home from work and set out all the
ingredients for fresh pesto: basil, pine nuts, olive oil, pecorino,
garlic, salt, pepper. Even though she still felt raw and wounded,
she wanted to make an effort. She looked at the pasta maker, wondering if she had time to hand-make pasta.

It was already six, so she decided to go with boxed fusilli, and
put water on the stove to boil. She texted Ezra: Hope your day
went well. What time will you be home?

She picked the smallest leaves off the basil so the pesto wouldn't
taste too minty and put them in the mortar and pestle they'd gotten for their wedding.

So sorry, Em. Hala just asked if I could take her call tonight—
her brother flew in to surprise her for her birthday. So I said
yes. Her night call goes straight into my call tomorrow, so it
looks like I'll be sleeping here tonight. Really sorry. See you
tomorrow.

Emily let out a breath, as if she'd actually been punched in the
gut. She wanted to talk to him. If he didn't come home, they
couldn't work through things, get their relationship back on
track, back to normal. If he didn't come home, that gnawing feeling inside her wouldn't go away, the one that made her feel off

kilter, like her life was sliding sideways. Then another text came through: I'm still trying to wrap my mind around everything, still thinking about us. This wasn't just about him doing a favor for Hala.

Emily stared at the texts. She'd really hurt Ezra—perhaps more than she'd realized. More than he'd hurt her, it seemed. She put the phone's cursor in the response box. She didn't particularly want to apologize—and honestly, she wanted him to apologize for not being there for her, for not telling her about Malcolm's death—but she would if it helped get him home, if it made him process all of this more quickly.

I'm so sorry I hurt you, she wrote. I just never thought those stories about my past would matter. What matters is now, what we have together. The past is the past. I was a different person then.

It felt like that. Like there was one Emily in college, and another one now. There were attributes they shared, but they were two different people. They made different choices, had different passions.

Emily typed again. I love you.

Then she stared at her phone, waiting for those three dots.

He didn't respond.

Which usually meant that some code had gone off in the hospital and he was rushing to a patient's bedside. But she wondered now if that was actually the truth.

30

EMILY WASN'T PARTICULARLY hungry after that exchange, so she turned off the boiling water and abandoned her pesto preparation. Instead of eating dinner, she poured herself a glass of wine and found her battered copy of *Anne of Green Gables*. She wanted something without any real romance. By chapter four, she was feeling better. By chapter five, she'd refilled her wineglass. And again at chapter ten. Once more at chapter fifteen. By chapter seventeen, she was having trouble focusing on the words.

If Ezra were home, she would curl up against him on the couch. If he were home, she wouldn't have had nearly an entire bottle of wine all on her own. If he were home, she would've eaten dinner. She looked at her list again. Even without Ezra there, she should eat dinner. She could eat dinner.

Emily got up and went into the kitchen. She pulled out the end of a baguette from the bread box and some cheese from the refrigerator and ate them both while looking into the bonus room. It was still a mess. She should clean it out, since she was home alone and it was barely eight p.m. What even was in there?

She hated the quiet of the apartment, so by force of habit she asked Alexa to play some jazz but then realized that was what Ezra liked best, not her, so she switched it to pop as she walked into the tiny, cluttered room. This was a good project for the night. She could feel accomplished, get something done.

Emily piled the items they'd gotten on their most recent trip to Costco in one corner, and already it looked neater. Then she found boxes of Ezra's medical journals and her notebooks from her PsyD program and separated them into their own piles. She'd get some pretty boxes for them, something she could stack in the living room as an end table or something. There were some winter clothes in a big garbage bag, which Emily brought to the front door to donate to Goodwill the next day. She'd been meaning to do that for the last eight months, but somehow when things got put in that room, they stayed there, in limbo. It was basically purgatory, where objects waited for her or Ezra to send them to their proper place.

Emily checked her phone. Ezra hadn't written her back.

There was a futon in the room that they'd planned to use when guests slept over, but the room had gotten so crapped up that no one had ever slept there. When Ari or her boys stayed the night, they pulled out the couch in the living room instead. Emily knelt down and looked under the futon. She found two wooden paddles and a ball that they'd used to play matkot at the beach over the summer. A Frisbee was there, too, and a croquet set that someone had given them for their wedding, possibly anticipating a move to the suburbs that hadn't yet happened and that Emily hoped never would. There was a long black duffel bag under there, too. Emily tugged on it, immediately realizing what it was: her keyboard. In spite of everything, she'd never been able to get rid of it. When the movers brought it in, she just pointed them to the spot under the futon. Ezra hadn't even seen it.

Emily remembered how it had felt to play at the fund-raiser at the Gregory Hotel—as if something wound tight inside her had loosened, as if she were finally doing the thing her body did best. She took a deep breath and unzipped the black case.

As she looked at the keyboard, memories came rushing back to her: practicing in her dorm room with Rob, performing with him on stage, writing the harmonies to his melodies late into the night. That keyboard had become an extension of who she was back then. It was part of her. But now it wasn't. She should give it away. Someone in their building would probably be thrilled to find it with a *Take me! I'm free!* sign in the laundry room. It might become part of them; it might help them create memories like hers.

She liked that idea.

But maybe she should play it one last time. Emily picked it up out of its case and brought it into the living room, where she propped it up on the dining table. Then she went back for the cords and plugged them all in—the power cord, the damper pedal. She didn't have her amp anymore. There was a pair of headphones she could've plugged in, but she decided against it. Instead, she told Alexa to stop playing Ed Sheeran.

The apartment went silent.

Emily was holding her breath when she flicked the keyboard on, worried all at once that it wouldn't work. But the green light started to glow, and Emily pressed down on middle C. The keyboard was top of the line, with perfectly weighted keys and a beautiful, resonant sound. She ran her fingers up it in a scale, as if she had to wake it up, get the keyboard to clear its throat before she could really start playing.

She tried a few chords. Then found some books to adjust the height of the keyboard. And she began to play. First it was just some arpeggios. Then she fingered the melody of the Ed Sheeran song she'd just turned off. Everyone but Rob had always been impressed by how easily Emily could hear a melody and then play it back afterward. Rob hadn't been impressed because he could do it, too. "I love that you're a member of the club," he'd said, when she'd played a new melody he'd just sung, soon after he'd bought her the keyboard in college.

From Ed Sheeran, she started playing their old medley, the finale of her and Rob's shows, the pièce de résistance, a review in their college paper had called it after going to one of their performances. Emily hadn't thought about that review in years. Had locked it away with the rest of her memories. But now, like the music, which had been living inside her, waiting to be reawakened, it came back. *Rob Barnes and Emily Solomon play music together like it's what they were born to do.*

Emily switched into "Crystal Castle," playing it the way she did at the hospital fund-raiser, emotions channeled through her fingers, her body rising and falling with the melody. When she finished, she was crying. All her feelings about Ezra and her miscarriage, the ones she'd been trying to bury all day, came out, as did the long-hidden ones about giving up music, about losing two loves at once—Rob and her keyboard. It was something she thought she'd made her peace with years ago, but now she realized she hadn't. She'd never forgiven herself for what happened to her hand, for breaking up with him, for breaking up the band. She wondered if Rob had ever forgiven her.

Maybe that was why he wrote the song.

Emily walked over to her laptop on the couch and searched for the Austin Roberts website. She found Rob, staring at her, smiling, light brown stubble on his cheeks and chin, his thick head of hair now peppered with a tiny hint of gray at his temples. She clicked on the word *bio* and started to read.

Austin Roberts has spent the last twelve years composing musical scores for film and television, for which he's been nominated for an Oscar and three Emmys. He lives in Los Angeles with his black lab, Freddie Mercury, and his two young daughters. Austin credits his divorce for his runaway hit, "Crystal Castle": "It made me reevaluate my life," he said, "and think about what could have been. This song is about a woman I loved and remember still. She's the one who got away." Austin will be on tour promoting his new album this fall. Click here for tour dates.

There was too much for Emily to process. Rob had been married. (To whom?) He had two daughters. (How old where they?) He was now divorced. (When did that happen?) And he was still thinking about someone who got away . . . someone who might be her.

Emily took a deep breath and clicked on the link for tour dates. She wasn't prepared to see the black-and-white photo he'd put up on that page: him, on stage at twenty-one, singing to her. Only you couldn't see her face, just her hair, braided in a crown around her head. The caption read: *The one who got away.*

It was her. The song was really about her. No question.

Emily scanned the tour stops. He had started in Los Angeles, then he'd gone to Oakland, to Portland, to Seattle, to Chicago, to Kansas City, to Austin, to Atlanta . . . she kept scanning the list. This was a huge tour—but his song was huge, too. It was everywhere—playing on the radio in the grocery store, Duane Reade, the deli. He must be filling venues all over the country with the play it was getting.

Where was he now?

When she found the day's date, she sucked in her breath. He was there. In New York City. Playing that night at City Winery.

She had to go.

She couldn't go.

Could she?

xxiii

I'D BEEN SEEING *Dr. West for six months, crying in her office about you, about your dad, about my mom, about all the things that would never be, could never be, when she suggested I start a journal. I could write it to someone I missed—maybe to my mother, she suggested—and tell my story, get everything out, get it all down, how I felt, what I thought, and in doing so, I could figure out a way to keep my whole life moving forward. I bought a notebook thinking I would write to my mom, but instead, once I sat down, I started writing to you. I'm still not sure why. But it has helped. It really has.*

Though I guess this is as much for me as it is for anyone. In some ways, I've been writing to myself, telling myself my story, looking at the details and making sense of them through a lens of distance and time. That probably was Dr. West's intent all along.

Now I only dream about your father sometimes, instead of every night. And I dream about you even less. I cringe to write that, but it's true. I didn't think I'd feel guilty for healing. But I guess, in some ways, I do.

31

EMILY STARED AT the computer screen. The show was starting in half an hour. Maybe she could go, stand in the back, leave before it was over. He'd never know she was there. She'd get to see him perform, get to hear him, and then, her curiosity satisfied, she could go.

And if it was too hard, if it made her think too much about the life she didn't lead, she could leave even earlier. After one song. That would be fine, too.

Emily made a deal with herself. She'd call the box office for tickets and if one was available, she would go. Put it in the hands of the universe. Her mom's voice popped into her mind then: *Everything happens the way it's supposed to happen.* She'd see if this was meant to happen.

As she called, she wasn't sure what she wanted the outcome to be. Would she regret it if she didn't go? Regret it if she did?

"I'd like a bar stool ticket to Austin Roberts's show tonight," she said. "If there are any still available."

"You're in luck," the woman on the other end of the line said. "We've got two left."

"I only need one," Emily replied, and gave her name and her credit card information.

The universe had wanted it to happen.

She got up from the couch, her mind still round around the

edges from the bottle of wine. She chugged a glass of water. Was she really going to do this? She should tell Ezra. But he still hadn't responded to her last text. She pulled out her phone: I'm going to listen to some live music tonight. Just wanted to let you know, she typed. Hope everything's okay over there. If he asked who was playing, she'd tell him. If he didn't, she wouldn't.

This was the kind of logic that had gotten her into this position, but the idea of telling him now, over text, seemed like a bad one.

For a moment Emily thought: *If I can't tell my husband what I'm doing over text, maybe that means I shouldn't do it.*

But then he responded with a K. Not even a *have fun* or *are you going with some friends?* And she thought: *Screw it. I'm doing this.*

A few seconds later another text came through with Love you, too. He'd finally read her earlier message. Finally responded. Why did he wait so long? Maybe it was on purpose. Or maybe work was just chaotic. It was hard to know with him. Usually, she didn't question it, but now it was so difficult not to.

Emily walked to the mirror in her bedroom. She looked responsible, respectable, like a working professional, in a pair of black slacks, ballet flats, and a patterned silk blouse. Nothing like the queen she was in college, with her tight pleather pants and heels. Her hair had been twisted up into a chignon and clipped in place all day, but now it was coming undone. She unclasped the clip and let her hair fall in waves to her shoulders. She looked at herself the way Rob might, if he saw her. She looked older, for sure, tired, sad. She shook her head. Well, it was a good thing he wouldn't see her.

She slipped on her suede jacket—a subdued one, not like the leather moto jacket she used to wear—and headed for City Winery.

32

EMILY GOT THERE a little late, and Rob was already on stage. The room felt electric as she entered it; he'd already worked his magic and had the audience mesmerized. Her ticket was for a bar stool in the back, so she turned and walked toward the bar, glad the house lights hadn't been completely dimmed.

She took off her suede jacket and folded it across her lap, then faced the stage. She couldn't believe it was really him. His voice was slightly deeper, more resonant than she remembered. He was telling a story about getting to town and walking by some of his old favorite haunts. "All y'all know this Texas boy went to college in New York City," he said, and the audience cheered and clapped their approval.

He'd deepened his Texas drawl, changed the structure of his sentences, she realized. He was exaggerating himself, creating a persona for the crowd. Or maybe that was who he was now and it wasn't put on at all.

"I don't know if y'all have heard the rumors, but I'm here to say they're true. It was a New York gal who broke my heart all those years ago and inspired my hit song."

"They're brutal, man!" someone in the audience shouted.

Emily caught her breath. Had she been brutal? Perhaps she had.

Rob looked like he was scanning the audience for something, someone. He stopped moving when he was facing her directly.

"Queenie?" he said into the microphone, his voice filled with disbelief. "Is that you back there by the bar?"

Emily looked up at the stage. Someone on the light board had found her and focused the spot on her. It shone bright in her eyes, and she tried to shade them with her hand. She couldn't see Rob anymore, but she knew where he was, of course. Her heart pounding, she gave a small wave toward the stage. The spot dimmed and she could see again. In the half-lit theater, everyone was staring at her.

Rob turned to the audience. She had no idea what he was going to say. Her pulse raced.

"An old college friend of mine came to watch me play tonight," he said. "I can't tell y'all how glad I am to see her."

Emily could feel herself blushing. She dipped her head as the audience clapped, grateful she'd left her hair down so it could swing in front of her face. Grateful, too, that Rob didn't out her as the woman who broke his heart. The brutal one. Though she wondered if the audience was putting it together. Or at least turning the question over in their minds.

"Queenie, don't you go walking out of here without saying hello to me after the show," he said from the stage as Emily readjusted herself on her bar stool.

She lifted her hand in acquiescence.

He had just changed her plans entirely. No more sneaking in and out and satisfying her curiosity. She tried to calm herself, get her sweaty palms to cool. It would be fine. They'd say hello, and then she'd go home. Maybe more than fine.

She took a deep breath and got lost in Rob's music, in his voice, and rode on the wave of his energy, just like she used to. Then she was remembering him backstage after shows, high on adrenaline. Magnetic. Powerful. And all of a sudden there was a pit in her stomach. What would it be like to see him again? How would she feel? Would it expose cracks in herself she didn't even know were there?

33

WHEN THE SHOW ended, a woman dressed all in black came over to Emily and invited her backstage.

"It's okay," Emily said. "I can wait for him out here." She was trying to keep her distance. Trying not to get too swept up in the drama of the evening, the choreography of the night. She could wait here, with easy access to the door.

"Are you sure?" the woman asked. "He really wants to see you."

"I know," Emily said. "I promise I won't go anywhere."

SHE SAT AT the bar drinking a club soda, wondering if she *should* go, despite her promise. If she should leave before she saw him. There was so much between them that she'd buried in her journal, so many healed-over wounds that she didn't want to open up again. But he'd written a song about her. And she'd promised she'd stay. And she should at least tell him how much she enjoyed his show. Plus she was curious. *Curiosity killed the cat,* her father used to say. But her mother would shush him. *Curious people are the most interesting,* she'd say. Emily hadn't been curious about much in the last few years, but she was curious about Rob. About what he wanted to say to her.

She was playing with the straw in her soda when she heard his voice, deep and warm, behind her. "You're still here," he said. He'd dropped the drawl. Sounded more like himself.

She turned around. "I'm still here."

His face had aged like hers had—more visibly in person than on the headshot on his website—and he carried sadness in his eyes, too.

He pulled her in for a hug, and it took everything she had not to rest her head against his shoulder before pulling away. He smelled exactly the way he used to. Pine-scented soap mixed with hair pomade and something else that was entirely him. The scent transported her into her former self, into an overwhelming rush of memories. She focused on the now.

"I've been scouring the internet for you," he said, looking at her as if she were a mirage, about to disappear when he blinked. "But I couldn't find anything more recent than two and a half years ago. At every show I've played, I've been wondering if you would walk through the door, wondering if you'd heard the song, and if you had, if you'd known it was about you. That's why I asked them to keep the house lights up, so I could scan the audience for you."

Emily's palms felt clammy. She hadn't expected that he'd be so honest, so direct.

"How could I not know it was about me?" she said, refamiliarizing herself with his easy smile, with the width of his shoulders, the jut of his chin. It felt surreal to be there, like she'd woken up inside a dream, like she was in an alternate version of time, where things had gone differently, where they'd always known each other, never been apart.

"You look like you but grown up," he said, not taking his eyes off her. "Not quite as I imagined, but close."

"You too," Emily said, though until recently, she hadn't really imagined him at all. She'd managed to keep him out of her head, out of her heart, for so long, but now that he was in front of her, all of those feelings came sliding back. The longing, the guilt, the passion—not just for him, but for everything. For life.

"Can I treat you to a drink?" he asked her, not taking his eyes from her face.

Emily glanced down at her phone, where she'd left it on the bar. Nothing new from Ezra. He hadn't changed his mind and decided to come home.

"How about a coffee?" she said. "I'm not used to these late nights anymore."

Rob laughed, a sound she had forgotten, but that, once she heard it, felt as familiar as if they'd laughed together that morning.

"Coffee it is," he said. "Let's find ourselves a diner nearby."

They'd eaten in so many diners back then. All over the city. The one they called the Disco Diner that played disco music and served French fries covered in melted cheese and gravy. The one they called the Pie Diner, because once a guy had walked in who seemed totally high on something and ordered six pieces of cherry pie and proceeded to eat all of them, while Rob and Emily watched in awe.

"Sounds good," Emily told him, still in shock that this was happening, that she was there with him, that he'd written a song about her, that she'd just watched him perform it, that she agreed to get coffee with him, that they were both slipping into the rhythm they shared more than a decade ago.

The two of them walked out into the New York City night, and it felt like she was reconnecting not only with Rob but with who she had been when they were together.

xxiv

IT'S BEEN A *while since I've written in here. I feel like I'm getting further and further away from the person I was when you were inside me. I'm healing the wounds that made that version of me the broken woman she became. But I'm afraid I'm losing some of the good things, too, some of the things I liked about myself then.*

And I still can't bring myself to play the piano.

34

ROB AND EMILY were sitting in the diner they found on Waverly—one of the few places still open at one a.m. that wasn't a bar. Emily had ordered a coffee and a corn muffin. Rob had gotten the works—scrambled eggs, toast, bacon, hash browns, orange juice, and coffee.

"I'm always starving after I perform," he said, after the waiter walked away.

He was saying it like this was new information, but it wasn't. Not to Emily.

"Because you're too hyped up to eat beforehand," she said.

Rob's face lit up. "You remember."

"Of course I do," Emily said. "So tell me about you. What have you been up to?"

This was all so bizarre. For a brief moment, Emily wondered if maybe she was in some sort of medically induced coma and living another life while she was asleep. She kept looking at him and then looking down at her wedding band, as if her brain couldn't quite process how he and Ezra existed in the same space-time continuum.

Their coffees arrived and Rob took a sip. "I've been writing film scores out in LA for the last twelve years. After a year on the road, I don't know, it wasn't doing it for me. If I'm honest, I think

I'd so clearly imagined you and me on the road together, that anything else seemed . . . kind of a letdown of sorts, I guess. And James, you remember James?"

Emily nodded. Rob's friend. Their bass player.

"He was doing some sound engineering out in Hollywood and this guy he was working with died in the middle of scoring a small indie film—no joke, I think it was a heart attack or something—and he recommended me. So I wrote some music in a pinch, and it turned out I wasn't bad at the whole movie scoring thing, so I stayed. I got nominated for an Oscar and three Emmys, but I haven't won. Yet."

Emily laughed. "Yet, huh," she said. A piece of the guilt she'd been feeling for the past thirteen years dissipated. She hadn't ruined his life by breaking up the band, by leaving him and their budding music career. "It sounds like you've been doing really well. I'm happy for you."

Rob grinned. "Yeah, it's been good."

"I got married, too," he added, as their food arrived. "Corinne, an actress who never quite acted in anything substantial. The more successful I got, the worse our marriage got. It ended up being real shit, but we don't need to get into that now. She and I divorced last year—probably should've done it sooner. But we made two of the best kids on the planet. Samantha and Melanie. They're eight and six. They sing together all the time, and they're good, Queen, they're really good. Sam just figured out harmony, and I'm telling you, these kids could book gigs, if I let them make a demo."

Emily had wondered, back then, what Rob would be like as a father. And now she knew. He was just as over-the-top in love with his daughters as he was with music, as he had been with her. It seemed like no matter what he loved, he loved it hard.

Before Emily could respond, Rob had pulled up a video on his phone and passed it over to her. "Listen to them," he said. "They're going through an *Aladdin* phase."

Emily hit play and two girls with matching aqua-colored eyes and polka-dot bathing suits sat on a lounge chair in front of a swimming pool, holding hands and singing "A Whole New World." Their connection reminded Emily of her and Ari. And Rob was right, they really could sing. And the little one had his stage presence, her face as animated as the original cartoon.

"They're great," Emily said when the song finished, and she handed his phone back.

"My best creations," he said.

Emily couldn't help but think about what the baby they'd created would have been like. Was it a girl? Would she have been able to sing like that, too?

"How about you?" Rob asked.

Emily pushed down her thoughts. "I'm married, too. Ezra's a doctor. No kids yet." Her voice caught on the last sentence.

"Hey," Rob said. "You okay?"

Emily wiped the corner of her eye. "I had a miscarriage earlier this week," she said, surprised that she'd said it but then immediately not surprised. There was still such an easy intimacy between them. And they'd been through so much together.

"Oh, I'm so sorry," Rob said. He walked over from his side of the table to envelop her in another hug, this one tighter than the last. Emily pulled strength from it. It felt so good to have a pair of arms around her.

"Thanks," she said, her mouth next to his ear. She could feel his hair flutter against her cheek.

"I'm a therapist now," she added, ending the hug, leaning back slightly. "I have a doctorate in psychology."

"Dr. Queenie," he said, with a smile. "I found a paper you wrote with some other people about—what was it? Social—"

"Social cognition in college students," she supplied.

"Interesting focus." He took a sip of coffee, looking at her over the rim of the mug.

She laughed. "I guess so."

Emily cut her corn muffin in half and lightly buttered one side.

"Remember . . ." Rob said, and then let his voice trail off.

"Remember what?" Emily asked, picking up her corn muffin.

"Remember when we went to that clinic before . . ."

"Yeah," Emily said. How could she forget?

Rob drank some of his juice while Emily realized how his brain had gone from her recent miscarriage to them, back in college, talking about pregnancy and babies. "There's a clinic like that not far from where I live, and years ago I asked them to give me a call whenever protesters show up. If I'm around, I head over with my guitar and my amp and I play so damn loud that the women can't hear what the protesters are saying. It doesn't help the signs, but . . ." He shrugged.

In the shrug, in the story, Emily saw the man she loved thirteen years ago. And she realized that their shared experience affected him, too. Maybe not to the degree that it affected her, maybe not the same way, but it changed him, too. It changed how he thought. It changed how he acted.

"That's the best story I've heard in a long time," she told him.

They finished eating soon after that, and Emily took out her wallet.

"Please, let me," he said, laying a twenty on the table. "You hardly ordered anything. Plus you inspired my hit single, so the least I can do is thank you with a corn muffin and a coffee."

Emily was going to protest, but instead simply said, "Thank you."

As the waiter came to pick up the cash, Rob said, "So can I invite you and your husband out tomorrow night? My guests? It's a secret, but I'm going to show up at an open mic night at Tony's bar in New Jersey."

"Tony our old drummer?" Emily asked.

Rob nodded. "Yeah, he's got a kick-ass bar in Hoboken. And he made me promise I'd come by once he heard I'd be in town. I told my manager I needed another day here, and he worked it all out."

"Huh," Emily said. She really had never wondered what those guys had gotten up to. A deplorable lack of curiosity on her part. Or perhaps a defense mechanism. A form of self-preservation.

"I've gotta confess, I have an ulterior motive," Rob said. "I'm not sure how many people will come and want to play. So I'm hoping I can convince you to get up there. You still play, right? You writing your own stuff yet?"

Emily felt bad admitting that she didn't, that she hadn't. Though she had played last night at the fund-raiser. So she settled on, "I don't play often. And I told you I'm not a songwriter."

He laughed at their longstanding argument. He'd always said that one day she'd write something herself, instead of just harmonizing his songs. "Well, think about it," he said. "It'd be fun to hear you play again, even if it's not your own stuff. And I'd love to meet your husband."

When he said it, he genuinely seemed to mean it, but Emily wondered what it would be like for him to see her with someone else, especially after he'd just gotten divorced. Even though she was the one who ended things years ago, and even though she knew his marriage was over, she still felt a pang of jealousy that he'd loved someone else enough to marry her, to have kids with her. She knew she had no right to be jealous, but the feeling was there.

"I'll talk to him," Emily said, knowing that after their argument last night there was close to no chance that he'd agree to come. Or that she'd even ask. Once he got home tomorrow night, hopefully they'd be able to talk. Put things back to normal. She missed him.

"He must be on call tonight?" Rob asked.

Emily nodded. "Life of a doctor's wife," she answered.

Rob stood up. "Here," he said, "why don't I give you my cell number. Then you can let me know whether to expect you two."

Emily hesitated for a moment. She shouldn't have his number in her phone. It would be too easy for an innocent text to turn into something more. But it seemed rude not to give him the phone—and like it would telegraph the message that he meant more to her than he did. Besides, she could always delete the number after she told him they weren't going to make it tomorrow. She handed him her phone so he could type in his number.

As he was typing, a text message chimed.

Rob looked up. "Ezra said his parents need help moving some furniture in their house, so he's going to go home with them tomorrow and spend Sunday in Princeton. He'll be home on Monday after work and you can talk then."

"Oh," Emily said, not finding a better word than that. Not wanting to explain what they were going to talk about or why her husband was texting her that information.

"So, I guess tomorrow night's invitation is just for you, then," he added, looking like he wanted to say something more but held himself back.

"I guess so," Emily answered.

Rob handed her back her phone. She could feel the tension rising between them.

"You know how my mom always said things will be okay in the end?"

Emily nodded.

"Well, if things aren't okay, it's not the end. For you, either." He looked at her meaningfully.

Emily knew what he was dancing around, what he was trying to say. And if she were smart, she would tell him that everything was fine. But that would feel like a lie. And he'd know it. So instead she said, "Thank you."

"Let me know about tomorrow night, okay?" he said.

"I will," she told him. "And . . . if I don't make it tomorrow, it was great to see you. Truly."

He bent toward her and hugged her, and held on tight.

She wanted to hold him just as tight.

But she didn't.

XXV

YOUR AUNT ARI *got married today. I keep thinking that you would've been five years old. You could've been the flower girl or the ring bearer. You would've been dressed up fancy, pink-cheeked and smiling in the photos. Or maybe you would've been scared, hiding behind my leg or clinging to my skirt. Ari's husband, Jack, has a sister with two kids, and seeing them run around—I haven't thought about you this much in years. It was like you were at that wedding with me, in my heart, in my mind.*

I wish your grandma could've been there. Ari asked me to walk her down the aisle along with our dad. She said that since we were such a team, it wouldn't feel right for me to walk with someone else on her wedding day. So she had one of us on each side. When we got up to the front of the aisle, and we walked ahead of her underneath the chuppah, Jack whispered to me: "I promise you I'll never get between you and your sister. She loves you so much."

"She loves you, too, Jack," I told him. "And I'm so happy to have a brother."

It would've been nice to have a date to their wedding, but I haven't dated anyone since your dad. I kept telling myself it's because I've been working so hard in school, but the truth is, I've been scared. I'm still scared. So scared that I'll get hurt again. So scared that I'll hurt someone else.

I don't want to spend the rest of my life alone, though, thinking about what might have been. I'd thought I was healed, but I'm not healed enough. I'll get there, though. I will. And when I do, I'm sure I'll imagine you on my wedding day, too, what it would've been like if I'd asked you to walk me down the aisle and stand with me as I brought someone new into our lives.

35

THE NEXT MORNING, Emily headed to the East River path for a run and thought about Ezra. The two of them often ran down the side of Manhattan together, his feet pounding the pavement with slightly longer strides, so she had to turn her legs over faster to keep up. Once they'd gone about four and a half miles down to Battery Park, they'd usually slow down and stop for a smoothie before taking the subway home, dripping sweat but relaxed and happy.

Instead of getting a smoothie after her run, Emily sent Ezra a text: Hope it's not too rough at the hospital. He didn't respond. But, she reasoned, maybe that text didn't invite a response. Or maybe it *was* rough at the hospital and he couldn't text with her just then. That had happened before. But she was feeling so insecure right then that she couldn't stop turning his nonresponse over and over in her mind.

She wished she knew what to do. She wished she knew the right words to say, the right move to make. But the one thing she did know was that if she pushed too hard, he'd just pull away even more, roll himself into a ball like a pangolin and stay that way until he was ready to move forward again, on his own terms and his own time frame, nobody else's. Was he not thinking about how his actions affected Emily? Was she asking for too much right now? She didn't know. All she knew was that she wished she understood what was going through her husband's mind but truly had no idea.

TO DISTRACT HERSELF, Emily called Ari, but her sister didn't pick up. A minute later, her phone lit up with a text: Hi Auntie Em, it's Tyler. Mom wants to know if you're okay, but she's driving so she gave me her phone.

Hey hun, Emily wrote back. I was just calling to see what was going on with you guys today. She'd been hoping maybe she could hang out with them for a while. There were friends she could try, too, but when she was sad or confused or feeling out of sorts, it was still only Ari she wanted to spend time with.

I'm playing travel soccer, came back over the phone, which is why Mom is driving. Then tonight we're going to Sophia's bat mitzvah. From next door. Mom said I can drink as many Roy Rogers as I want.

Sounds fun, Emily wrote back. Good luck at the game. And enjoy the Roy Rogers!

She'd talk to Ari tomorrow. No need to interrupt her crazy day of plans with the story of her meeting last night with Rob. It would keep.

EMILY SHOWERED AND got dressed and then walked into the living room, where the keyboard was still sitting on the dining table. She wasn't planning to go to the open mic in New Jersey, but she liked the idea of playing at one someday. She turned on the keyboard. What would she play for an audience, if she had the chance?

She fingered a few melodies with her right hand. There were some people, like Ezra, who strongly preferred one kind of music over another—he loved jazz and the Beatles; that was pretty much it. Rob had a slight penchant for 1970s British artists, but he was more like she was, appreciating all kinds of music, depending on the mood she was in. But she'd never really had a chance to choose what she'd play herself, she realized. Her piano teacher chose, her mom chose, Rob chose. What would she play, if she could play anything, any genre, any song?

It wasn't just the melody, she realized, or the musicality of the song that pulled her toward one or another, it was the words, too, and how the lyrics and the music played with each other. She fingered some Peter, Paul and Mary—"If I Had a Hammer." There was something about the way those words danced with the song's rhythm that worked so well. The hammering of the guitar.

There were other songs like that. One that she'd loved when she first heard it in high school, even though it was more than ten years old by that point: Tracy Chapman's "Fast Car." The insistent pulsing of it felt like riding in a car, and when Tracy started in with the repetition of the phrase "be someone," it felt like the car was revving its motor, picking up steam. Emily fingered the melody on her keyboard and then started adding in chords with her left hand. Once she had that down, she sang along with the chorus, tentatively at first, and then full out, as if she were on stage. Her voice wasn't as strong as it used to be; there were all those muscles involved in singing that she hadn't been exercising for years. But she wasn't as bad as she thought she'd be, either.

Emily pulled up the lyrics on her phone and rested it on the music stand at the back of the keyboard. They didn't have smartphones like this when she used to play, and it felt funny to see her phone there. It used to be charts that Rob hand-wrote for all of them, his music notes perfect little ovals, something James used to tease him about.

She started singing again, from the top, and lost the next hour to music, the way she used to. She only stopped when her phone rang, and she realized then that she felt a twinge of pain in her hand but not nearly as bad as it used to be—not as bad as she'd assumed it still would be. She saw that Priya was calling and picked up the phone.

"Hey," she said. "What's going on?"

"Just wanted to see how you were doing," Priya said. Emily could hear cars and wind behind Priya's voice. She was probably headed somewhere, walking near the river in Brooklyn Heights, where she lived.

"I'm doing okay," Emily said. "I rediscovered my old keyboard and have been playing all morning." Somehow the music really did feel healing.

"Sounds like a nice morning," Priya said. "I didn't know you played."

"Yeah," Emily said. "I used to perform, but I haven't in a really long time. I've been thinking that maybe I should again. The music feels really good."

"You should!" Priya said. "That would be so much fun. And I'd love to come hear you perform."

"Yeah?" Emily asked. "You'd want to listen?"

Priya laughed. "Of course," she said. "Why not? Were you thinking about playing somewhere special?"

Emily hadn't really been thinking that far ahead, but the answer was easy.

"There are some open mics around the city. Whenever I'm

ready, I'll probably find one of those. An old boyfriend actually invited me to one tonight, but Ezra's out of town and I didn't want to go alone." That wasn't completely the reason she was staying away, she realized, as the words tumbled from her mouth. Even if Ezra *were* in town, she probably wouldn't go. Actually, if Ezra were in town she a hundred percent wouldn't go. Maybe she would've played her music for him. And they would've sung together. And talked everything through. And she wouldn't feel quite so unbalanced. But knowing that didn't change the fact that the more she thought about the open mic night, the more she wanted to go.

"I'll go with you," Priya said, automatically. "Neel can spend the night with Anika. Do some father-daughter bonding."

Emily thought how nice it was that Priya offered. The two of them had met only a few years ago, when Priya came to work at NYU, and they didn't really socialize outside of the office, but maybe because they were in that consultation group with Reuben, their relationship felt deeper than it would appear from the outside.

"I don't know," Emily said. "It's more complicated than I'm making it sound."

"I'm intrigued," Priya said. "And would love to hear more about what that means. But if you want to do it, I can handle complicated. Up to you, of course."

Emily thought about it. If Priya were there with her, it wouldn't be quite as complicated. She could sing "Fast Car," say hi to Rob and Tony, take a step back into music before she convinced herself not to. It would distract her from obsessing over Ezra and his text messages. And she'd get to spend time with Priya, which she always wanted to do more of outside the office anyway.

"Oh hell," Emily said. "Let's do it. It's in Hoboken at eight."

"Let's meet at seven, then," Priya said. "We can take the PATH train together and have time for a drink before things get started. You can fill me in on why you think this is more complicated than you're making it sound."

Part of Emily couldn't believe she was doing this, but another part felt like it was inevitable. Like it was meant to happen.

"That works for me," she said. "I'm looking forward to it."

"Me too," Priya said. "See you later."

Emily clicked to the text messages on her phone. What's the address for tonight? she texted Rob. My friend Priya and I are coming.

That was it. There was no backing down.

XXVi

IT'S BEEN YEARS *since I've written in here, but I was thinking about you today. I started a new job. My very first as a psychologist. After getting my PsyD, after a year of internship, after getting my license, I'll be working at NYU, helping the students there the way that Dr. West helped me. I'm looking forward to it, but I'm—I can't quite figure out the right word. Nervous? Scared? Concerned? Worried? Afraid, maybe. I'm afraid I won't be good enough, I won't help enough, I won't be able to find the right words, ask the right questions to make a real difference. All of a sudden it feels like a lot of pressure, a lot of responsibility.*

And I'm afraid I won't be able to handle listening to some of it. Some of the stories that are the most painful, that expose the basest parts of humanity.

All of this thinking made me wonder how I would've done being your mom. Would I have felt the same fear? The same concern? Would I have messed things up so badly that you'd have had to go see another psychologist to repair everything inside you I broke?

It's such a responsibility.

I wonder if I'll ever have a child, if I'll ever be a mom to anything more than a constellation of cells in my uterus. I honestly think I might not. Ari always knew she wanted to be a mother, but I never felt that way. I still don't. Maybe you're all I'll ever have. Maybe that's how it should be.

36

EMILY LOOKED AT the clothing hanging neatly in her closet, pants with pants, blouses with blouses, skirts with skirts. She'd become such an adult. Initially she'd changed her wardrobe to make sure she looked older than her patients, to make sure they respected her and didn't treat her like just another friend. Soon that look permeated her weekend wardrobe, too. And Ezra liked it—the crepe pants, the silk tops, the tailored skirts. So did she. The clothing made her feel strong, in control, put together, like she always knew what she was doing. But now she wished she still had a pair of leather pants or torn jeans in there.

She took out a pair of regular jeans, the tightest ones she owned, and put them on with a black cami, one she usually wore under a blazer. But she left off the blazer, and added a pair of heels. Then she walked to the bathroom and braided half of her hair into a crown, something she hadn't done in thirteen years. She was a bit more heavy-handed with her makeup than usual. And went to her jewelry box to find a pair of old silver hoop earrings to complete the look. While she was there, she saw the four-leaf clover necklace that Rob had given her years before; she'd never been able to give it away.

Emily looked at herself in the mirror again and smiled. She looked like a musician.

It felt good to be Queenie again.

xxvii

I MET SOMEONE *today, in the elevator at work. I'd seen him around before, but he never noticed me. He never seemed to notice much of anything, he was so absorbed in his own mind.*

It turns out his name is Ezra. Dr. Ezra Gold. And he works in pediatric oncology. When he started talking about his job, all I kept thinking about were the babies who wouldn't make it and how difficult that must be. Every time. I don't know if I'd be strong enough to handle it.

"I'm impressed," I told him, when he told me what he did. "It must be hard."

"You know," he said, "I was just talking to my students about quality of life during illness. And I think that's important in any medical field, but especially when you work with children. If these little people only have three or seven or eleven years on this planet, I want to make sure that the time they spend here is as easy and fun and happy and painless as I can make it."

I think I may have fallen in love with him right then, right there in the elevator. I don't think it was love at first sight, but maybe love at first listen? It's so rare to find someone whose head and heart, whose intelligence and empathy are so connected, so in line with each other.

I told him I'd love to hear more about his job, and he invited me out for lunch.

I haven't ever been this excited about a lunch date.

I haven't been this excited about another human being since I met your dad.

37

EMILY MET PRIYA at the PATH train. Her suede jacket was open over her cami.

"Look at you!" Priya said, when she arrived.

Emily laughed. "Is it too much? Should I tone down the makeup? Take down my hair?"

Priya shook her head. "Not at all, you look great."

As the women sat on the train together, Priya said, "I feel like we're going on an adventure. Crossing state lines."

"It does kind of feel like an adventure." Emily felt almost giddy, happier than she'd been in the five days since she lost the baby, since her fight with Ezra. But still not happy. She thought about the maxi pads she'd stuffed into her purse. She was still bleeding. Her husband was still gone.

"So tell me about this ex-boyfriend business," Priya said. "And why it's so complicated."

The PATH train was jostling them along. Emily took a deep breath. She wasn't completely sure where to start.

"So you know that song 'Crystal Castle' that's been playing everywhere?" she asked.

"Of course," Priya said. "*I built you a castle in my dreams, with something and something and la la la la la la la seems.* That one."

Emily laughed. Rob would crack up if he heard that rendition of the lyrics. "Yeah," she said, "that one. So, it's about me."

"What?!" Priya said, her eyes wide in surprise. "You? How do you know? How do you know that guy?"

"College," Emily said. "We were in a band together and crazy in love."

Priya shook her head. "You contain multitudes," she said.

"Don't we all?" Emily said back.

Priya laughed. "I guess we do. But wait, you were in a band with this guy, what, twelve years ago, and he's still so in love with you that he wrote a song about you? What does Ezra think?"

Emily looked down at her fingernails, at the half-moon crescents at their base. "He hasn't come home since I told him," she said. "First he wanted a night alone, and then he took on an extra overnight call as a favor to a friend, and now he's spending a night with his parents in Princeton to help them move furniture. They all seem reasonable reasons to stay away from home but . . . taken together . . . and after we fought . . . and knowing how Ezra processes things . . ."

"That feels like an overreaction to me," Priya said. "Is this triggering something else? Something from his past?"

"Well," Emily answered, "he didn't know about the band or even that I played piano as well as I do and . . . on top of that I ended up telling him that Rob—I mean Austin Roberts—and I got pregnant in college and I had a miscarriage then, too. I perhaps didn't handle it as well as I could have."

Priya looked at her for a moment. "I'm just your friend right now," she said.

Emily nodded. "You're not a therapist. Just my friend."

Priya smiled. "Okay," she said. "As your friend, I'll say: He's a little old to give someone the silent treatment. I bet he's done things that you don't know about, too. Things he was ashamed to tell you or felt were private."

"That's what I said," Emily told her. "But he was still hurt. And I do understand. But he hurt me, too. He basically walked out on me. I've been grieving our lost child without him. And I get that all of this at once is a lot—a patient of his died a few days after the miscarriage, and the mom blamed him, and then I put him in a bad spot, playing piano at a fund-raiser when he didn't know I could do it, and on top of that he found out things about my past I hadn't shared before—and then I told him how much it hurt me that he wasn't with me more after we lost the baby and that he was dismissing my feelings. It was a bad conversation. And I think you're right—so many of those things are triggers for him. He takes so much on himself, blames himself, hates to disappoint anyone—but I . . . I want him to come home so we can talk it through. We need to be able to make mistakes and hurt each other and then fix it, you know? He can't just run away. Otherwise this marriage will fall apart. We need to be able to come together when things are difficult. To forgive each other and become stronger."

"Like how a bone is stronger after it heals," Priya said, as if it were something she'd thought about before. Emily realized she probably had, if not in her own life, then with her patients.

"Exactly," Emily told her. "Exactly."

Ezra should understand that more than anyone.

"Can you rewind and tell me more about this band, though?" Priya said. "Because I, for one, am intrigued."

And Emily did, talking about the performances, about the songs they used to sing, and remembering how happy she was on stage, how it defined so much of who she was back then. How different she was now.

38

PRIYA AND EMILY walked into the Snare, Tony's bar, the name of which had made Emily laugh. Tony always used to call his snare drum a real boyfriend snare. Whenever he soloed on it during shows, he'd have tons of men trying to buy him a drink afterward, once he'd let their fans know that he was into guys and not girls.

"Which one is he?" Priya whispered, as they walked through the door.

But Emily didn't have to answer. Rob was at the door in a second and a half. "Queenie!" he said, bending in for a hug. "Your hair is back!" He turned to Priya, sticking out his hand. "And you must be Priya; it's so nice to meet you. Do you play, too?"

Priya shook her head. "I wish. I'm just an appreciative audience."

Rob smiled. "Well, I hope we'll give you a show to appreciate tonight."

Emily took him in. He looked pretty much the same as he had the night before, but his energy was different, relaxed and keyed up all at once, like he was really delighting in being in this bar about to perform at an open mic.

"You wanna open the show, Queen?" he asked her.

Emily shook her head. "No chance. How about third?" That felt comfortable to her. She'd realized on the walk to the bar that the last time she'd performed all alone was her piano recital in eighth grade. Throughout college, she'd always been part of the group—either with the whole band, or just with Rob. She didn't want to have to kick things off by herself.

"You got it," Rob said. "Tony's got some friends who can start us off. He and I'll close the show. And we'll see who else we get along the way."

"Sounds good to me," Emily said. She was starting to feel that pre-performance energy. She'd forgotten how it felt—like her whole body was ready, her muscles were alert, her mind was starting to focus. Her blood felt like it was moving through her body faster, oxygenating every part of her, making everything sharper, brighter, louder.

Priya and Emily headed over to the bar, and after they ordered vodka tonics from the bartender, Priya turned to Emily. "Why does he call you Queenie?"

"The first time we met, he called me a crystal queen, and then he wrote a song about me back then called 'Queen of All the Keys.' After that, it stuck for a while. And Queen became Queenie. A nickname of the nickname, I guess." Emily shrugged. She was simultaneously embarrassed by and proud of the name. It was fun to be a queen.

"I'm still not over this," Priya said. "We're in the same room as Austin Roberts. And he hugged you. And shook my hand. And called me by name. This is kind of nuts."

Emily laughed. "He's just a person like everyone else," she said. "I always thought he'd be a star one day."

The two women sat down at a bar table for two as the room started filling up. Word must've gotten around that Rob was there. When the bar was packed to the point that people were lining the walls around the small stage, Tony came by to say hi. Emily wouldn't have recognized him if she'd seen him on the street. In college he had long hair that he'd worn layered and wavy. Now his head was shaved and it seemed like he worked out pretty hard.

"You look great, Tony," she said, when she hugged him.

"You too, Queen," he said, looking at her. "I've always wondered if you'd pop up again. I searched for you every now and then on social media, but I never found you. I did find a lot of other Emily Solomons, though."

"I'm not on it," Emily said. "I'm a psychologist, and I didn't want my patients to be able to find out too much personal information about me."

"Huh," Tony said. "I never would've pegged you as a shrink. Well, I'm glad you popped up tonight. We'll have to get all three of us back together up there. A reunion show minus James."

Emily nodded. "Sure," she said. "I bet I could still follow Rob's lead."

Tony hugged her again. "Really great to see you, Queen," he said.

As he walked away, Priya started laughing. "This Queen business is too much."

Emily laughed, too. "I guess we're all just used to it."

THE SHOW STARTED. One of Tony's friends came out with an acoustic guitar and sang a beautiful rendition of "Fire and Rain." Then another came up, plugged his guitar into the amp, and sang "Bad Moon Rising."

"Meh," Priya whispered to Emily. "The first guy was better."

"Are you covering this for the *Times*?" Emily whispered back.

"Maybe for the *Washington Square News*, if the kids'll accept an article from university staff," she answered.

Emily smiled at her. Then the room started clapping, and it was Emily's turn. She went to the bar's piano and adjusted the microphone.

"Hey," she said, and listened to her voice reverberate through the bar. "I'm Emily Solomon and I'm gonna play some Tracy Chapman for you."

She realized, a second after she said it, that she'd used her maiden name instead of her married one. She hadn't introduced herself as Emily Solomon in years. Consciously made sure she didn't. But being on stage threw her backward, somehow.

She looked out into the crowd. Because of the way the stage lights were set she couldn't really see the audience. She knew where Priya was sitting and could make out her shape, sort of. She knew where Rob and Tony were sitting, too, and turned her head in their direction for a second before she started. She'd practiced enough that she knew the lyrics by heart now, and knew what her fingers needed to do, too.

Emily slipped them onto the keys and began to play the intro before she started in about a fast car and a ticket to anywhere.

SHE THOUGHT ABOUT the words and thought about the time in her life when she felt them acutely. When she wanted out of her house as her mom was dying, when she wanted out of the situation she and Rob had created in college, when she wanted out of dealing with the pain of her miscarriage the week before. Without even thinking about it, she channeled all that emotion into the music, through her fingers, with her voice. When she got toward the end, as she started singing those insistent *be someone*s, she felt that emotion coming back at her from the audience. When Rob played the night before, the room was riding on his energy. Here, the room was riding on her feelings, responding to her heart. She could feel them transfixed by her, no one moving, no one fidgeting.

When the song ended, the piano resonated for a moment, and then everyone began to clap. Rob got to his feet, and then Priya did, too, as Emily said thank you and then walked off the stage, past where Rob was standing. He reached out and touched her arm.

"It's a crime that you're not on stage anymore," he said. "Come tour with me."

Emily's only response was to squeeze his hand, because she knew that if she opened her mouth, there was a good chance she would say yes. She hadn't realized how much it meant to her to play, to share her music with other people, to make that emotional connection. How much she really missed it, really needed it to feel like herself.

"Wow," Priya said, when Emily got back to the table. "You're really good. Like, *really* good. I had no idea you could perform like that."

"It was fun," Emily said. "Want a drink?"

"You really do contain multitudes," Priya replied. "I'll take another vodka tonic."

The women sat together drinking and listening to music, and then it was time for Tony and Rob to close the show.

"So as most of y'all know," Rob said, "I'm Austin Roberts, and Tony here, the owner of this fine establishment, is my friend from college. So he offered to come up and play drums while I sing my *Billboard* hit—I still can't even believe I'm saying that—'Crystal Castle.'"

Tony whispered something to Rob.

"Oh! And Tony says that our friend Emily—you remember her from her kick-ass Tracy Chapman before—promised she'd come play with us for old times' sake. Queenie?"

Emily stood up and walked up on stage with them and sat down at the piano.

"You remember the chord progression for 'Queen of All the Keys'?" Rob said to her off mic. "It's the same."

She nodded, not telling him that she'd already figured that out.

The three of them started playing, Rob started singing, and Emily offered some harmony lines that matched the ones she used to sing in "Queen of All the Keys." It only took them a couple of measures to get their groove back. And then they rocked it. Emily followed Rob's lead, the way she always did, and listened for Tony's beat, and the three of them were totally in sync, playing together as if they hadn't ever stopped.

When the song ended, Rob turned to Emily and mouthed, *Please come on tour.*

Emily smiled at him and stood up from the piano bench, but he shook his head. She sat down again, not sure what he had in mind.

"Since we've got our band back together again, we're gonna play one more song for y'all, the finale we used to jam to thirteen years ago. So please give us a break if we don't remember all the words."

He turned to Emily. "Only love can break your heart," he said.

She smiled at him, wondering if she would actually remember any of what she was supposed to sing.

He kept going, and she responded without even thinking about it until the duet started in earnest.

It all came back to Emily, almost as if the song had shortcut her brain and somehow appeared in her fingers and in her vocal cords. She stood up, nudging the piano bench to the side with her foot, and was flirting with Rob on stage the way they used to. They were laughing and teasing each other, and then they got to the final bit they sang together, facing each other. They sang about how wonderful life was because they were both in the world.

And Emily realized all of a sudden that the part that came after that was a kiss. Rob raised his eyebrows at her, and a piece of Emily was tempted to nod, to say: *Yes, kiss me.* To feel his lips against hers again, to turn back time, to rewind to the days before they'd played Webster Hall, before she'd gotten pregnant, before she'd fallen and broken her hand and broken up the band. But she was an adult now, and she couldn't go back. She shook her head, and instead the two of them hugged, Rob swinging his guitar to the side, so it wouldn't get caught between them.

"I really am so glad you're in the world," he whispered into her ear. "It makes it more wonderful to me."

"I'm glad you're in the world, too," she whispered back. "I really, truly am."

xxviii

I KNOW I said that I wasn't sure if I wanted to have children, but meeting Ezra has made me reevaluate that. I think I might want Ezra to be the father of your brothers or sisters. He's the best man I've ever met. He's just . . . good. He's a deeply good person. And he makes me want to be better, to focus more on other people, on helping them, on being like Dr. West. He has a quote stenciled around his living room, traveling from wall to wall, just under the seam where it meets the ceiling, that says: "Do all the good you can, by all the means you can, in all the ways you can, in all the places you can, at all the times you can, to all the people you can, as long as ever you can."

When I first got to his place, I didn't notice it. In the dim light, I thought it was a design, some kind of decorative border on the top of the wall. But once he turned the light on, I could read it. I turned in a circle following the phrases to their end.

"Weird for a guy who was raised Jewish to have John Wesley's quote on his wall, I know," he said. "But my mom's dad was Methodist, and before I was born, my parents stenciled it like this around my bedroom. I grew up with those words, and I really believe them. So when I moved here, my parents came and helped me stencil them here. It reminds me what I want to do with my life."

I stood in his living room and read the quote again. "It's beautiful," I said. And I vowed then that I would always do the same. I wanted to follow him into this world of trying to help people. Of consciously choosing good. Of that ideal being the motivating factor of my life. I know I said that Dr. West changed my life, and that's true, but Ezra changed it, too.

We sat down on his couch then, and Ezra popped up to offer me a glass of water or wine. I took the wine. I hadn't slept with anyone since your father. It had been years. Eight of them. And I'd been afraid—afraid that I'd do it again: break someone else's heart, break my own. But I thought there was no one in this world I'd met who was better than Ezra. And the idea of losing him, of not having him in my life, overwhelmed my fear of getting hurt, of hurting someone else.

"Did you ever watch Mister Rogers' Neighborhood?" I asked him when he came back with the wine. "When you were a kid?"

He nodded as he sat back down next to me. "I loved the Neighborhood of Make-Believe. There was a guy who lived in a clock with no hands because make-believe was whatever time you wanted it to be. I tried to take the hands off the clock in our living room after I saw that."

"Daniel Striped Tiger," I said. "He's the one who lived in the clock."

Ezra's eyes lit up. "You loved it, too!"

I smiled. "Maybe not as much as you did, but I always remembered the episode where Mr. Rogers said that if the news gets too scary, you should look for the helpers in the story. The police officers and firefighters and doctors and the regular people who reached out to give other people a hand. When I was older and my mom was sick, I remembered that. I looked for the helpers, and things felt a little more manageable."

Ezra put his arm around my shoulder and squeezed.

"You're one of the helpers," I said to him. "You're one of the people who makes life less scary."

He put his wine down and kissed me. Then he whispered, "You are, too."

I hadn't thought about myself that way before. Ezra gave me a gift in that moment. He let me see myself through his eyes. And made me realize who I wanted to be. I wanted to be one of the helpers, just like he was.

I put my wineglass down and kissed him back, running my fingers over the soft button-down shirt he was wearing, first down his back, then down his chest.

"Do you want to see my bedroom?" he asked. "I mean, we can stay here if you want, but it might be more comfortable—"

I cut him off with a kiss and then stood, reaching my hand down for his. He got up and led me to the bedroom, which I could just make out in the dim light. The bed was made; there was a glasses case on the nightstand on the left side, with a lamp, a digital clock, and a book I couldn't read the title of.

We sat down on the edge of the bed, and then we were lying on it, and then our clothing was off and we were touching each other, skin to skin. His body was tighter and thinner out of clothes than he looked while he was wearing them.

"Look at you," he said, pulling back for a moment. I felt seen, almost too seen, and wanted to pull my shirt back on, but then I took a deep breath and gave him the gift of my vulnerability.

He leaned over and ran his tongue around my nipple and I remembered how wonderful it felt to be intimate with someone, how powerful the connection could be when it was something you both so wanted.

He slid his finger inside me and moaned in anticipation of what was to come. I flashed back to you, to your dad, to that one time. "Do you have—" I started.

He reached into his nightstand drawer. "This?" he asked, holding up a square of foil.

"Yes," I breathed, as he ripped it open.

When he slid inside me, it felt like the first time all over again, like my desire had been reawakened after lying dormant for so long.

Afterward he said, "I guess this means I have to marry you now."

I looked at him, not sure how to respond.

"Just kidding," he said. "Bad joke."

But I wasn't sure if he really was joking. And, actually, I kind of hoped he wasn't.

If I married him, I could always be the person he saw me as. I could always look at myself through his eyes. I could be the helper, not the one who needed help.

The idea made me feel strong. And I wanted to feel that way forever.

39

EMILY AND PRIYA and Rob stayed while Tony closed up the bar. There had been so many people there, and it took Tony a few announcements of "final call" and "closing time!" before he could get them all to leave.

"I feel like I should give you a cut," he said to Rob, after he locked the door.

Rob shook his head. "My pleasure, man. It was fun."

Tony took the cash out of the register and put it in a lockbox. "When I first opened this place, last call was at two a.m., and I always had to deal with some drunk or other who didn't want to leave, and I got home at nearly four. It messed up my whole schedule. So I decided a year or so in that last call would be midnight. It made everything so much saner." He locked the box with a key from the ring attached to his belt loop. "And honestly, the till wasn't that different, once you factored in the staff I needed to pay to keep this place open. We do much better at happy hour, pre-dinner stuff."

"Plus now you can go out after your night ends," Rob said.

Tony shook his head. "Not anymore. I've got my dogs to walk in the morning, and then a personal training session at nine."

Rob looked shocked. "You serious?" he asked.

Tony nodded. "Same reason I stopped drinking. I decided I hate feeling like shit in the morning."

Rob nodded. "Respect," he said, finally.

Then he looked over at Emily and Priya, who were talking quietly a little farther down the bar and pitched his voice so they could hear. "Can I interest you two ladies in a post-performance celebration? Because, to be honest—"

"You're starving," Emily said.

Rob laughed. "And predictable, it seems."

Priya looked at her phone. "I can stay for maybe another twenty minutes," she said. "But then I should get home. I promised Neel I'd spend tomorrow morning with Anika so he could go on a bike ride with some friends. And that girl gets up with the sun."

"Queenie?" Rob asked.

Emily nodded. "I'll go back with Priya, so you've got yourself twenty minutes of eating."

"There's a late-night pizza place down the street," Tony said. "It's on the way to my car. I can walk you."

So the four of them left the bar, locking the door of the Snare behind them. A few Austin Roberts superfans had stuck around and Rob took selfies with them before setting off down the block.

"Are you used to that yet?" Tony asked Rob.

He shook his head. "Does anyone really get used to that?"

PRIYA AND EMILY were walking just behind Rob and Tony. "So are you considering it?" Priya said quietly, continuing the conversation they'd started in the bar about Rob's invitation to tour with him.

Emily shrugged. "Not really," she said. "A piece of me would love to be on the road, performing every night, but my life is here.

At NYU, with Ezra. I made my choices, you know? Years ago, I chose this path."

Priya looked at her critically.

"It's okay, I haven't paid you for a session," Emily said, laughing, recognizing in Priya the same struggle that she had sometimes when talking to friends.

Priya laughed, too. "Okay, okay," she said. "I'll stop. But . . . choices are made all the time," she said. "One choice doesn't have to define a life."

Emily grabbed her friend's hand and squeezed it. "I know," she said.

She thought about her mom's belief that we all made the choices we were supposed to make, we just didn't know what they were supposed to be until we made them. She was supposed to be here tonight. She was supposed to see Rob again. But what was she supposed to do after that?

"YOU LADIES READY for some pizza?" Rob called back, as they neared the restaurant.

Eat pizza. The next thing she was supposed to do was eat pizza.

xxix

EZRA AND I *were dating for three months when he asked if I wanted to meet his parents. We were at his place, making breakfast together after a lazy morning in bed where we'd twined ourselves around each other, holding each other close, both before and after sex. I think we needed those moments of physical contact.*

"You know, touch is analgesic," Ezra said to me, as he wrapped both arms around me, pulling me even closer to him. "It's the oxytocin."

"So you mean if I have a headache, I can either take Tylenol or hug you?" I asked, pulling him toward me, tucking my head under his chin.

"We should try that," he said, "next time you have a headache. But we can see it on the monitor at work: patients' heart rates slow when their hands are stroked, when someone climbs into bed with them and holds them tight."

It made sense to me. Ari and I felt better holding each other's hands when our mom died. I felt better curled with her on the couch when I lost you, when I lost music, when I lost your dad. And I felt better in Ezra's arms than I did nearly anywhere else.

"Does holding me like this make you feel better?" I asked.

"It does," he said. "It makes me feel more ready to take on whatever comes my way, to face whatever challenges there are ahead of me."

I nodded against his collarbone. "Me too," I said.

———————

WE GOT UP *after that and made an omelet. I took an egg to crack against the edge of the counter but then stopped to watch him. He was tapping the top of a second egg with a butter knife until it cracked, then sticking the tip of the knife in the crack and turning it slowly and steadily to make a hole big enough for the yolk and albumen to flow out.*

"I've never seen anyone crack an egg like that," I said, fascinated.

"No possibility of shell," he said.

I left the eggs to him and started chopping peppers and dicing tomatoes, wondering if he had some magical way to cut those, too.

"So I was thinking," he said, as we tossed everything together in a bowl, "my parents are coming to town next weekend. And I'd love for them to meet you. What would you think about that?"

He was concentrating on pouring milk as he spoke, and looked up at me when he was done. "I just think . . . what we have is special and . . ."

"Of course," I said. "I'd love to meet your parents." Ezra talked about them enough that I was curious. I knew they were all really close, that he was their only child. And with my mom gone and my dad planning a wedding in Santa Fe, I loved the idea of being wrapped up in a tight-knit family again.

I loved the idea of being wrapped up with Ezra.

40

"I FORGOT ABOUT East Coast pizza," Rob said, finishing his second slice. "Is it terrible if I go get thirds?"

"You mean New York pizza," Priya said. "I grew up in Boston, and the pizza there is nothing like this."

"But we're in New Jersey," Emily pointed out. "Is the pizza really the same here as in New York City? That feels like some sort of blasphemy."

"Well," Rob said, "I'm staying at a hotel in Manhattan. Shall we taste-test? Pizza crawl? I did one of those with my girls when I flew home to see them last week. I was surprised how much pizza two tiny kids could eat."

"Is it hard to be away from them?" Emily asked, still amazed that Rob was a father.

"It is," he said. "But they're with their mom for the school week even when I'm home, so we're used to FaceTime."

Emily nodded. His voice was light, but she could see in his eyes how much he missed them.

"So. That pizza crawl?" Rob asked, redirecting the conversation.

Priya looked at her phone. "I've already stayed out longer than I should. I'm afraid I can't. But I have to say, this is the most fun night out I've had in a long time."

Rob looked at Emily. "Let's all head back then, and maybe

I could convince you to stop off at one more pizza place before you head home? Just, you know, to compare? Answer this very important culinary question?"

Emily wanted to. But wanting to do something didn't mean you should. "Let's head back," she said. "I'll see how tired I am when we get there."

Rob smiled. "So does that mean I should get you a shot of espresso before we leave?" He pretended to look around for a waiter.

Emily smiled back. "Cute," she said.

Priya looked at them both. "All right," she said. "Enough flirting, you two. Let's go."

Emily blushed. She wasn't sure if Rob did, too, because she wasn't looking at him anymore. She was staring down at the crumpled napkin on her grease-stained paper plate, hoping no one saw her reaction.

They walked down the street with Priya in the middle, but it was hard to deny the tension crackling between Emily and Rob. It was like an ember had been glowing for years, and now someone was fanning it, blowing on it, waiting to see if it would burst into a roaring flame once more.

THE THREE OF them took seats on the PATH train.

"So how did you two meet?" Priya asked.

"Funny story," Rob said. "I was sitting all alone one night in a folk music club my junior year of college, minding my own business, when this stunning woman comes over and asks me if I want to share her popcorn."

Emily laughed. "Not true!" she said. "I walked into this folk music club my sophomore year of college, minding my own business, when this guy with the biggest smile I'd ever seen offers to buy me a drink. So I figured it was only fair to offer him some popcorn in return."

"I think I offered to buy you the drink after you offered me the popcorn," Rob said, winking at her.

"Well, if that's what you need to tell yourself," Emily said, "I won't argue. But we both know the truth."

"The truth that it was love at first sight?" Rob said, raising an eyebrow, Groucho Marx–style. He was joking but not joking. Teasing but being serious, too.

Emily was quiet for a moment, stopping the banter completely. "Yeah," she said softly. "Maybe it was."

WHEN THE PATH let them off at 33rd Street, Priya gave Emily a hug. "It was great to see you so happy tonight," she whispered. "Be careful with him, though. He wants a lot from you."

Emily hugged her back. "I will. Thank you for coming."

Then Priya said good-bye to Rob and hailed a cab.

"Good night!" Rob and Emily chorused, as Priya shut the car door behind her. Then Rob looked at Emily. "Another slice, Queen? Or are you going to leave a stranger in this city to eat pizza all by his lonesome? One who might even end up at a terrible dollar-a-slice pizza joint, if left to his own devices?"

Emily shook her head at him, laughing at the same time. This night felt like a moment out of time where she could laugh and flirt and share her feelings through her fingers and her voice. It was a moment she didn't want to lose quite yet. "Come on," she said. "There's a great pizza place not far from here. Don't let anyone ever say New Yorkers aren't friendly, staying up late to help a stranger in need find some pizza."

As they walked, Rob lightly caught her hand with his. She didn't stop him. And they walked to the pizza joint, fingers clasped, arms swinging, just like they used to.

XXX

EZRA'S PARENTS RENTED *a house on the Jersey Shore the summer after he and I started dating. We decided to spend Labor Day weekend with them out there before both our schedules got crazy again, when all the students came back to campus. We were walking along the beach at sunset and Ezra pointed toward a lifeguard stand. It was late enough that the lifeguards had gone home for the day, so the chair was empty.*

"Let's check out the view," he said.

I looked up at the height of the chair. "I'm glad neither one of us is afraid of heights," I answered.

He kicked off his sandals and so did I, and we climbed up the chair together, finding handholds and footholds where we could.

Ezra was quiet, which I attributed to how seriously he was focusing on not falling off the side of the chair. When we got up to the top, we sat next to each other, watching the sunset.

"It's beautiful," I said, as the wind pulled strands of my hair out of its bun. I tucked them behind my ears.

"Not as beautiful as you," Ezra said.

I turned to look at him, and he was angled toward me with a ring box, open, in his hand.

"Will you marry me?" he asked.

My stomach flipped. I felt, for a moment, like my consciousness had left my body, like I was watching myself. The moment felt so strong, so powerfully emotional that I couldn't process it right then. And then I was back inside myself and smiling wider than I thought my face could even manage.

"Of course," I said, giddy with happiness. I know Ezra isn't perfect, I know I'm not perfect, but ever since we've met, we've just felt perfect for each other.

There was this time a few months after we started dating when I got bronchitis. I was home, cocooned in some blankets and watching television, napping in the middle of one episode of Law & Order and waking up in the middle of a different one, so nothing quite made sense. He came over. It was just after we'd exchanged keys, and I heard him fumbling with his key in my door but didn't manage to get up off the couch before he made it inside.

"You stay there," he said to me, after kissing my forehead.

He set up a humidifier and took VapoRub out of his backpack.

"You're like a medical Mary Poppins," I told him.

He laughed, but I tried not to, because I knew laughing would turn into coughing and would make it hard to breathe.

"Just wait until you see what else I have in here," he said.

Then he walked to the part of my living room that had the kitchen area in it, and he began dicing onions and throwing them in a pot with some olive oil, which he'd also pulled out of his backpack.

"What are you doing?" I asked, watching him from my place on the couch.

"Chicken soup," he said. "It's a Gold family recipe. And there's actually scientific backing to why it'll make you feel better. Bone broth is good for you—it has iron, zinc, amino acids; so is garlic, it's an antioxidant with diallyl sulfide; liquids are always good to keep things moving around in your body; and the heat will break up mucus."

"So I'll be healed up in no time," I said, watching him cut up the chicken.

"That's the plan," he said, smiling over at me. "But I'll come and take care of you as long as you need me to."

It might have been the fever, or the fact that I'd been feeling sick for days, but when he said that, it brought tears to my eyes. When I was a kid, I always tried to take care of myself, whenever I could, because moving around was hard for my mom, especially when she had a flare-up. And Ari and I tried to take care of each other if we couldn't manage it alone, especially after my mom got really sick. It was hard for her to do much caring for anyone else—and your grandpa was so preoccupied with her. I felt bad when I needed them and tried not to. Now that I'm thinking about it, that's probably why I never told your grandfather about you, about how messed up I was that year. But Ezra acted like taking care of someone wasn't a big deal. He said he'd do it for as long as I needed him to.

"I love you," I told him from the couch that day. It was the first time I said that to him.

"I love you, too," he said. "But maybe you'd already noticed."

I hadn't. Or maybe I had. But hearing it was so wonderful. Knowing that I didn't always have to fend for myself—or count on Ari.

THAT WAS WHAT popped into my head when he took my hand and slipped the ring on my finger. Somehow he'd figured out my size. And that, too, was perfect.

"It's three diamonds," he said. "For our past, our present, and our future."

I looked down at my hand, and there they were, three round

diamonds all lined up, all the exact same size. His promise to me that we'd be with each other forever.

We kissed then, on the lifeguard chair, with the waves crashing, the wind in our hair, both smelling like sunscreen and the sea. I never wanted that moment to end.

When we got back to the house, Ari was waiting with Ezra's parents, a celebratory bottle of champagne chilling in a bucket of ice.

As soon as I saw her, I flew into my sister's arms. "He asked my permission instead of Dad's," she whispered to me. "And waited before he proposed to find a weekend I could come out to celebrate afterward. You've got yourself a keeper."

I hadn't cried until then, but those words did it. I'd found a man so kind, so caring, so thoughtful, someone who knew how much my sister meant to me and made her part of our union. A man who I knew would be a great dad to your future brothers and sisters. I vowed to myself then that I would do everything I could to make him feel loved, understood, inspired—the way he did for me.

41

WHEN THEY GOT to Little Italy Pizza, which was incongruously located in Midtown West, Emily said, "I know it doesn't look like much, but it's open twenty-four hours and is the New Yorkiest New York pizza around."

"I'm in," Rob said, letting go of her hand to open the door for her.

"Thanks," she said, walking in front of him, forced to slide inches from his chest as she stepped through the door. The nearness made her feel like a magnet, her body pulled toward his, her willpower alone keeping them apart.

Rob ordered a pepperoni slice, and Emily found herself hungry, too, so she got plain cheese and sat down at a booth. Rob paused when he got there, as if he wanted to slip in next to her, but then thought better of it and sat opposite. Emily noticed one woman nudging the man she was with and pointing at Rob. Would Rob be able to go out for pizza like this much longer without a baseball cap covering his face?

"You know I was serious," he said, "when I asked you to come tour with me. You're so talented. You should share that with the world."

Emily had been blotting the oil off her pizza with a napkin and looked up at him. "That's sweet of you to say, but I'm not that talented. Not like you."

Rob shook his head. "I don't think you understand." He pulled out his phone. "Here," he said. "I want you to watch yourself perform. Pretend it's someone else."

"Rob—" Emily started. She didn't want to watch herself. She knew it would be embarrassing to see. She probably made ridiculous faces or did something strange with her eyebrows. Her voice probably wasn't as melodic or rich as she'd hoped it would be, her piano playing not as sharp.

"Just watch it," he said. "Please. For me."

She wiped her fingers on a paper napkin and took his phone, pressing play on the video. And she saw herself. She saw herself as he saw her. She looked smaller than she imagined, on that stage, playing the bar's upright piano. Her hair shone copper in the spotlight, where it glinted off the peaks of her braid. Then she started to play, her body rocking with the music, her hands strong against the keys. The music sounded bold, powerful. And then she started to sing. And her own voice almost brought tears to her eyes. She was mournful, passionate, hopeful. Rob was right. She hadn't known, hadn't realized.

She looked up and felt a tear slide down her cheek. She wiped it away with the back of her hand. "I guess I'm not so bad," she said.

"Queenie," he answered. "You're transcendent."

Before Emily realized what he was doing, he'd pushed his paper plate across the table and slid in next to her in the booth. She moved over to make room, but they were still only millimeters apart.

"We could be huge," he said. "The Sonny and Cher of our generation. The Johnny and June Carter Cash."

She smiled, remembering those words from years before. "Could we still?" she asked.

"You're only thirty-three," he said. "After we broke up, I never thought I'd write a song that hit the *Billboard* charts, but here we are. Anything's possible, Queenie."

Emily stopped to consider it, really consider it. What would that be like? Leaving her life in New York, her patients? Living apart from Ezra? Traveling the country, maybe the world, playing with Rob? Being recognized at pizza joints? She'd be living out the dream they'd had when she was twenty. But not the dream she and Ezra shared. The one they'd been building these past years.

Rob was watching her think. "You don't have to answer now," he said. "It's a big decision. But think about it. They're sending me to Mexico next. Then Miami. Top hotels, everything comped . . . if you were there, too, I bet we could book even bigger venues, reach even more fans."

"I'll think about it," she said, but she wasn't sure if she meant it.

Rob slipped his arm around her shoulders, and Emily let herself lean against him, marveling, as she always did, at the analgesic property of human touch. She felt calmer, less anxious, more hopeful. New paths had suddenly opened up for her, paths she'd long ago thought had been blocked off and closed down. She didn't know if she wanted to travel down them, but knowing that they were there felt good somehow. Like the world was more open than she'd thought it was.

"I've been listening to Beethoven's Fifth Symphony recently," Rob said.

"The Fate Symphony," Emily answered, its name popping into her mind from the Music Humanities class they'd both had to take in college. Part of the core curriculum.

"The Fate Symphony," Rob echoed. "And you know the motif—"

"Ba-ba-ba bum." Emily sang the opening bars softly.

"Right. Short-short-short long," Rob sang back, replacing her sounds with words. "It's amazing to me how he keeps that motif going, throughout. The melody's not the same, but in all the movements, it's there. Short-short-short long."

Emily nodded, remembering the second movement as one they'd focused on in class.

"I was thinking about my life—my career—as a symphony the other day. And I think you're the motif. The first movement was in college, when we played together, when we made magic on the stage. And then when I was composing scores, even though you weren't there, you were. I kept thinking, 'How would Queenie harmonize here? What would she do on the keys?'"

"You did?" Emily asked, too surprised to say anything else.

"I did," Rob affirmed. "And now we're in the third movement, the scherzo, and you inspired the song that put me on the map. I want you here with me, in the third movement."

She looked at him, his eyes were intense, looking right at her.

"And then we can write the fourth movement together," he said.

"Of your career?" she asked, sliding into psychologist mode, clarifying, making sure she knew what the subtext was.

"Of anything," Rob answered. "My career or . . . anything."

Emily thought about Rob's analogy, about what the motif of

her own symphony would be. It wouldn't be him, she was sure of that. But it wouldn't be Ezra, either. It would be, she decided, loss. The loss of her mother, of her first child, of Rob, of music, of her dad, in a way. Loss was what propelled her to follow the path she did, to become a therapist, to connect with Ezra. But now two of the things she'd lost were being returned to her. What did that mean for her fourth movement?

xxxi

EZRA AND I *got married! Last week! I felt like I should let you know. Or do you somehow already know? Your grandfather's wife had too much chardonnay and told me that my mom was watching me, looking down on the moment, and I rolled my eyes and walked away from her. Because how does she know? How does anyone know what happens afterward? What happened to your grandmother? What happened to you?*

I wonder sometimes if souls really can be reborn, like Ari suggested when you were inside me. Were you reborn as someone else's child? Will you come back to me if Ezra and I have a baby together? Or is it over for you? Has your story been told, the ending complete? And that's it?

In graduate school I read about psychiatric patients who believed that they had lived past lives. The details they knew were so specific, it was hard to come up with other ways to explain the phenomenon. But if souls are recycled like that, then it's possible your grandmother's soul was already recycled, in which case she wouldn't be watching our wedding. You, either.

WE HAD A *really small wedding, a really quiet one, not like Ari and Jack's black-tie extravaganza. Your grandfather offered to pay, which actually surprised me, since his life in Santa Fe seems to have* somehow eclipsed his life as Ari's and my father. We hardly ever see him, now that he moved. And we talk about once a month—but the conversations aren't real. They seem more out of duty than out of a real desire to connect. But I've always had Ari. And now I have Ezra.

Ezra and I had talked about your grandfather's offer, and we decided that we wanted to basically elope with our families. So I asked your grandfather if he would rent us all a huge house on the Riviera Maya for Memorial Day weekend and fly his rabbi down to marry us.

He said he'd pay for everyone's flights, too, since it would still be less expensive than Ari's wedding. So that's what we did. Though Ezra's parents insisted on paying for their own flights. And a chef, too.

It was so beautiful. We got married on the beach, under a canopy, behind this gorgeous house that had a swimming pool and palm trees with hammocks and swings hanging between them. It was called Villa Corazón, which is part of the reason we chose it. With the chef there all weekend, no one had to cook. And Ezra and I wrote our own vows—one set of vows that we would share, words that we would each vow to the other.

We vowed to love, honor, and respect each other always.

We vowed to choose each other, every morning, every afternoon, and every night.

We vowed to support each other in the hard times and in the wonderful ones.

And we vowed to do all we could to give each other our best selves until the end of our days.

Then, feeling the sand under my bare feet, I stepped forward so he could slide a ring on my finger and declare, "By this ring, you are consecrated to me as my wife by the laws of Moses and Israel."

And then I slipped a ring on his finger, saying, "I am my beloved's and my beloved is mine."

The rabbi read our Ketubah aloud, and then our parents and Ari and Jack and their kids each came forward to bestow one of the seven blessings upon us. After that, Ezra slipped a shoe on his right foot—a shoe he'd brought down to the beach just for this purpose—and smashed a glass we'd wrapped in a napkin, symbolizing that our love would last for as long as the glass was shattered, which is to say, forever.

And then we kissed as the sun set, and the chef served us a Mexican feast on the beach. It was a perfect night.

When we were on our dessert course, your grandfather said, "I think the two of you need a first dance."

We had some music piped in from the house, a playlist Ezra had made on his computer that we connected to the sound system.

"We didn't choose a song for that," I told him.

"I have an idea for one," your grandfather answered. Ari pointed the remote control toward the house and turned off the jazz. And then your grandfather started singing about the night coming and the land being dark and the moon being the only light we could see.

I hadn't heard him sing for a long time. Not since the day before I fell, when he sang with me and your dad in the living room. And I forgot how effortless his voice sounded, how calming. I stood up and reached for Ezra's hand. He stood, too, and we danced in our bare feet on the beach in the moonlight to your grandpa's song.

Ezra laid his cheek against my head as we danced.

"Emily," he whispered, while your grandpa sang, "I just feel so grateful right now. So grateful that you married me, that our families are here, that we have so much ahead of us."

"I'm grateful for you," I whispered back. "For everything you've given me. I love you so much."

"You too," he replied. "There haven't been words invented yet for how much I love you."

And because there really weren't words, I kissed him.

Maybe one day soon we'll make a little brother or sister for you. I hope it happens soon.

42

WHEN THEY FINISHED their pizza, Emily and Rob started walking east, in the direction of his hotel and, beyond that, her Kips Bay neighborhood. Even though he had an early-morning flight, neither one of them seemed in a hurry. They stopped to look at the moon, perfectly framed by two skyscrapers.

"Manhattan really is something else," Rob said.

"Do you miss it?" Emily asked, as they kept walking, acutely aware of his hand dangling next to hers, not holding it, but so close.

"Some of it," he said, "I miss who I was when I was here, the strength of my convictions back then. Manhattan is so tied up in us, though, for me. The mind-blowing amazing parts—"

"And the shitty parts, too," Emily said.

"They were pretty shitty," Rob said. "I don't think I handled things the way I should have. The way I would, if it were now, if I'd been older, more mature. I'm sorry I didn't try to understand more of how you felt."

A taxi stopped next to them, the driver asking if they needed a ride. Emily shook her head, and the driver sped off.

"I'm sorry, too," Emily said. "For not giving it more time, for breaking up everything, for taking my grief out on you. I was such a mess. I made everything a mess."

Rob reached for her hand and squeezed it.

"I was angry with you for a while," he said. He didn't let go of her hand.

"I was angry with myself," Emily said. "All I kept thinking about was what I lost and how it was all my fault—you, music, the . . . the baby we made together."

Rob stopped walking and looked at her. He grabbed her other hand, so their bodies were connected in a circle, nothing beginning, nothing ending. "I'm sorry I was such an asshole about that. I'm sorry I said it wasn't real. I thought about it when Corinne was pregnant with the girls. I thought about what a jerky thing it was for me to say. To believe. It was easier, I guess. But it made everything worse. I should've been better. I should've been there with you, you know? We could've felt it together." He took a deep breath and shook his head. "That would've been one awesome kid."

Emily couldn't speak, because she knew if she tried, no words would come out. Just sobs.

Rob could tell and let go of her hands so he could wrap his arms around her. She laid her head against his chest. "It's okay," he said, like he used to, when she would tumble into grief about her mom. "I got you."

His touch was so calming, so soothing. She took a deep breath. Tears had made it to her eyelashes but didn't travel any farther. "I'm okay," she said softly. "I'm okay now."

He pulled back to look her in the eye. "Yeah?" he said, his breath soft.

"Yeah," she answered, looking back at him, seeing the depth of his concern in his eyes. "I really am."

"Emily," he whispered.

She felt it. The smoldering ember had become a flame. Heat

crackled and popped. It danced inside them, between them, around them.

They were close enough that their breath mingled. In that moment, kissing him seemed inevitable. He leaned forward just a fraction and she met his lips. His passion filled her with warmth, with hope, with desire. She felt loved.

Their lips broke apart. "My Queenie," Rob whispered, as if in awe of what had just happened.

"My R—" was on the tip of her tongue, but then Ezra's words came to her. The ones he said at their wedding. *I will do all I can to give you my best self until the end of my days.* And she'd said them back. They were vows they both took, that they both wrote together. This was not her best self.

She stepped away, her lips no longer a whisper from his. "I can't," she said. "I'm sorry. I can't."

And that was when she started to cry.

"Queenie," Rob said. "Emily." He looked like he wanted to hold her again, comfort her, find whatever had just been lost, but he knew he shouldn't. His arms hung, useless, at his sides.

Emily felt panicked, her heart a hummingbird against her rib cage, her stomach twisting with guilt. "I've got to go home," Emily said, mascara running down her cheeks. "This was all a huge mistake."

There were so many things Rob wanted to say, but he chose the simplest. "Okay," he said. "I'm sorry if I pushed too far. If I read into something that wasn't there."

He hadn't. That was the problem. He hadn't.

But she wouldn't tell him that.

Instead she said, "Thank you for showing me another way to see myself. But this is the life I chose." It was all she could do to keep her voice from shaking, to keep from falling apart completely.

He nodded, not taking a step closer, staying where he was, hands still at his sides, as if it took every ounce of his concentration to keep them there. "If you ever . . ."

She took a deep breath. "You know how to get back to your hotel?" she answered.

He nodded. She wiped her eyes, smearing makeup across her cheek. His hand rose, just a hair, as if he wanted to fix it for her, but then it rested back at his side.

"Sleep well," she said, biting her lip to keep her composure.

"You too," he answered. He watched her walk away. And just like last time, she took a small piece of him with her.

43

EMILY HAILED A cab and got inside. She felt shocked by what she'd done, and guilty. Even though it was two o'clock in the morning, she called Ezra. She couldn't wait for him anymore. She needed him. She needed to talk to him. She needed not to go looking for love somewhere else. She was still hurting from the miscarriage—mentally and physically—and she needed him. She needed him to care for her like he used to. He didn't pick up, but she wasn't surprised. He was probably sleeping after his double call. He often turned his phone off when he could, when he knew the hospital wouldn't be calling him. She left a message. "Can you please come home?" she said, her voice thick with tears. "I miss you. I love you. I choose you. I want you to choose me."

Then she got out at their building and walked inside alone, her phone in her hand, waiting for him to wake up, hoping it would be soon.

Instead of going to bed, Emily went back into the second bedroom and rummaged through a box of her old notebooks to find her journal. The one she'd started years before at the recommendation of Dr. West, a way to tell her story, process it as she explained it to someone else. She hadn't written in it for years. Not since right after she'd gotten married to Ezra.

When she found the notebook, leather-bound and navy blue with gold on the edges of the pages, she brought it, along with a pen, to the couch in the living room. Instead of reading it over, which she used to do sometimes—when she needed grounding, when she needed reminding of who she was—she opened it to the next blank page and flattened it in front of her.

I want to feel whole again, she wrote. And then looked at the words. What did that even mean? *I want to feel loved again.*

Her phone vibrated and she looked at the screen, expecting Ezra. But instead there was a text from Tessa. For a moment, Emily couldn't remember how in the world Tessa had gotten her number, but then recalled the lunchtime of babysitting, which seemed forever ago now. A sense of dread filled her. There was no good reason that Tessa would text her in the middle of the night.

She clicked open the notification and read: I don't know who else to reach out to. I need help. Are you there?

Emily wasn't usually up at 2:27 in the morning, but today she was. She was there.

Yes, she wrote back, What's wrong?

Emily's heart raced. She was worried about Tessa. Worried that she didn't feel she had anyone else. Where was Chris? Where were her friends? Her family?

I keep thinking Zoe would be better off without me. And I can't stop coming up with ways I could make that happen.

Emily had dealt with patients who were experiencing suicidal ideation only a handful of times before, but never when they were in the middle of a crisis like this. Never when it was a patient she cared about as much as Tessa. Her heart raced, knowing that everything she chose to say could have life-or-death repercussions. She took a deep breath. She really wasn't in the right frame of mind to be strong for anyone right now. But she would do it. For Tessa, for Zoe. Did something specific happen to make you feel this way? she typed. She thought about calling, but if this was how Tessa had felt comfortable reaching out, this was how she would respond. She didn't want to risk calling and then Tessa not picking up and going silent. She didn't want to be too intrusive.

Chris left us today. I can't do this alone. I'm staring at a bottle of sleeping pills right now. I just need someone to take care of Zoe.

Adrenaline raced through Emily's body. This was even more serious than she'd first thought. She'd seen Tessa on Friday. She had seemed like she was struggling but not like she was suicidal. Emily needed to risk a phone call. She needed Tessa to hear her voice. I'm going to call you, Emily typed. Please pick up. She pressed the button that would call Tessa's phone.

"Dr. Gold?" Tessa said, after the phone rang once.

Emily breathed a sigh of relief. "Tessa," she said. "I'm here. We'll figure this out. Can you do me a favor, though? Can you walk into another room?" She knew easy access to things like weapons or medications made suicide more likely. Would Tessa leave the room and leave the pills behind?

There was the sound of movement on the other end of the line. "Okay," she said. "I'm walking into the bedroom."

"Great," Emily said. "Thank you." Her mind was scrolling through options. She could tell her to go to the ER. She could meet her at the ER. But what if Tessa didn't go? What if she hung up after that suggestion and Emily never heard from her again? She could call the police, but she didn't want to put Tessa on hold and risk losing her completely. She knew she wasn't supposed to do it, but the only choice that felt right was going to Tessa in person. Assessing her when they were face to face. She didn't care if she was breaking protocol. She was too afraid of what might happen if she didn't. "Will you tell me where you are? I'm going to come over and help you." Emily worried Tessa wouldn't answer. That she'd hang up.

But Tessa gave her address, which wasn't far. "I'll be there in ten minutes," Emily said. "But let's stay on the phone until I get there. Do you want to tell me what happened today?"

Tessa started telling her about the argument that she and Chris had gotten into the night before, about the fight that continued in the morning, about how he left . . .

As she told the story, she seemed to calm down slightly. Emily jumped in a cab, moistening her thumb and rubbing the mascara from her cheeks and under her eyes, knowing she had to look presentable if she was going to try to counsel Tessa. She got out a few minutes later, still listening to Tessa talk. Still so glad Tessa was talking, that she was on the other side of the phone.

When Emily finally walked into the apartment building, she asked to be buzzed in and went upstairs.

Tessa opened the apartment door and fell into Emily's arms. "I'm so afraid," she said, over and over. "I'm so afraid, I'm so afraid I'm going to do something terrible."

"It's okay," Emily told her. "You didn't do anything terrible, you called me, you did the right thing, and now we're going to get you help."

She hugged Tessa close, felt her tears on her shoulder. The irony that Rob had been comforting her not long before wasn't lost on Emily. Sometimes you were the one who needed support. Sometimes you were the one who gave it. She wondered if, years ago, Dr. West had ever gone through anything in her personal life that she had to push aside for her patients.

"I need help," Tessa said.

Emily was so glad that she was going to be able to get it for her. That she had been there when Tessa called. That together they'd made it to this point, the point where Tessa was alive in her arms. With all the doubts she'd been feeling, she was glad she had been able to do at least something right.

44

BEFORE TESSA AGREED to go to the ER, she wanted Emily to promise that she wouldn't call Chris and that she wouldn't let anyone take Zoe except her mother. But Chris still had parental rights. Emily had to call him.

"I'm not going unless you promise," Tessa said, through tears. "I don't want him to have her. He didn't ever want her."

Emily hesitated. "I promise," she finally said, holding Tessa close. "I promise. I'll keep her with me until your mom can make it here." It wasn't the right choice to make, but it was the right choice to make for now.

Tessa nodded, her breath shuddering. "Okay," she said. "Okay."

And while Tessa was being evaluated by someone from psychiatry, Emily sat with Zoe on her lap, rocking the baby back to sleep when she cried. Emily thought about the choices people make and what those choices lead to down the line. And she thought about the choices that people have thrust upon them. Things that aren't actually choices at all. Tessa hadn't chosen for Chris to leave, to have a mind so close to the breaking point that this crisis was the result of that nonchoice.

Emily hadn't chosen to have a miscarriage, or have a song written about her by an ex-boyfriend, or have Ezra disappear for a few days. But she had chosen to go to Rob's show, have coffee with him afterward, perform in the showcase, and let him hold her hand as they walked to get pizza. She'd chosen to accept his arms when they offered her comfort. She'd chosen to let his lips meet hers. But she'd also chosen to stop. She'd chosen not to go to his hotel with him. She'd chosen to call Ezra, to honor the vow she'd made to him.

Life was a blend of choices and not choices, things that we had control over and things we didn't. Her mom had once told her that it's not what happens to you but how you respond that determines your path in life. Emily had thought of it then in terms of her mother's acceptance of her disease, of the honest way she existed while knowing she was going to die—sooner rather than later—and her determination to spend each day she could in the best way possible, no matter what constituted "best" at that time.

But now, Emily realized, it was a philosophy that covered all of life, not just when you're faced with tragedy. Things happen, and you react, and those reactions determine your path. If she had acted differently back in college, she could be living a different life right now. Maybe in Los Angeles as a working musician, or maybe in a New York suburb, giving piano lessons to kids like she once was. Maybe she and Rob would've become stars, traveled the world, bought a house in some place with a romantic-sounding name like Aix-en-Provence and raised four children there off the sales of their albums. Or maybe they would have failed dramatically and ended up in a downward spiral of drugs and depression. There were infinite possibilities.

And infinite possibilities for Tessa, too. And for Ezra. How he would respond to her now, in the future. And for Zoe, asleep in Emily's arms. There were so many lives that could unfurl ahead of her. So many choices other people would make for her and she would make for herself.

Tessa came out with one of the psych nurses to say good-bye to Zoe for at least a few days. She'd decided to check herself into the hospital. Emily agreed it was the best thing for her and for Zoe. She gave Tessa a hug and left with her mother's phone number and instructions to call her once it became morning for real. "I don't want her to have to wake up in the middle of the night to this. I'm here. I'll be better soon. And you're keeping Zoe safe. Tell her that."

Emily said she would and promised again that she wouldn't let Chris take Zoe, and then she picked up the diaper bag she had hurriedly packed at Tessa's apartment and headed home. More choices lay ahead for everyone. And more things would happen that nobody chose at all.

xxxii

EZRA AND I *moved in together today, officially. I know it seems old-fashioned, to wait until after we were married, but between his jobs and my job, and all the things you have to do to plan even the smallest wedding, figuring out our living situation seemed like the last on our list of things to do. We stayed together all the time, sometimes in his place and sometimes in mine, but actually packing up our things, finding a place we both wanted to live in together, as our first home, we did that when we got back from Mexico.*

Initially, Ezra wanted me to move into his place because it was bigger than mine and it would be easier than finding a new place to rent until we had enough money for a down payment, but I liked the idea of us starting fresh together, finding someplace that we could decorate however we chose, a mishmash of him and me, an embodiment of us.

So we went hunting for the right place. And Ezra really got into it, the way he does anything he's planning.

"I highlighted a map yesterday when I was between patients," he told me, while we were getting ready to visit some open houses. "If we live in this area, we can both walk to work."

I knew that he wanted to live within thirty minutes of the hospital, so he could be on call and still be home, if he chose. He often preferred to stay in the hospital anyway but liked having the option. It was something his parents had done. One of the things I've realized about

Ezra is that he seems to see his parents' choices as gospel—the right way to exist. He spends so much time trying to live up to what he thinks they want, trying to make them proud, trying to be good enough for them. I'm not as sure about his father, but I'm pretty sure his mother would think he was perfect even if he weren't a doctor, lived in a different city, and failed at everything he tried. Maybe one day I'll find a way to tell him that. And that, truly, I'm sure his father would come around, too. But in the meantime, I just try to make it easier for him to do what he thinks he needs to. I want to be someone who enables his happiness. It's one of the things I can give to him, the way he can give his safety, his stability, to me.

"I don't mind having to take the train," I told him. "If it means we can get a nicer place."

He looked down and grabbed a highlighter, adjusting his map. "Here, how's this?" he asked.

"Looks good," I told him.

In the end, we found a one-bedroom with a dining nook that came with a storage unit in the basement. It's funny, we didn't really ask each other what we were putting in the storage unit, just moved our boxes and bags in there, promising to go through them all eventually, when we bought our own place in a year or two.

My keyboard went in there, in its black carrying case. He didn't ask me what it was. I'm not even sure if he saw it. If he did, if he asked why I kept it, I'm not sure what I would say. I haven't spoken to Ezra much about my time in the band or as a musician. In fact, I haven't spoken to him about them at all. Even though I combed through them and untangled them with Dr. West, they still seem like a knot in the chain of my life, like when you have a necklace that somehow gets tangled so badly that you can undo most of it, make the necklace wearable, but there's still a small kink in the chain that you can't undo without risking the integrity of the entire thing. The necklace looks fine, beautiful even—you just have to put the knot behind your neck so no one sees it.

I know it's supposed to be healthy to talk about trauma, to make it part of the narrative of your life. It's what I tell my patients. But I have trouble doing it myself. I have trouble integrating that experience with who I am now.

Instead, it's a knot in a necklace that I won't let anyone see. Not even Ezra. Not because I don't trust him, but because I don't trust me. Once I start trying to untangle that last bit of the knot, I don't know what will happen. I don't think I'll ever be able to work through it completely, which means even if I start talking about it, I'll end up just having to pull the knot back tighter in the end.

Dr. West and I fixed almost the whole chain. And it's easier just to wear the necklace the way it is.

45

WHEN EMILY GOT home with Zoe, she was surprised to find Ezra sitting on the couch in the living room, his phone to his ear. But the minute she saw him, she was able to breathe easier. He was here. He was home. She looked at her watch. It was six a.m.

"Good morning," she said as she dropped her keys on the entry hall table. "I didn't know you were coming home today."

He looked up. His face went from concerned to relieved to confused.

"Em, where have you been? You asked me to come home. I just got here and you were gone. I was starting to get worr—" He saw Zoe. "Whose baby is that?"

"This is Zoe," she said, bringing the baby to Ezra. "She belongs to one of my patients, who just checked herself into the psychiatric unit at NYU. It's been a long night. I . . . hadn't heard differently, so I thought you weren't coming back until tomorrow night."

He looked at her. She was sure he was thinking about the fact that she should not have her patient's baby, but he didn't say anything about that. Instead he said, "You called me. You asked me to come home and it sounded like you'd been crying. When I woke up to use the bathroom and heard your message I called you back, but your phone went straight to voice mail, so I figured you'd gone to sleep. I couldn't fall back asleep, though, so I took my mom's car and drove into the city. And then you weren't here. And your phone still wasn't ringing. What's going on?"

She sat down next to Ezra, still holding Zoe, still with a diaper bag on her shoulder. Her body ached and her mind felt like she was thinking through pea soup. "I'd been waiting for you to call, and then Tessa did, and I had to handle that." She yawned. "And at some point my phone died. I'm guessing before you started calling. I'm sorry. I haven't slept all night."

Zoe started to whimper. Emily looked down at her. "I think she probably needs a bottle. Or a new diaper. Or both."

Ezra looked at her. "Explain to me again how you have your patient's baby? This seems like a breach in ethics."

Emily was so tired. She could barely process what he was saying. "It was the only way she would agree to stay in the psychiatric unit If I promised to take Zoe and keep her until her grandma could get here. I have to call Zoe's grandma."

Zoe's whimpers turned into wails and Emily tried to rock her. "It's okay," she said. "You're okay. We'll get you a clean diaper soon. And how about a bottle?"

"I'll take the baby," Ezra said, after a moment. "You call the grandma."

Emily handed Zoe over gratefully and then plugged her phone into the wall and dialed once it had enough power to light up again. Her stomach knotted, knowing what was about to come next. When she introduced herself and started explaining where Tessa was and why, her mother started crying.

"She's going to be okay," Emily said, echoing the words she'd just used with Zoe.

"I'll be on the next flight from Cleveland as soon as I can book it," she said.

"Okay, we'll be here waiting for you," Emily said, and gave the woman her address.

They hung up, and Emily went back to Ezra and Zoe, feeling completely drained.

Ezra had made a bottle for the baby from the powdered formula in the diaper bag and was sitting on the couch feeding her when Emily walked in. She couldn't stop her brief smile when she saw him like that. But it disappeared when she remembered what she had to tell him. What they had to talk about.

"Hey," she said.

He looked up. "How was the grandma?"

Emily shrugged, not sure how she even got through the call. "About what you'd expect. At least I was able to tell her that her daughter was still alive. That her granddaughter was safe."

Ezra nodded. "At least she didn't blame you."

Emily sat down next to him. "That wasn't fair of Malcolm's mom," she said. "And it wasn't true. You know that, right? Want me to take Zoe?"

"Zoe and I have a good thing going," he said, looking down at the baby. Emily wondered if there was an added analgesic quality to holding a baby, if Zoe made Ezra feel calmer. "We're okay over here. And technically it was true. I didn't save him. If I had figured something else out, he would've lived."

Emily leaned against Ezra's shoulder. If Zoe's touch didn't help, maybe hers would. Feeling his body against hers certainly helped Emily. "Or maybe you gave him an extra three or four years that he wouldn't have had otherwise, if he'd seen a different doctor, gone to a different hospital."

"It's just . . ." Zoe had finished the bottle, and Ezra lifted her upright to burp her. "I go over every single treatment decision I made each time a patient dies, wondering what the outcome would've been if I'd done something different. And for Malcolm's mom to say that . . ."

Zoe burped loudly and Ezra laughed. Then the baby did, too, reaching for Ezra's glasses.

He let her take them, and Emily looked at him. He always seemed so vulnerable to her without his glasses on. As if a piece of his armor were missing.

"She seems like an easy baby," Ezra said.

"I guess comparatively," Emily answered. "But I don't know if any baby is really easy. At least, not for a college kid at this point in her life."

Emily leaned back against the couch and closed her eyes. She was past the point of exhaustion. She hadn't slept in more than twenty-four hours.

"When you called me," Ezra started, "was it because of your patient?"

Emily opened her eyes. "No," she said, too tired to tell him anything but the complete truth, the words forming slowly in her brain. "It was because I was afraid I was going to lose you. I need you, Ezra."

Ezra reached out his hand and stroked her hair. "We need to talk," he said. "I need you, too. I realized that the minute I woke up and heard your voice on my voice mail. You're the most important person in the world to me, and I let myself forget that."

"I choose you," Emily said. "Every morning, every afternoon, and every night."

"I choose you, too."

Ezra wrapped his arm around Emily and she laid her head on his shoulder, closing her eyes.

"You need to sleep," he said.

"Mm-hmm," she answered, almost asleep already.

"Go take a nap," he told her. "I'll change Zoe and let the hospital know I'll be in late today. Then Zoe and I will hang for a couple of hours while you sleep."

"Okay," Emily said.

When she woke up four hours later, she still felt tired but at least coherent. She got out a clean pair of jeans and a cotton top, and, when she changed her underwear, realized that she had stopped bleeding. Her baby was all gone.

46

ON HER WAY back to the living room, Emily stopped to wash her face and brush her teeth. Through the bathroom door, she could hear Ezra reading a *New York Times* article out loud to Zoe as if it were a picture book. The rise and fall of his voice seemed incongruous with his words about the increasing price of prescription drugs.

She walked out of the bathroom and down the hall. Ezra and Zoe were on the floor on a towel, and she was chewing on a teething ring Emily had thrown into the diaper bag.

Ezra looked up at the sound of Emily's steps. "She seems to like the sound of my voice," he said. "And her grandmother texted you to tell you that she'll be here around ten thirty." He looked at his watch. "So not much longer."

Emily sat down on the towel next to Ezra and picked up Zoe, cuddling the baby against her chest. Emily looked down at her. Zoe stuck her fist in her mouth and started sucking on it. "Are you hungry, sweet girl?"

"Do you know if she's eating solids?" Ezra asked. "How old is she? Five months? Six?"

"Six," Emily said. "And I know Tessa's been trying, but last I heard, Zoe wasn't so into it." She looked at Zoe as she put her back down on the towel. "You like formula better, don't you?"

While Emily walked into the kitchen to make Zoe a bottle,

her mind flashed to an alternate future in which she was making bottles for their baby in this kitchen. Before her eyes could start to tear, she walked back into the living room and picked Zoe up again, slipping the bottle into her puckered lips. As Zoe drank, Emily started singing the first song that came into her mind: "Teach Your Children."

She walked to the couch and sat down with Zoe, singing the part about how those of tender years can't know the fears their elders grew by.

"Crosby, Stills and Nash," Ezra said, smiling. And he started singing along with her. She let him take the melody and sang the harmony. Even though the reason she'd started singing was to stop herself from crying, her tears fell anyway.

"This is what I want," Emily said. "You and me, singing to a baby. Singing to *our* baby."

Ezra leaned his head against hers. "I was afraid," he said. "When you miscarried, I was afraid I wouldn't be able to handle the heartbreak if I let myself feel anything at all. It was too much to bear, on top of everything else. I was afraid I would shatter." Emily looked at her husband, and he was crying. "But this is what I want, too."

The buzzer went off, startling all three of them. Zoe started crying, and while Emily tried to calm her, Ezra picked up the white phone next to their front door. "Thanks," he said to the doorman on the other end of the line. "You can send her up."

Then he walked back into the living room, where Emily was giving Zoe her bottle. "Her grandmother's here," he said.

Emily took a deep breath and wiped her eyes, preparing to be Dr. Gold again.

47

THE DOORBELL RANG, and Ezra opened it to a woman that Emily recognized immediately as Tessa's mother. She had the same ski-slope nose, the same round cheeks.

"Where's my grandbaby?" she asked.

Emily stood up with Zoe in her arms and walked toward the door. "Right here," she said.

"Dr. Gold," Tessa's mom answered. "Thank you for keeping her. And thank you again for helping my daughter last night. And last year."

"I'm sorry I couldn't do more," Emily answered, handing Zoe over, thinking about the other ways this conversation could be going. The version where Emily hadn't reached Tessa in time, where Zoe lost her mom.

"You kept both of them safe," she said. "That's enough." She shook her head, too overcome with emotion to say more.

But had she? Emily wasn't so sure. It had worked out okay but so easily couldn't have. Were there signs she'd missed the last time Tessa was in her office? Questions she should have asked? Was she not as perceptive because she was thinking about her own loss? Not as focused because she was jealous of what Tessa had?

Ezra brought over the diaper bag, which Tessa's mom slid over her shoulder. Then she looked back at Emily. "What do I do now?" she asked.

Emily looked into her eyes, which were the same deep brown as Tessa's, and saw the love there.

"Go visit your daughter. Let the doctors there treat her. And then, if she were my daughter, I'd take her home. To Ohio. Take her and Zoe home with you, and make sure she knows that she's not going through any of this alone."

Tessa's mother nodded. "I'll take both my babies home."

Emily put her hand on Tessa's mom's arm. "They're lucky they have you," she said.

Tessa's mom smiled, thanked Emily again, and left.

Once the door closed, Emily leaned against Ezra, his strength keeping her upright.

"What a day," he said.

"What a weekend," she answered, not completely sure how she'd just managed to hold it together.

"What a week," he answered back. "I love you."

"I love you, too," she said, rising up to kiss his cheek, not focusing on the fact that he left, just focusing on the fact that he was back, that he came when she called, that he was here, now, when she needed him.

He turned and she was kissing his lips, and then his arms were lifting her off the ground and gently laying her on the couch. He knelt down next to her. "How are you feeling?" he asked, compassion in his voice as he stroked her hair.

"I stopped bleeding," she said. "But I'm not—"

"I know," he said. "Not yet."

He climbed onto the couch next to her, wrapping his arms around her, kissing her forehead. And then a phone on the living room table vibrated. Ezra turned and reached for it. "It's yours," he said, handing Emily her phone.

She looked at it, wondering if it was Tessa or her mom or Ari or one of her boys. But it wasn't. It was Rob, his message visible once her phone unlocked at her touch. Just wanted to make sure you're okay, it said. I'm sorry if I fucked stuff up last night.

Ezra looked at Emily and, his voice even, measured, said, "What's that about?"

Emily knew she had to tell him the truth but was worried about what his response would be. "You promise you won't run again?" she asked.

He winced. "I promise."

"Short story: Rob is Austin Roberts, who wrote the song about me. He was in New York and invited me to an open mic night. So Priya and I went, and I played. And then he tried to convince me that I should go on tour with him. And . . ." She bit her lip. "He hinted at wanting more than that. From me."

"But you said no?" Ezra looked ashen. "No to touring and no to . . . more?"

"I said no," Emily affirmed. "And I left. And called you."

"And you left me that message, asking me to come home."

"Right."

His body was still pressed against hers, but he'd pulled his head back so he could see her whole face, her whole expression. "So . . . why did it sound like you'd been crying?"

Emily's first instinct was to avoid, but she knew she couldn't do that now, not with Ezra, not after everything. She had to tell him the truth. "Because a piece of me wanted to say yes, and . . . and we kissed. Afterward I was afraid and ashamed and started to cry . . . all my emotions have felt so close to the surface ever since—"

"You wanted to say yes?" Ezra asked. "And you kissed him."

Emily bit her lip, trying to figure out how to make him understand. "I missed feeling loved. And I miss music. I miss sharing
music. I miss being on stage and finding a way to play my emotions. The idea of being able to do that again . . . it made me feel . . .
electrified." She looked up at him, the thoughts she'd been having for weeks coalescing in a decision she was sure was the right
one. "I think I want to take a leave of absence from NYU. It's
been too much, recently."

"Why would you leave your job? You love your job."

Emily shook her head. "I don't anymore," she said. "And since
Tessa called last night, I can't stop thinking about how I'm probably screwing up—missing things. And what could happen if I
do. I'm absorbing so much pain, all the time. I need to set it free,
not take it in."

"You're not making any sense," Ezra said, his face shutting
down.

"I think I need to do something else for a while," Emily said.
"To become a musician again."

Whatever empathy Ezra had felt earlier, whatever closeness
they had achieved, seemed to dissipate. "So you're saying you *do*
want to go on tour with this guy who wrote a song about you."

"That's not what I said." Emily wanted so desperately for him
to understand her. "I just want music back in my life. I want
something different. I want to be different."

"But I married a ther—" Ezra started.

"You married *me*, Ez, without any preconditions," Emily said
softly. "And I don't know if I want to be a therapist anymore.
I don't know if I can handle it, especially while we're trying to
have a baby, when I'm so focused on that. I'm afraid I missed
something—with Zoe's mom. What if I miss something again? If

one of my patients died because I didn't see the signs, I don't know if I could live with myself afterward. I know your patients don't always make it, and you can handle it, but I don't think I can."

"Are you saying that I—"

"I'm not saying anything about you, Ezra. I'm talking about me," Emily said. "And . . . I want music in my life again. I want to be on stage and share—"

Ezra moved away from her on the couch. "It's hard for me, too," he said. "But I don't give up. I stick it out. It's the kind of sacrifice you make when you have the ability to save lives. We both have that ability, Emily. It doesn't matter if it's hard for us. That's what Golds do. That's what *we* do."

Emily twisted her hair into a bun and considered her husband. "You know," she said. "If you want to do something else, I'm not stopping you. Golds can . . . we can . . . do other things."

"That's not what I meant," he said. "I meant that we've been given a gift, and you're talking about throwing it away."

"But don't I matter, too?" Emily asked. "Doesn't it matter how I feel? What using this gift, as you call it, is doing to me?"

He was quiet for a moment. "Who do you save," he asked, "the one or the many?"

Emily sat, shocked into silence. He was putting everyone before her. Literally every patient's well-being was more important than her own. How was this the man she'd vowed to spend her life with? How was this her kind, empathetic husband? The one who always took care of her? What had happened? It felt like his heart had enough compassion in it for everyone but her right now.

"You kissed him?" Ezra asked, after she went silent.

She'd said it already. He was going to make her say it again. "I did, for a moment, but then I stopped. I shouldn't have. I just . . . he'd just apologized for how he'd reacted to the miscarriage we had in college and I was crying and he was there and you'd gone and . . . It's not an excuse, but maybe an explanation."

"So it's my fault?" Ezra said to her.

"I didn't say that," Emily answered, sitting up on the couch.

"Yes," he answered. "You did."

Emily took a breath. Was he right? She had no idea at this point, her thoughts so infused with feeling it was hard to be objective, to stay logical. "I want to call NYU today and tell them that they should start looking for someone else. I'll stay until they do. This week is fall break anyway, so—"

"I don't think you should do that," Ezra said, standing up.

Emily closed her eyes for a moment and then opened them again. "It's not your choice," she said. "It's mine. It's my job, and I get to choose if I want to keep doing it."

"Take some time," he said. "Really think this through. Once you've slept some more."

"I'm not going to change my mind," she told him. And she knew it, deep inside her, she knew that something had shifted, that no matter what happened, her future today was different than her future yesterday.

"Em," he said. "Please listen to me."

"I need you to listen to *me*. To believe me. I need you to trust that I know my own mind, that I know what I need to do."

He looked at her, his eyes shining with unshed tears. "That's the problem, isn't it," he said. "I don't think I do."

She stared back at him. She had no idea what to say.

"I feel like I don't know you anymore," he said.

She felt exactly the same way. What they'd experienced so

recently had changed them, and it seemed they hadn't yet figured out how to love these altered versions of each other. She didn't respond.

After a moment of silence, Ezra said, "Maybe *we* need a break. From each other."

Maybe he was right. What was true was that this conversation was going nowhere, and there was no way they'd be able to coexist comfortably together in the apartment right now. "I'll spend the night with Ari," she said, picking up her phone and heading to the bedroom to throw some things in a bag. "Let's both take some time and come back with clearer heads." Clearer hearts, she thought.

When she got into the bedroom, she saw her journal where she had brought it earlier when she retrieved it from the couch. She went to stick it at the bottom of her T-shirt drawer, but then had an idea. She wasn't sure if it was a good one, but before she could second-guess herself, she grabbed a piece of paper and a pen from her night table drawer and wrote: *This might help you understand me better.* She was sharing every secret, every fear, every hope she'd had for the last decade-plus. If he read it, he would truly know her.

And maybe then he would understand.

48

EMILY WALKED THROUGH Grand Central Terminal toward the ticket machines to buy one on the next train to Ari's place in Connecticut. As she walked, one of her thoughts put itself to music. *He has compassion in his heart for everyone but me.* That had never happened before. Like Rob had reminded her, she'd never written the melody to a line of lyrics. She'd always written harmonies, added to what was already there. But she'd never created a song from scratch. She sang the line quietly under her breath. "He has compassion in his heart for everyone but me." A second line came. *He drops his anchor in the ocean while I swim in the sea.*

Did that line make sense? She wasn't sure, but she did know that she was writing a song. Her own song. A song born of the love and pain and confusion she was feeling. A song born of herself.

Emily fished her phone out of her bag to type out the lyrics. She found Rob's text from earlier, which she'd forgotten about in the midst of her fight with Ezra, and responded to his apology with the words: I'm writing a song.

In an instant, her phone was ringing. She picked it up and Rob was on the other side. "You're okay?" he said, the moment she answered.

"Not completely okay," she responded.

"Because of last night?" he asked, tentatively.

"In part," Emily answered.

She heard Rob breathe out on the other end of the phone. "I'm so sorry," he said. "I didn't mean to . . ."

She could hear the sympathy in his voice and the guilt. But it wasn't all his fault. She didn't want him to think it was. Emily pulled herself out of the foot traffic in the station and leaned against a marble wall.

"It's not just you. Something happened with one of my patients after I went home, and then Ezra came home and . . . there's just a lot going on," she said.

"I'm sorry things are rough." A couple laughed loudly as they passed by her. "Where are you?" Rob asked.

"Thanks," Emily said. "I'm in Grand Central—headed to Ari's."

"I see." Rob paused. "Did you say you're writing a song?"

Emily smiled. "I am," she said. "I'm writing my very first song."

She heard him laugh on the other end. "Well, good for you," he said.

Emily could hear something in the background, where Rob was. Maybe waves? Wind? "Where are you?" Emily asked.

"Cancun, Mexico," he answered. "Just checked into my hotel. I'm doing a show here tonight and tomorrow. It's the start of fall break."

Of course. That made sense. If NYU had break, then so did the other schools. And he'd mentioned Mexico last night.

"Are you on the beach?" she asked. "Do I hear waves?"

"I'm actually on my private balcony overlooking the beach," he said.

She imagined it—the sun, the sand, the palm trees. "That sounds wonderful," she told him.

Rob was quiet for a moment and then said: "Come. Flight's on me. I've got a villa, and there's a whole empty bedroom and an extra bathroom with your name on it. More fun than Connecticut. And you can play with me, if you want, on stage. We'll make you the special guest. You can work on your song. Let's be the Sonny and Cher, the Johnny and June Carter Cash of our generation—even if it's just for one night."

Emily imagined herself in Mexico, on the beach, in the sun. She imagined herself on stage again. She imagined making music with Rob. The counseling center was open over break, but almost all the students had canceled. They were going to do some professional-development thing that she could easily miss tomorrow—especially if she was taking a leave, which she was still planning to do, whether Ezra liked it or not.

She passed by the S train, which would take her near Penn Station. From there it was easy to get to JFK. She imagined herself on a balcony overlooking the beach and felt the tension she'd been carrying in her shoulders release.

"There's a separate bedroom and bathroom?" she confirmed.

"There is," he said. "The villa is two floors, one's on each."

"And I would play?" She wondered if this was her chance to give it a try, to see how she felt performing, to figure out if pursuing music was worth risking her marriage, risking the life she'd built for the last decade.

"For as many songs as you'd like," he answered.

Emily found herself nodding. Maybe she'd try it and hate it, and then she could go back to Ezra and tell him that he was right, that she'd figure out how to get her focus back at NYU, that she'd find a way to work through her fears and her failures. *Every choice you make is the one you're supposed to make* rang softly in her head.

She cleared her throat. "Okay," she said, glad that she'd grabbed the duffel bag that she always traveled with, the one that she kept her passport zipped into so she'd never forget it in a desk drawer, like a friend of hers in grad school had once done on a trip to Morocco. "I'm coming. But I've got my ticket. I don't need you to pay."

"Are you serious?" Rob asked, his voice surprised. "You're really coming?"

"As serious as a dirge," she told him. "I'll call again when I know what flight I'll be on."

"I'll be waiting," Rob answered.

Then they hung up. Emily almost couldn't believe what she'd just agreed to. But she needed this. She needed to see. Without giving herself a chance to change her mind, she opened up the web browser on her phone and bought herself a ticket to Mexico with the debit card for her solo account. Then she stared at her phone for a moment, not actually believing she'd done it. What was she thinking?

Music, she reminded herself. She was thinking about music. She was going to perform on stage. In Mexico. With Rob. And then she'd know how it felt. If it was as powerful now as she thought it would be.

When the confirmation email arrived, Emily texted her sister. Change of plans, she wrote. I'm going to Mexico for a couple of days. I'll call from there. Love you. Then she turned off her phone. She knew Ari wouldn't approve, knew she'd ask questions that Emily wasn't ready to answer. She'd call Ari when she got there.

Emily swiped her MetroCard for the shuttle and started her adventure.

49

EMILY WAITED IN line to board her plane, still convincing herself that this was the right choice. She'd told herself that when she'd showed up at JFK, when she quickly checked in for her flight, when she raced through security. And she kept telling herself that when she made it to the end of the line just as her boarding group was called.

Sitting in row 17, seat B, she was still having second thoughts.

But the music was calling to her. She needed to find out if she should really resurrect her dream. If this life was what she wanted.

She wondered what Dr. West would make of this. What would Emily herself think if a patient had told her this story? Reckless behavior, poor decision making. She'd wonder about bipolar disorder, but she didn't fit the rest of the criteria for that. Maybe some sort of postmiscarriage hormone imbalance. Or a not-quite midlife crisis. Or maybe she was simply calling out for attention, calling out for help.

She should go back into therapy. When she got back, she would. She needed help, the same way she did when she was in college. But that was for later. For now, she was going to play music in Mexico.

She turned her phone back on to call Priya before takeoff, not looking at or listening to the messages from Ari. She left Priya a voice mail: "I'm going to be gone tomorrow, maybe the next day. There's a lot to talk about. Sorry I'm missing the staff development thing. I went to Mexico." Then she turned her phone off again.

Emily wondered if Priya would guess the truth, that she was somewhere with Rob, or if she would assume that Emily and Ezra had gone for a quick trip together to patch things up after losing the baby. That was what she should be doing. But the thought of fighting with him right now was too overwhelming—what if they reached the end of the argument and she lost him completely? What if their relationship changed in a way she didn't want? She knew that difficult circumstances either pulled people together or broke them apart. That two people had to consciously decide to make things work. Was she deciding not to make this work? Or was this just a step on her journey of figuring out what she wanted to make work? How to make things work?

Even if she chose Ezra over music, he'd have to choose her.

After everything he said, she wasn't completely sure if he would.

50

THROUGHOUT THE WHOLE flight, Emily kept thinking about Ezra. She kept thinking about the feeling that had inspired the beginning of a song, the one she was writing, the one that was her own. She gave herself over to it, and let it grow and change. As the plane traveled farther from New York, the melody and lyrics kept evolving. She wished she had a keyboard so she could really hear it and start arranging it as she wrote. But even without a keyboard, by the end of the flight she had something.

He has love in his heart
For everyone but me
He floats on a river of compassion
While I swim in the sea.
When I reach for him
He just doesn't see
Because there's love in his heart
For everyone but me

And you say he's kind
And you say he's good
And I know it's true
For you, for you

It wasn't a whole song. It wasn't even a good one. But it had a verse and a chorus. Or maybe a chorus and a bridge. She needed to work on it. But channeling her emotions into a song . . . it made everything feel like somehow it would be okay. She was transforming her pain into something else. And in doing so, she was transforming herself.

Plus, focusing on that meant she could ignore the feeling that her life was coming undone. Things were falling apart. The center was shifting off course. And she wasn't doing anything to pull it back. At least not yet.

She might even be pushing it further afield.

51

WHEN EMILY CROSSED the jet bridge into the airport in Cancun, she could feel the damp warmth of the beach penetrating the building—and her, too. Her bones felt warmer. But her heart cracked a little when she realized the last time she stepped off a plane into this airport it was with Ezra by her side, a few days before their wedding. Things had felt so different then. So solid, so secure, like nothing could ever tear them apart, the threads of their relationship woven from iron. But iron rusts and crumbles. Was that what was happening now?

As she got through customs, she saw someone in a baseball cap and sunglasses holding a piece of hotel stationery with her name scrawled on it. Had Rob sent her a driver? She'd told him not to but actually wouldn't mind not having to figure out where and how to get a taxi. She walked toward the man and realized, as she got closer, that Rob hadn't sent anyone. It was him under the *MEX* baseball cap and aviators. He broke out in a grin when he spotted her moving in his direction.

"*Bienvenidos a Cancún*," he said, when she was within earshot.

Emily started to laugh. Her question at the pizza place had been answered. "So you're getting recognized now?" she whispered.

"It's been getting worse at each tour stop," he said under his breath. "There was a crowd waiting for me when we landed this time around. Diana insisted I wear a disguise to come get you. Thank goodness for hotel sundry stores."

"Diana's the tour manager I met in New York?" she asked. "The woman who asked me to come backstage?"

Rob nodded. "Did you check a bag?"

"It was a bit of a spur-of-the-moment decision," Emily said. "So I haven't got much. I'll need to buy something to perform in. And maybe some flip-flops."

Rob nodded. "Our car is outside. We can make a stop before we get to the hotel—there's a little shopping village in the hotel zone."

Emily and Rob walked outside, where a black Suburban was waiting for them. The driver got out as they got closer and opened the door.

"Thanks," Emily said, as she got inside. Then she looked at Rob, who was taking off his hat and sunglasses. "Do you always have a personal driver now?" she asked quietly, so the driver wouldn't hear.

Rob shook his head. "Not always. Raúl works at the hotel. He drives people to the airport and back, sometimes out to dinner. That sort of thing."

Emily nodded, impressed—and also proud of Rob that he'd gotten here, achieved what he'd dreamed of when he was in college.

"We need to make a quick stop at a shop where Emily can get some clothes," he told Raúl. "Can we go to that little shopping village across the way?"

"Of course, sir," Raúl said.

The seats were leather and the air conditioner was on full blast. Emily leaned back and closed her eyes.

"So what happened?" Rob asked. "Seems like something big for you to be here."

Emily opened her eyes, not wanting to relive it but knowing she owed him an explanation. Knowing that Rob would understand. "I told Ezra I wanted to take a leave of absence from NYU and his response was not what I would have hoped."

"Ah," Rob said. "But it's not his decision."

"Right." Emily leaned farther back into the plush seat. "Not his decision."

"I learned that the hard way when we were in college. I can make my own decisions, but I can't make anyone else's. I couldn't make yours, as much as I'd wanted to."

She turned toward him, feeling again like she had to apologize. "My decision seemed like it was the right one at the time—to give you up, to give music up—and I truly believed it was for years. But now . . . I'm not so sure. Playing on stage again—it felt like it reawakened something in me that is . . . I don't know . . . maybe essential to who I am. Like in making that decision years ago I'd lost part of myself."

"I can't speak to the music, but I think in the end, us breaking up was the right choice at the time," Rob said, reaching across the middle seat to put his hand on top of hers. "It's like the butterfly effect. If you'd chosen differently, we might not be here. I might not have a hit song, or two gorgeous girls, or this chance to reconnect with you. I'm real happy with where I ended up, so no reason to second-guess, at least not on my behalf."

Emily felt her eyes start to fill with tears, because she wasn't quite sure she was happy with where she'd ended up. She was second-guessing on her own behalf. Second-guessing the decision to allow her pain to dictate her life.

"I'm glad," she said to him. "I really am. And . . . I hope I'll be able to say that same thing soon."

He gave her hand a small squeeze. "Me too, Queenie," he said. "Me too."

As the car drove past palm trees and hotel driveways, she wondered how long it would take before she *was* happy where she ended up. She hoped not another thirteen years.

52

EMILY FLIPPED THROUGH a rack of pants, realizing that what she wore when she performed in New York would feel out of place here. Instead she pulled out a short black tank dress and a sheer blouse. Its pattern was a whirl of green and amber that she knew would bring out the green in her hazel eyes. Holding them, she felt excitement pulse through her body.

She walked to a small dressing room and shut the door, hidden from Rob's view. As she undressed, the air felt different on her skin. She pulled the dress over her head. It skimmed her body, ending midthigh, the thin straps accentuating her shoulders and collarbone. She tied the blouse just under her breasts and left the dressing room to check out the outfit in the store's three-way mirror. She looked like a new version of herself. Not like she was trying to re-create her college image, but like someone she could be now. She noticed Rob reflected behind her, quietly watching. She turned around. "What do you think?"

"I think yes," he said, his eyes focused in a way that brought heat to Emily's cheeks. "I like the boots."

She looked down at her feet. She'd thrown on the first pair of shoes she'd seen in her closet before she left her apartment, and they were a pair of cowboy boots she had gotten when she and Ezra spent a long weekend in Nashville last year.

"It'll go with your whole down-home Texas thing. Howdy," Emily said, imitating his on-stage twang. "I'm real glad y'all are here tonight."

Rob laughed. "The audience eats it up. And it's *all* y'all," he said, still laughing. "I've gotta make sure I include everyone."

"I'll remember that," Emily said, walking to the dressing room.

"You said you wanted some flip-flops, too, right?" Rob asked. "Did you bring a bathing suit?"

Emily stopped. "I didn't," she said. There was a sale rack of bathing suits to the left of the dressing rooms. She walked toward them and started flipping through the options. She pulled a green one-piece off the rack for a closer look.

"How about this one?" Rob asked. He was carrying a black bikini with white piping. "Didn't you have something like this the summer we were first together? You wore it when we went to Coney Island."

Emily hadn't thought about that bikini in years, but she remembered it now. It was strapless—a bandeau top and a low-rise bottom that tied together on the sides. The bikini Rob was holding was cut differently. This one was a halter and the bottoms were a little more modest.

"What do you think?" Rob asked.

Emily took the bikini and looked at the price tag. "I think this is a little more than I want to spend . . ." she said.

"My treat," Rob said. "The outfit, too."

"I couldn't—" Emily started.

"Why don't you try it on first?" Rob said. "We can figure out who pays afterward."

———

EMILY WALKED INTO the dressing room with the bikini and the green one-piece.

She put the bikini on and looked in the mirror. The suit was a bit more revealing than the ones Emily had at home in New York, but it was beautiful. She turned around. Maybe she could get used to this.

"So?" Rob asked, though the door. "Do you need me to help you tie anything in there?"

Emily blushed, imagining him imagining her in the suit. Imagining him imagining her out of the suit. That wasn't why she was here.

"It fits," she said. "But I think I'm going to go with the one-piece."

As she took off the swimsuit, her heart felt like a yo-yo, going back and forth between enjoying her time here with Rob and feeling bad about her fight with Ezra, feeling like maybe she shouldn't be here. It was as if she'd forgotten, for a moment, what had happened, what she and Ezra said to each other in New York, and in that moment of forgetting, happiness and joy snuck in, but then she'd remembered again and the space for joy disappeared.

The song she'd worked on during the plane ride morphed in her head:

There's love in your heart
For everyone but me
You row across the water
While I drown in the sea

When I reach for you
You just don't see
Because there's love in your heart
For everyone but me

And they say you're kind
And they say you're good
And I know it's true
Because they say the same
About me to you

When you look for me
Have I already flown?
When you want me there
Are you all on your own?
When you reach for me
Can I just not see?
Is there love in your heart
That is there for me?

"Hey," Rob called from the other side of the door, "how are you going to wear your hair for the show?"

Emily hadn't thought about that yet. "It's a surprise," she called back, as she buttoned her jeans. "I'll show all y'all tonight."

Rob's laughter on the other side of the door made her smile. The yo-yo was still spinning, still flying up and down and up and down. She wondered if it would ever stop.

53

"YOU SAID IT'S just two shows here?" Emily asked Rob as he unlocked the hotel's private villa.

"That's right," he said, holding the door open for her. "Show tonight, show tomorrow night, then I'm off to Miami for three more shows after that. Then home for a couple of days to see my girls."

Emily walked into the villa and looked around. "Wow," she said, taking in the plush carpeting, the gauzy drapes, the view of the ocean, and the plunge pool just outside.

"Not bad for a kid who grew up on the wrong side of the tracks in Austin, huh?" Rob was looking around as if he still couldn't quite believe it.

"Not bad for anyone," Emily said seriously, pausing in front of the window leading out to the pool. "I hope you really understand what you made happen—with your music, with your talent."

"With your inspiration," Rob said, coming up behind her. "I'll never be able to thank you enough."

Emily shook her head, embarrassed, and put her bag of new clothing down on the floor. "My inspiration was breaking your heart," she said. "That doesn't quite seem like something I deserve thanks for."

Rob stepped closer, both of them looking out the window at the ocean, so close their cheeks were nearly touching. "You deserve thanks for loving me in the first place. For showing me what love was, for teaching me about desire and what it means to feel connected to someone else so profoundly. I mean it. Even if I never saw you again, even if you never wanted to speak to me again, I would be grateful that you made me feel that way."

Emily turned toward him.

Then he turned, too, the air between them electric. But Emily remembered how she'd fallen apart last time their lips met. How guilty she'd felt. It seemed he remembered it, too.

"Want to go for a boat ride?" he asked, his breath warm on her cheek. "We have about an hour and a half to kill."

"Sure," she answered, fearing that if they spent more time together, alone in this villa, they would end up doing something she would regret. "Which room's mine?"

Rob pointed across the living room. "I took the one upstairs, so the one down here's yours. Just through that hallway."

"I'll be out in a minute," Emily said, and went to change.

The room was beautiful—just as perfectly decorated as the room in the Gregory Hotel she and Ezra didn't spend the night in together. The sheets felt like silk, and there was a towel in the shape of a bird sitting on the bed. Emily pulled out her phone and turned it on. She saw a new text from Ari. Did you make it to Mexico? Are you okay? And then saw that there were seventeen more. Instead of reading them or listening to Ari's voice mail, she gave her sister a call.

"What's going on?" Ari said the minute she picked up the phone. "Are you leaving Ezra?"

Emily took a breath. "No," she said. "I'm not leaving Ezra."

"So what are you doing in Mexico?" Ari asked. "Are you at a yoga retreat or something?"

"I'm with Rob," Emily answered quietly, cringing, waiting for her sister's disapproval.

"You're what?!" Ari said. "So you're not leaving Ezra, but you're having an affair?"

"No!" Emily said. What could she say to make her sister understand? "I'm performing. When I saw Rob, when I played on stage, it was like I finally became my whole self again. And Ezra basically said he doesn't want me to change. So when Rob invited me to play with him, I came to see if pursuing music was worth potentially giving up my husband. If it really would feel like I imagined."

Ari was quiet for a while. "I want you to be happy, Em. But . . . are you sure this is the way to figure this out?"

Emily stared out the window at the ocean waves crashing against the sand. "I don't know," she said, honestly. "But I needed some way to figure it out and . . ." She shrugged even though her sister couldn't see her. "I think Ezra and I needed some time apart. We can't seem to connect right now. We don't understand each other. And . . . and he told me I should sacrifice my own happiness for other people's."

"Well," Ari said. "I don't agree with that."

"Yeah," Emily said. "Me neither." There was a couple on the beach asleep together on the same towel. That used to be her and Ezra.

"Do you think he really meant it?" Ari asked.

The man on the beach rolled slightly closer to the woman.

"I think he did in the moment," Emily said. "Once he has time to think about it, I hope his feelings will change."

"Me too," Ari said. Then after a moment she added, "Where are you staying?"

Emily braced herself for her sister's disapproval again. "At his villa," she said. "But in a separate room. With a separate bathroom." She didn't tell her sister how she could sense Rob's presence, even through the closed doors.

"Em," Ari said. She said it the way she said Emily's name through their whole lives when Emily made a choice her more-responsible sister wouldn't have chanced.

"I'll be fine. It'll be fine," Emily said. "He's sleeping upstairs, and I'm sleeping downstairs."

"And neither one of you knows how to climb stairs?" Ari said.

"We're adults," Emily told her sister, watching the waves crash against the shore.

"I wasn't questioning your age," Ari said. "Just your decision."

Emily knew her sister was trying to look out for her, the way she always did. "I love you," she told her.

Ari sighed. "I love you, too," she said. "And if you need me, for any reason, just call. I can get on a flight to Cancun pretty quickly from up here."

Emily smiled. "Thank you," she said.

"You ready?" Rob called out.

"One second!" Emily called back.

"I've got to go," she told Ari as she slipped off her clothes, "but I'll call you soon."

"Okay," Ari said. "And really, if you need me, I'll be there."

"I know," Emily answered. "And same goes for you. Always."

Emily slipped on the green bathing suit she'd gotten in the shopping village and threw on the cover-up and flip-flops she'd found, too. Then she opened the door. "I'm ready," she said.

Rob was standing there in a pair of short swim trunks and a tight white T-shirt.

He looked at her, his eyes intense, and shook his head. "Not for what I'm ready for," he replied.

She rolled her eyes at him. "Come on," she said. "Don't we have a boat to catch?" But she felt it, too. That outfit, his smile. She felt lighter around him, happier, more alive.

She should go home. But even though she knew it was what she *should* do, she also knew it was not what she *would* do. She wanted to see this through. She wanted to play tonight. She wanted to recapture at least a small piece of who she'd been.

"What time do we have to be back to get ready for the show?" she asked, as they walked out the door.

"We've got an hour and twenty minutes." he said.

"Then let's go!" she said, and took off running across the sand, the breeze in her hair and the salt air in her lungs a balm to her heart, just like she knew the music would be.

54

SOON EMILY FOUND herself on a twenty-four-foot bowrider
bobbing peacefully in the water. Rob was driving the boat—he
had passed on the additional offer of a chartered captain—and
had cut the motor and dropped anchor. There was nothing to see
but deep blue water lapping at the boat all around them.

Emily walked to the front of the boat, sitting down on one of
the padded seats in the bow. The wind whipped through her hair.
A seagull cawed over head. She wished Ezra were there with her.
And then she didn't. Her heart kept up its yo-yo.

"Are you sunscreened?" Rob asked, sitting across from her in
the bow. He'd taken his shirt off and his chest was more defined
than she remembered. He was rubbing sunscreen into his shoulders and down his arms.

She shook her head. "Can I have some?"

"Sure," he answered. "But would you mind doing my back?"

Emily hesitated, then picked up the bottle of sunscreen from
the floor of the boat and squeezed it into her hands. It'd been sitting in the sun, so it was warm to the touch. She walked over to
sit behind Rob and started rubbing the lotion into the sun-kissed
skin of his back. His muscles rippled underneath her fingers, so
different from Ezra's lean frame. She heard his breath catch, but
she ignored it. She ignored her own racing heart.

"All done," she said, when she rubbed in the last bit of lotion.

"Want me to do you?" he asked.

She hesitated again, but she didn't want to be sunburned for the performance.

"Thanks," she said, turning around so her back was facing him, glad for a reason not to look at him.

His guitar-player fingers were strong as they kneaded her back. They moved from the skin below her shoulders to the skin above her waist, where bathing suit fabric started again. As he rubbed in the lotion, Emily felt a shiver run through her. This was the first time anyone other than Ezra had done this for her in years. Rob brought his hands to her sides, rubbing the last bits of lotion down her ribs to her waist. She felt cared for, precious.

He squeezed more sunscreen out of the bottle and leaned back to massage it onto her neck, her shoulders, down her arms, and then, his arms reaching around cradling her, his breath soft on her neck, he gently worked the sunscreen into the backs of her hands and down the length of each finger. She thought to say it was okay, he could stop, she could do this part, but her mouth wouldn't form the words. She realized she'd closed her eyes, reveling in his touch. She felt lost in time and space.

When Rob pulled his hands away, she felt their absence. He lay down on the padded bench beside her. It was just wide enough for two. "Want to join?" Rob asked.

Emily lay down next to him, her whole body tuned to his. He shifted his arm, and she rested her head on his biceps.

"Comfortable?" he asked.

"Mm-hmm," she said, closing her eyes, feeling the sun on her face, breathing the warm ocean air. They lay, inhaling and exhaling together.

"Do you think about it often?" Rob asked, softly.

"About what?" Emily asked.

"About . . . the baby we lost."

She heard a seagull cawing and then opened her eyes to watch it dive down into the waves.

"I used to," Emily said. "Every day. Less often now, but I still do. He—or she—would've been in seventh grade this year. Can you believe it?"

"That's incredible," Rob said, his arm tightening around her, rolling her head onto his chest.

"I know." Emily closed her eyes and drifted off to sleep in the late-afternoon sun, dreaming about Rob, dreaming about their baby.

55

BACK AT THE villa, Emily and Rob stood on the balcony, each with a cocktail. It was the calmest Emily had felt in days—in months, actually.

"I can't believe this is real," she said to him.

He looked at her. "Me neither," he answered. Then he glanced back at the clock in the living room. "We've gotta get ready," he said. "I'm gonna jump in the shower."

Emily waited for the butterflies in her stomach. But they weren't there. She was excited, but she wasn't nervous. "Me too," she said, and then clarified. "My own shower."

Rob laughed. "I figured."

ONCE EMILY WAS dressed, she went back into her bathroom and applied the kind of stage makeup she used to wear. Thick eyeliner, three coats of mascara, foundation under powder under blush. The application came back to her just like the piano had. She dried her hair and looked at herself in the mirror. Instead of the thick braided crown she used to wear, she made four small braids, two at each temple, that she pulled back, leaving the rest of her hair loose and wavy.

"Want to meet me at the venue?" Rob called from the living room. "I should head over now."

Emily walked out of the bathroom and shut off the light. "I'm ready," she said, as she arrived in the living room.

"Are you ever," Rob said, looking her up and down. "You look great."

She smiled. "You too," she told him. He had on jeans and a soft white V-neck T-shirt with his own pair of boots. Even the way he inhabited his clothes exuded confidence.

"Let's go check out your keyboard. I gave Diana the backline specs, and I'm sure she found something perfect."

"Let's do it," she said, wondering what Rob had specified.

The butterflies still weren't there. Just excitement that pulsed with every beat of her heart.

56

THAT NIGHT, EMILY watched most of Rob's show from the wings with Diana. She was amazed by how many fans there were, how many of them knew all the words to his songs, even the ones that weren't played on the radio as often as "Crystal Castle." She had a chance, for the first time, to really listen to his lyrics—the songs were filled with beauty, with desire, with hope, with regret. He was there in all of the songs. There was nothing he was hiding; Rob was singing himself, sharing himself with everyone who came to his concerts, everyone who listened to his words. Maybe that was why she was so drawn to him right now—the doors of his heart were thrown wide open. She wanted hers to be.

Soon Rob was announcing her, telling everyone who she was. "All y'all know that 'Crystal Castle' was inspired by a woman I knew a long time ago, a woman I always thought of as the one who got away. Well, she's here with us tonight!"

The crowd started to cheer.

"Let me introduce you to Emily Solomon!"

Emily walked out on stage noting that Rob went back to her maiden name, turned her into the person she'd been before. She wondered if it was on purpose or was just how he thought of her, a slip like the one she'd made at the open mic.

"Ready to play, Emily?" he asked.

"Always," she answered, as she stepped behind the keyboard

Rob's team had set up for her. She had a mic threaded through her hair, taped in place, and it was live now.

They played the same rendition of "Crystal Castle" that they had at Tony's bar but without the drums. There was something even more soulful about it this way, the two instruments entering into a conversation, her vocals underscoring his. And the audience was responding to it. The room felt electric, just like it had so many years ago when they'd played at Webster Hall. Emily felt like the past and present were combining, like what was wrong had been set right. Like she had rediscovered the magic she had lost.

When the song finished, the audience erupted in applause and shouts and whistles. Emily felt the crowd's emotion surge through her body. It left her breathless, sure that this was what she had to find some way to do—over and over again for the rest of her life.

"Thank all y'all for coming tonight!" Rob said, his guitar raised in one hand.

"One more song!" the audience chanted. "One more song!"

Rob looked at Emily and raised his eyebrow.

She knew what he was asking and nodded.

He strummed a few chords on the guitar and the audience quieted down. "We got a real old one for you," he said. "Emily and I used to play this in college."

Then he started the medley of love songs. The audience laughed and cheered and clapped at all the right moments. And then they got to the end, with Rob inches from her, that place in the performance where they used to kiss.

There was a spotlight on only them. The rest of the room was dark. And it felt like everyone there was holding their breath.

"Do it!" someone finally yelled. "Kiss her!"

Emily lifted her face toward his, offering her permission, and he bent forward and softly kissed her, a small peck on her lips. The crowd started clapping and wolf whistling. Rob looked at Emily. She could tell there were words he wanted to say, but his mic was still on. Hers was, too. So he turned back toward the audience, slipped his fingers into her hand, and raised them both high in the air. "Thank you!" he said. And they walked off the stage together to applause that echoed throughout the room.

Emily felt like she was flying, like she was a comet orbiting the solar system; this was what she loved doing. This was where she felt most like herself. This was what she had to do. She turned to Rob, grinning. He took a step toward her, the joy she felt reflected in his face, and he wrapped his arms around her in a spontaneous hug, holding her tight.

"That was awesome," she said against his chest.

"Totally awesome," he replied, his lips moving against her hair.

She could hear the applause roaring in her ears, the appreciation for her music. It was a sound she wanted to bottle and keep with her always, something she could open up and drink in when she needed it.

BEFORE THE SOUND guys came over to unhook her mic, Emily pulled her cell phone out of the bag she'd left backstage, wanting to text Ari, to let her know how fantastic it was to be on stage. But when she looked at her screen, she was met with a missed call from Ezra and two texts: one from Ari saying that Ezra had called looking for her, since she hadn't picked up her phone, and Ari had told him that she was in Mexico. The second was from Ezra confirming that she actually was in Mexico. All it said was: Are you really in Cancun?

I am, she typed back. Just for a couple of days.

She held on to the phone for a while, while her mic was unhooked, but he didn't write back. She thought about adding on to her previous message. Telling him how great it felt to play music on stage, how much it meant to her, try to make him understand, but she didn't have the words.

Then Diana came over. "That was fabulous," she said to Emily.

"Thanks," Emily answered.

"So, I haven't spoken to Rob yet, but his PR team would love this story. Would you be up for some media interviews in Miami? And how long are you staying on tour with us? The more advance notice, the better."

Emily swallowed. This seemed like too many decisions at once. She looked down at her phone to see if Ezra had written her back. Her words got stuck in her throat.

"Are you bothering Emily?" Rob asked, coming over and wrapping his arm around her shoulders, as if he were protecting her from Diana. "I told you she was off-limits. No questions."

"We need to talk then," Diana said.

"Tomorrow," Rob answered. "I'm hungry."

Emily smiled at him. "Me too," she said.

57

BACK IN THE villa, Emily was in her room alone, changing into a T-shirt that Rob had loaned her. The flannel pajama pants and thermal top she'd packed for her sister's house in Connecticut were sweltering. Rob's T-shirt was threadbare—the kind that had been through the wash so many times that the logo on it had nearly disappeared. Emily couldn't quite figure out what it had once been. The T-shirt reached her midthigh. She contemplated putting on her flannel pajama pants, but it was just so hot and he'd already seen her in her swimsuit. So she walked out in the T-shirt.

Rob was outside in the dining area, looking relaxed in a T-shirt and workout shorts. In front of him was a room service feast: ceviche, marinated pork, rice, plantains, fish. And a bottle of tequila. He was sipping it from a glass.

"Want some?" he asked, lifting up the bottle.

"Sure," Emily answered, sitting down next to him and surveying the food in front of her. She'd taken her braids out, and her hair was framing her face, resting on her shoulders.

He handed her a generous pour of tequila and then raised his glass. "To making music," he said, and they both clinked glasses and took a drink.

"That's the best tequila I've ever had," she said, looking at the label.

"That's what I asked room service for," Rob answered. "A bottle of the best tequila on the menu."

Emily laughed. Even with all the trappings of this successful musician life, he was still Rob.

He started serving himself some food, but Emily just sipped the tequila. She was thinking about the text from Ezra. He still hadn't responded to her. Had there been something he'd wanted to say when he called Ari's house? When he called her cell phone earlier?

They'd had ceviche at their wedding. And a bottle of tequila, though not one quite as good as this. The night after they had gotten married, when they went back to their room alone, Ezra had whispered to her that he'd never been happier than he was in that moment. She'd whispered the same, and it had been true. She tried to remember that feeling. It was hard to recapture.

"You're not eating," Rob said, a piece of shrimp speared on his fork.

Emily focused in on him again. "Sorry," she said. "Just thinking. How's the ceviche?"

"Delicious," he answered with a smile.

Emily put some on her plate and took a bite.

Rob refilled her tequila glass and his, which they'd both drained. "You okay, Queenie?" he asked.

"You called me Emily so many times during the show, I wasn't sure if I'd lost my nickname," she said, avoiding his question, picking up her glass.

"Well," he said. "It seemed like I should introduce you to the audience properly."

She took another sip of tequila. "You used my maiden name," she said.

He took a sip. "I didn't even realize," he said. "I can introduce you differently tomorrow night. You're staying for tomorrow night?"

She could see how gingerly he was stepping around this question.

"For tomorrow night, but then I think I have to go home." She'd have loved to stay—for Miami, for whatever city came next after his break in LA, but Diana was right. If she did that, she'd become part of the show, part of the story. And she wasn't ready for that. Even as good as it had felt to play with Rob tonight, even if it might be a way to repay him for the choices she'd made in the past, it meant too much for her future. It meant she'd be pushed into making decisions she wasn't quite ready to make.

He nodded. "You know you're welcome to tour with me as long as you want."

"Thank you," she said. Maybe it was because of what he'd been through in the last couple of years, or maybe it was because they hadn't been together for so long and he was surprised she was here with him again, that he was being so careful, so thoughtful. His support felt unconditional—the opposite of how Ezra's felt at the moment. It wouldn't stay that way, she knew. At some point Rob would ask for more, but right now, he just seemed happy that she was there for however long she would be, in whatever way she could be.

He refilled their glasses again.

"This is my last one," she said, realizing her words were starting to slide into one another. "I'm cut off after three." She hadn't felt this tipsy in a long time.

"Yes, ma'am," he said, and then passed her a plate of plantains.

"Friendly suggestion that you should eat your dinner instead of just drink it."

She dutifully spooned some plantains onto her plate and ate one.

His face was in his hand, and he was smiling as he looked at her.

"What?" she asked.

He shook his head. "I just can't believe you're here with me, in my hotel room, in my T-shirt, drinking tequila."

"Your villa," she corrected him.

He laughed.

"I can't really believe I'm here either," she said. The tequila had blurred and sharpened her vision at the same time. The villa seemed fuzzy in the background, but every centimeter of Rob's face was in hyperfocus. She could see a fan of tiny creases at the corners of his eyes. She reached out and touched them.

"Queen?" he asked.

"It's a new part of you," Emily tried to explain. "There are parts of you that I haven't really met yet."

She ran her fingers through the side of his hair, where a few silver strands broke up the brown. That was new, too.

"I smashed my finger in a car door," he said, holding out the pointer on his right hand. "About six years ago."

Emily held his finger and looked at the scar. "Did it hurt?" she asked.

"A lot," he answered.

She pressed the scar against her lips. "All better," she said.

"You want some water?" he asked.

"I want you to kiss me all better," she said. "Can you kiss me all better?"

"Oh, Queenie," he said. Then he stood and gathered her in his arms, carrying her to her bedroom. He laid her on the bed and kissed her forehead. "There is nothing I'd like more than to kiss you all better, but not like this. I'll leave some water and Tylenol on your table. Sleep well, beautiful."

Emily closed her eyes, and the world started to spin. She opened them again as Rob put pills and a glass on the table next to her.

"I love you," she told him.

"I've always loved you," he answered.

A few moments after he left her room, she heard guitar chords strumming. Then Rob was singing:

Kiss me all better
You said
You said
Kiss me all better
As I tucked you
Into bed

Emily closed her eyes again and this time his music grounded her and made the world stop spinning off course. She fell asleep cradled in his song.

58

THE NEXT MORNING, Emily woke up at dawn with a headache. She looked over and saw the water and Tylenol to her left, took both pills, and drained the glass. It had been a long time since she'd woken up hungover. It made her feel like she was in college again. She didn't want to be in college again. She turned over and went back to sleep.

A FEW HOURS later, she woke up again, feeling more like a human. She ambled out of the bedroom to get some more water and a cup of coffee and found the villa empty. There was a note on the table from Rob: *Meeting with Diana, be back soon.*

She wasn't sure when he'd left, so she wasn't sure what *soon* meant. She twisted her hair up into a messy bun that she secured with the pencil he'd left next to the note, then brushed her teeth and washed her face. She felt like she'd traveled back in time to the days of waking up late after drinking too much the night before. She remembered the roar of applause, the on-stage kiss, her off-stage request, and Rob tucking her in. It really was like she was twenty years old again. But she wasn't. She was thirty-three.

"I am an absolute mess," she said aloud. She wondered if she should take some paper and start journaling again, write a letter to try to gain perspective. But instead she picked up Rob's guitar. He'd taught her the basics in college, and though she didn't remember much, she did remember the mnemonic for the strings: Elvis Always Digs Good Banana Eating. It was what his teacher had taught him, when he first learned to play. They'd spent a night once trying to come up with other sentences that worked. Everyone Always Dumps Garbage Bags Empty. Ellen Ate Dan's Great Big Elephants. Every Austinite Does Goddamn Big Erections. Then they'd gotten distracted by Rob's goddamn big erection and ended up in bed.

Ostensibly, knowing those notes, Emily should be able to make music somehow on the guitar. She plucked one string, moving her fingers down the frets, raising the notes a half step as she went. If she did that, she realized, she could use the guitar like a keyboard, using single notes to stand in for chords. She focused on the A string and started messing around with the song she'd been writing in her head for the last couple of days, changing the words again, trying to make them sound right.

There's love in your heart
For everyone but me
You row across the water
While I drown in the sea
And when I reach for you
You just don't see
Because there's love in your heart
For everyone but me

And they say you're kind
And they say you're good

And I know it's true
But they say the same
About me to you

When you look for me
Have I already flown?
When you want me there
Are you all on your own?
When I slip up
Is that all that you see?
Is there love in your heart
For everyone but me?

And they say I'm kind
And they say I'm good
But I know it isn't true
Because of how I treated you

There's love in my heart
That's waiting there for you
There's love in my heart
That's big enough for two
If we reach for each other
I hope you can see
That there's love there waiting
For you, from me

It would've been easier with a keyboard, but Emily was making do with the guitar. She incorporated more of the strings, slowly playing the whole chords she would have used on the piano. She'd started again, pulling the pencil out of her hair so she could write it down, when she heard the door open behind her. Rob was back.

Emily turned to face him. "Morning," she said. "I hope I didn't do anything too unforgivable last night."

He shook his head. "Nah," he said. "You were fine." His hair looked windswept and he was holding a bag of breakfast pastries. "I heard your song," he added. "While I was unlocking the door. It's beautiful."

He put the pastries down on the table.

"Thank you," she answered. "I—I hope it's okay I was using your guitar."

"Of course." Rob pulled a piece off a cinnamon roll, leaving the rest in the bag. "Are you writing a song about your husband?"

Emily nodded and all of a sudden felt guilty, like she was somehow betraying Rob by doing that. "It's the song I started in New York," she explained.

Rob sat down on the couch next to Emily, wiping his fingers on his shorts, and she handed him the guitar. "I write songs about you," he said, strumming a few chords, almost as if he didn't realize he was doing it, "and you write songs about him. Not about me."

She felt like she needed to apologize. "I might write a song about you one day," she said.

He looked at her, thoughtful, as if he were wondering if that statement was true or just something she said to placate him, and strummed again. The excitement of last night seemed to have bled out of both of them. "How are you feeling?" he asked.

"I'll be fine," she said. "Thank you for taking care of me last night. Are you feeling okay?"

"Not in the best shape of my career," he said. "I kept drinking after I put you to bed."

Emily stood. "Want some more coffee?" she asked.

He nodded and she walked over to fill two mugs with one of the one-cup machines.

As she was walking back to him, his phone rang. "It's my girls on FaceTime," he said. "Would you mind staying out of the frame?"

Emily put his mug on the end table next to the couch and walked, with her own mug, back to her room.

"Well hello there, lovely ladies!" she heard him say as she closed the door.

She missed Ezra. She missed Ari. Maybe she could jump on FaceTime with her sister. Coffee in hand, she walked over to her night table and found her phone there. Ezra had written back to her text: I read your journal. There aren't enough words.

Emily stared at what he'd written. What did he mean? Enough words for what? Enough words to speak to her again?

Her coffee churned in her stomach and she walked out onto the hotel's balcony to will the feeling away.

She dialed on her phone.

"Hello?"

"Priya?" Emily responded.

Priya's voice came through, warm and clear. "Hey there. How's your Mexican getaway? Are you and Ezra back on track?"

"Not really," Emily said. "It's . . . kind of a mess." The waves crashed in front of her, cresting and falling. "I'm here with Rob, actually. But not romantically. We're sleeping in different bed-rooms."

"Whoa," Priya said. "Well. I can do the thing where I pretend to be a normal person and support you even if you're doing some-thing problematic. Or we can really talk."

Emily laughed softly. "I think I might be beyond the normal-person response now. I feel like I keep making stupid decisions even though I know they're stupid. I convince myself they're right, that they're the thing I'm meant to do, but in my heart I know they're complicating everything even more."

"What do you mean?" Priya asked.

"I think . . ." Emily thought about it; she thought about her life as if it were someone else's. "I think Ezra disappointed me so deeply when he wasn't there after our miscarriage that I keep testing the boundaries of his love for me. Kind of like—will you still love me if I do this? Or that? If I fly to Mexico? If I become a musician? If I show you all of the really messed-up parts of my-self? I feel like I want him to prove to me that he loves me any-way, and he keeps showing me the opposite. So I push harder. I love him, but I think I'm afraid he doesn't love me—he loves a particular version of me, but when things get tough he runs. What if he doesn't come back?"

Priya cleared her throat on the other end of the line. "I could see how what you've been doing falls into that paradigm. And I think it's quite possible that you're doing some of this as a reac-tion to Ezra, but it seems to me that some of this is about your own happiness. For the last few months, you haven't seemed happy at work—I really realized it when you were talking about being a sin eater. I was going to talk to you, but then you had the miscarriage and it didn't seem the right time. Anyway, now you were given a chance to do something you used to love, so you went. You could've stayed, but you chose to leave, to go to Mexico and see if your dream was there. It's not all about Ezra."

Emily sat down in a little chair that had been placed on her balcony. "My mom always used to say that everything turns out the way it's supposed to, that the decisions you make are the ones you were supposed to make."

"Huh," Priya said. "So we think we have free will, but we don't?"

The sun shone down and Emily lifted up her face to feel the rays on her skin. "Yeah, that's what she thought. I've been using that as an excuse, though, I think. For years. I think I have to take responsibility for what I've done."

"Oh, Em." Priya's voice was full of sympathy. "I wish I were there to give you a hug right now."

"Me too," Emily said.

"Listen," Priya told her, "you've got a good head on your shoulders. Things are starting to come clear. I have faith in you. You'll figure it all out. You'll find a way to be happy."

"Thank you," Emily answered. "That means a lot. No matter what, I'll see you soon."

Emily sat in her room and worked on her song, pulling up a piano keyboard app on her phone to figure out the accompaniment until Rob knocked on her door.

"Hungry?" he asked. "It's way past lunchtime."

Emily nodded, and the two of them headed down to the beachside restaurant. They recaptured a bit of the fun they'd had the day before, laughing and smiling together, but it felt like an echo of yesterday.

"You still want to play tonight?" he asked as they were finishing up.

"If you'll still have me," she said.

He laughed. "Queenie," he said. "When will you realize that I'll always still have you?"

He stood up and reached out his hand for her. She took it and the two of them walked back to the villa to get ready for the show.

59

EMILY WATCHED AGAIN from the wings. Rob was still objectively fantastic, but there was something missing from this show, like he'd been slightly wrung out. If you didn't know him, you wouldn't expect anything else, but since she did, she could see it. Diana did, too.

"What happened?" she asked Emily. "Is he still pissed about what I said this morning?"

Emily pretended not to hear her. Rob hadn't shared his conversation with Diana, and she hadn't asked. She wondered if it had anything to do with her.

When it was time for the last song, Rob introduced her, this time calling her Emily Gold, saying she was a friend from a long time ago who inspired him, leaving out the line about her being the one that got away, playing that aspect of things way down. She walked on stage to a round of applause and waved, and then she heard someone shout, "Em!"

It was a voice she'd know anywhere. Ezra. He was here. She shaded her eyes and tried to look out into the audience, but she couldn't find him.

Before he could call out again, Rob was starting "Crystal Castle" and then Emily's fingers were on the keys and she was singing her part. She heard the crowd singing along with them, saw them with their arms around one another swaying. She felt the surge of the audience's love travel through her, grow within her.

Rob turned and winked, as if to say, *Even when we're off, we're on.*

She smiled and kept singing, kept playing. But thoughts of Ezra intruded. He was here. Somewhere out there. Did *There aren't enough words* mean that he was going to fly to Mexico? Was she supposed to have figured that out?

When the clapping started, Rob walked toward her on the stage, so their voices were drowned out by the audience. "Who called your name?" he whispered, even though she was pretty sure he already knew. "I saw your face. It's someone you know."

"It's Ezra," she whispered back.

She could see Rob thinking, and then he said softly, "Do you want to sing for him? Your song?"

"My song?" she echoed.

The applause died down. "Em!" She heard Ezra call again from somewhere down below. He wanted her to know he was there, that he'd come to talk to her. He didn't disappear this time, and he didn't let her disappear either. She wanted to send him a message, too.

She turned to Rob and nodded.

He turned to the audience. "We've got some'm real special for all y'all tonight. Our girl Emily here's been working on a brand-new song. And this is the first time anyone but me's ever gonna hear it."

The audience cheered. The stage went dark, except for a spot on Emily. She saw Rob sit down and sip a glass of water someone had stuck under a stool for him. Then she started to play.

When she got to the end, she had to push the song around the lump in her throat as she sang:

I hope you can see
That there's love there waiting
For you, from me

Just before the lights came up on the stage, she saw Rob wiping a tear off his cheek. Then the spot was back on him and he was saying, "I think we'll leave you there tonight. Thank you for being such a great audience."

The audience cheered and Emily and Rob headed into the wings to the mic guys. As they were getting unwired, Emily couldn't stop thinking about Ezra, about the fact that he was here, that he'd heard her song. She had no idea what he would think about it. Whether he would know it was about him, the same way she knew that Rob's "Crystal Castle" was about her.

The mic guys left, but Emily stood still.

"You're not happy together right now," Rob said, "but you still love him."

"I do," Emily said, looking into his green eyes. "And I'm not— we're not. But just because we're not happy right now . . . I'm not ready to give up. He and I need to talk. We've been through a lot and our marriage cracked. But I want to try to put our pieces back together. I owe him that. I owe myself that."

Rob leaned his guitar into its stand. "You know," he said, looking up at her, "sometimes the pieces don't fit back together."

"I know," Emily said, taking a deep breath, "but sometimes they do."

60

WHEN EMILY WALKED out the stage door exit, Ezra was waiting there for her.

"It was powerful," he said quietly.

"Hm?" Emily said, looking up at him.

"Listening to you play at the benefit last week. It's part of why I was so thrown. I could feel you in that song. I could feel the rawness of your emotions—your pain and your love and your passion and it . . . it was a part of you I didn't know, a vulnerability you never shared. It was that times a million tonight. When you sang . . . that was about me, right?"

Emily nodded. "It was. I'm sorry for . . . for screwing up, for making mistakes, for making them worse."

Ezra slid his arm around her back. "Can we find somewhere to talk? There's a lot I have to say. Too many words."

Emily led Ezra down to the beach. It reminded her of the night they got married, of the evening they got engaged, the waves lapping against the shore. The beach, she realized, was always their place. They took their shoes off and sat down on the sand.

"You gave me your journal," he said.

"I want you to know all of me," Emily said. "It felt like it was about time I did that. But I didn't know how you'd feel once you did."

"You wanted to be whole again," he said. "You wanted to feel loved."

The wind lifted her hair and briefly covered her face before it set her free again. "You read it all," she said.

EZRA BENT HIS knees up in front of him. "I did." He looked at her. "It was so hard for me to connect the story to you, but when I could, when I did . . . What . . . what you said about me . . . it seems like you were trying to tailor yourself to be someone who matched me, who did what I did and valued what I valued. But . . . I'd like to think I'd have loved all of you, Emily, if you'd given me the chance, if I hadn't been so shocked by what I learned."

"I—"

"Wait," Ezra said. "I came to say more than that, though. I came to tell you that I'm a hypocrite. That I expect things of you that I don't expect of myself. There are things I haven't told you, either, things I haven't shared. And that's not fair."

Emily tucked her bare legs underneath her. The sand was cool against her skin. "What didn't you tell me?" she asked, wondering what it could possibly be.

"When I was in medical school, I was almost engaged," he said.

"You were?" she asked, not because she didn't believe him, but because she didn't know what else to say. He'd kept the same kinds of secrets she had.

"I moved with her out to California for my residency. She

wanted to work in medical tech, figuring out how computers could make medicine better. Once we got out there, she changed her focus; she saw the money other people were making and wanted to go after it—success meant something different. It changed her. It changed us. It made me think that the kind of success I wanted wasn't something she'd be proud of anymore. I'd bought a ring but couldn't bring myself to give it to her. I finished my residency feeling totally at sea—the only thing that got me through it was my work. It's how I coped, it's how I cope, I guess, when things in my personal life are hard. But you're not me. And you're not Veronica, either. And I didn't take care of you the way I promised I always would."

Her name was Veronica. "No, I'm not her," Emily said. "But after hearing about that, it helps me understand why you reacted the way you did." She leaned her head against his shoulder. "I'm sorry. But I . . . I still do want to pursue music. And it might change me a little. It might change us. And I know you said it wasn't something Golds do, but . . . maybe we can expand the definition of your family. Of our family."

"I read *The Crack-Up*, the F. Scott Fitzgerald book, when I was in college. And there's this line where he says, 'In a real dark night of the soul it is always three o'clock in the morning.' When I read your journal and then found out you were in Mexico, when I realized you'd gone to perform with him, my soul felt like three o'clock in the morning. And I realized I wanted to fight for us. And I will. I'll do whatever it takes to fight for us."

"It felt like three o'clock in the morning for me, too," Emily said. She watched the moon play hide and seek behind a cloud. "When we lost our baby, when you weren't there with me. You heard my three o'clock in the morning when I played at the fund-raiser."

"I know," he said. "And I heard it again in your song for me tonight." He bent his head and kissed her. "Your soul is beautiful."

"It doesn't feel that way," she whispered. "It feels twisted and complicated and messy."

"There's beauty in that, too," Ezra replied. He kissed her again, then moved his mouth to her neck. "I want my life with you in it."

Emily lifted his chin up with her finger so the two of them were looking into each other's eyes. "I do, too. And I want to work hard to make that happen. But we need to fix things between us. Change them. We can't just go back to the way everything was before."

"I know," Ezra answered.

Ezra and Emily wrapped their arms around each other and stayed that way for a long while, breathing each other in, holding each other close. "Come on," he said, eventually. "Let's go home."

They got back to the hotel room he'd gotten for the night, nothing like Rob's villa but lovely just the same, with a small balcony overlooking the beach and a king-sized bed on plush carpet.

"I love you," he whispered, as they climbed into bed.

"I love you, too," she said.

He pressed his lips against her skin under the covers. It felt like he was kissing her body alive again. His touch, his love, his recommitment to their future altered how she looked at herself once more.

She kissed him all over, too, hoping her lips would awaken his body in the same way. That together, they could kiss away their pain and bring forth hope in its place, rising from the ashes of the past weeks.

For them, this was a new beginning. This was a new start.

61

ON THE PLANE ride home, Emily and Ezra negotiated a truce, a way to move forward.

"Will you stay at NYU for a while longer?" Ezra asked, holding her hand as they flew over Florida. "Until you find your footing in music?"

"Yes," Emily said. "I can do that." She already felt bad about leaving her patients; this would give her a little more time with them.

"Will you stop talking to Rob?"

Emily squeezed his hand. She thought of the confidence that Rob gave her, the unconditional support, the ability to see herself differently. She needed that. Now more than ever. And she'd promised him that they'd be friends. That she wouldn't disappear. "Please don't ask me to do that," she said. She looked into his eyes, willing him to see her, to see her sincerity. "You don't have to be jealous. He's just a good friend now."

That was what she and Rob had agreed when they said goodbye. That they would be friends, they'd talk, they'd exchange music, but that was where things would end.

Ezra looked out of the porthole window. "I guess I can live with that," he said.

———

WHEN THEY GOT home, they started therapy—together and on their own. They shared secrets, they told the truth, and they found news ways to compromise, a deeper understanding of what their relationship needed. All while Emily made music, wrote music, a whole album's worth that she sent to Rob. The ease with which the music and lyrics flowed was both a surprise and a salve. Some songs were about Ezra, some were about her mom, and some were about Rob. What she'd said in Mexico had been true.

EMILY AND EZRA didn't have sex for more than a month after the miscarriage; they just used their lips and tongues and fingers. And when they did make love again, they used protection. The idea of getting pregnant scared Emily, because it could be paired with another loss. And Ezra admitted how worried he was that he wouldn't be able to handle the heartbreak if something went wrong again, either. But two months in, something started changing for Ezra.

"I think we're strong enough," he said one night at dinner. "I think we should try again."

"I don't know," Emily answered. It wasn't only her fear of loss that was stopping her now. She had just rediscovered her passion, was changing her life, and she was worried about what a baby would mean.

Later that night, Emily played her new songs for Ezra for the first time.

"They're beautiful," Ezra told her. "Like you. Like our baby will be."

It was ironic, she thought, all that time that she was ready when Ezra wasn't, and now that he was ready, she needed more time.

A FEW DAYS later, just as she was putting on her jacket, heading out of the counseling center at the end of the day, Emily got a call from Rob.

"I have an idea," he said when she picked up. "Can you be ready to perform—a full set—in six weeks? I'll be doing a show in New York again, once we get this whole radius clause worked out, and this time I need an opening act."

"You mean it?" Emily asked, waving good-bye to Priya as she headed out the door. "You'd really want me to open your show?"

"Of course I mean it," Rob answered. "I sent your songs to my manager to convince him I wasn't crazy. And Diana put in a good word for you."

Emily walked down the steps of the building. "I don't even know what to say."

"Just say yes," Rob said.

If this had been two months ago, her saying yes would have meant the end of her marriage, she was pretty sure, but now, after all the talking they'd done, the secret-sharing, the work, she hoped Ezra would support her, even if it made him nervous. She hoped he would want her dream to come true.

————

THE NEXT DAY Emily officially went on leave at NYU. Ezra had said that even though he still didn't trust Rob, he didn't want to hold her back.

"You trust me, though," Emily said. "Right?"

"Right," Ezra said, a smile blooming on his face, as if he'd just then realized it. "I do trust you."

That night he took her out to dinner at the Clocktower, a restaurant they'd been saving for a special occasion. He ordered a bottle of champagne and toasted Emily. "To my wife," he said. After they sipped their champagne, he looked at her and said, "Em, I'm really proud of you."

It felt to Emily like the sweetest thing he'd ever told her.

62

"I BROUGHT YOU something," Priya told Emily a couple of weeks later, when she stopped by Emily's apartment to say hi. The show was a done deal now, and Emily spent most of her time rehearsing.

"Oh yeah?" Emily asked.

Priya produced a pair of green socks. "I know this may sound silly, but a friend of mine told me that green is the color of fertility, so when you wear green socks, it increases your chances of getting pregnant. And I wore green socks the day I got pregnant with Anika, so . . . maybe?"

Emily laughed and took the socks. "Thank you," she said. "I appreciate it." She put them down on the table in front of her, next to the two mugs and the teapot she'd set out there. "Though we still haven't been trying."

"No?" Priya said.

Emily shook her head. "I thought a baby was what I wanted more than anything, but now that I have a chance to perform again, I worry that . . . what if it derails everything before it's even begun?"

"It could," Priya said, slowly, "or it could jump-start your music in a different way. Inspire a hit song. Or your music career could take years to materialize. How long did it take Rob to write a hit?"

"More than a decade," Emily said, playing with the tag on the socks.

Priya shrugged. "Not that your life will follow the same path as his, but I'd hate for you to sacrifice one dream while you're trying to pursue another."

"I guess I should be grateful I have the ability to try for both." Emily sat down on the couch after filling her mug.

"You can be grateful, and it can still be hard," Priya said, filling her own. "But on a happier note, Neel and I have a babysitter booked for your show. He's flipping out that we got VIP passes."

Emily laughed, happy to focus on the show instead of on pregnancy. "Well, you're my Very Important People," she said.

Priya shook her head. "It really is incredible. Your life from a few months ago to now is a hundred percent different. How does Ezra feel, now that the show is getting closer?"

Emily thought about her answer. "He's happy for me. But I think he's worried, too, that all this work we've done won't last. Our relationship is so different than it was when we got married, but I think I like this version of us better. It's messier, but it feels stronger."

"And you and Rob?" Priya asked.

Emily leaned against the arm of the couch. "He's been a really good friend. And a huge champion. He made all of this possible. Ari thinks he has an ulterior motive, but I'd like to think that he doesn't. That he was being honest in Mexico when he agreed to be friends, nothing more."

Priya nodded as she added milk to her tea from the pitcher Emily had left on the coffee table. "I'd like to think that, too."

Both women were quiet for a moment.

Emily was so glad that she and Priya had crossed from work

friends to actual friends who would hang out together regardless of who worked where.

"How are my kids doing?" Emily asked. Priya had taken on a lot of Emily's patients when she left. She hadn't realized how hard it would be to leave them, and she still thought about them all the time.

"All trucking along," Priya said, taking a sip of tea. "Have you heard from Tessa?"

Now that Tessa wasn't her patient anymore, she sent Emily an email from time to time.

"Last I heard, doing well in Ohio. She and Zoe are living with her mom and she's taking classes at Cleveland State. Still working toward law school one day." Emily thought about Rob and his mom's saying, *Everything is always okay in the end, and if it's not okay, it just means it isn't the end.* She didn't believe it, not one hundred percent, but she understood what his mom meant by it. Things happen, and usually people can work through them; usually they can find a semblance of normal, a way to keep going, in spite of the pain. If they're lucky, they'll even find a way to thrive.

63

THE NEXT SUNDAY Emily and Ezra were walking through the city, bundled up against the December cold, when Ezra spotted a piano in the park.

"Is that one of the Sing for Hope pianos?" he asked. "I thought they were supposed to go to schools in September. What happened to this one?"

Emily walked over, too. The piano had been placed in a gazebo, safe from rain or snow. The change in temperature couldn't have been good for it. "Maybe they forgot this one," Emily said.

"More likely they left it here on purpose," Ezra answered, lifting up the cover on the keys to play a few notes.

Emily prepared herself to wince, but it wasn't as out of tune as she'd feared. She walked closer, running her fingers up the keys in a scale. "Not bad," she said.

"Any requests?" she asked him, sitting down on the bench, taking off her gloves.

Ezra leaned against the piano and looked at her. "How about one of your songs?"

Emily had been working on something new. Something about her and Ezra that she was calling "Dark Night of My Soul." She started to play and sing softly to her husband.

Lost in the blackness
When my soul felt bleak
When my heart felt broken
My body weak
My love for you
Reached its peak
It was the dark night of my soul

Ezra sat down next to her on the bench. "I think that one's a duet," he said.

She looked at him, her eyebrows raised in question.

"Will you teach it to me?" he asked. The vulnerability in his eyes touched her. Over the last couple of months their hearts had been slowly opening to each other again, and she saw his now, wide open, every door unlocked.

So she taught her husband the melody. And once he was able to sing it, she harmonized behind him. And then changed the words at the end of the chorus: *It was the dark night of our souls.*

He was right. The song worked fine as a solo, but it had an even deeper meaning as a duet. With the bare trees around them, sheltering them from the wind, it felt like they were in a bubble of their own in the middle of Central Park, the two of them, singing to each other, a healing of wounds they'd both inflicted. She felt her voice melding with his, her heart melding with his—it was a specific closeness that she'd only ever felt before with Rob. Emily's and Ezra's voices meshed perfectly together, and she poured her love for him, for the baby they had lost, and her hopes for a future together, into the music. Emily was grateful for the choices she had made, for her decision to be with Ezra. And for his decision to be with her, to stay. For the work they had done to come back from the dark night of their souls. They had been tested and they had survived.

64

WHEN THEY GOT home, before they even stripped off their hats and gloves and scarves, Ezra caught Emily by the arm and kissed her. His lips felt cold against hers, and she knew that hers probably felt cold against his, too.

"Making music with you is very, very sexy," he told her.

She smiled. "I hadn't quite expected that reaction," she said. "But I loved making music with you, too."

He smiled. "How about this reaction?" he asked, lifting her up so she was cradled in his arms, and walking with her, scarf and hat and gloves still on, into the bedroom. As Ezra carefully took off her gloves and unzipped her boots, all she could think about was how badly she wanted him.

She reached out and pulled the zipper down on his coat. He shrugged out of it and she grabbed for the waistband of his jeans. Once they'd undressed each other, once he'd had his head in her lap and she'd had her head in his, he reached for a condom, but she stopped him. "I don't think we need that." She'd spoken without conscious thought. It was an instinctual choice. An impulse that felt right.

He looked her in the eye, questioning, even as he smiled. "Are you sure?"

She nodded.

He kissed her hard, laid her down, and slid inside her.

"Yes," she said. "Yes."

65

A FEW DAYS later, after Emily spent the afternoon practicing her set in a rented studio space, she came home to find Ezra directing a man with a piano on a dolly about where to put it in their apartment.

"What's going on in here?" she asked, fighting the urge to throw her arms around him, because it was pretty obvious that he had just bought her a piano.

"It's your Hanukkah present," he told her, beaming. It was a white upright that fit perfectly against the wall next to the couch.

And then Emily did throw her arms around him. "Thank you," she said. "You have no idea how much this means to me."

He hugged her back. "I actually think I do," he said.

66

A COUPLE OF weeks later, Ari came to Manhattan and met Emily in SoHo to go clothes shopping.

"So what are we looking for?" she asked.

"Something simple, but cool, and not trying too hard," Emily said. "For the show, I want to look like a fancier version of me."

The sisters were carrying hot chocolates in their gloved hands, window-shopping on Houston Street.

"Do you have a store in mind?" Ari asked.

Emily shook her head. "I'll know it when I see it," she said. "How are things going on your end? How was your ski weekend?" Ari and Jack had just taken the boys up to Vermont.

"It was fun," Ari said. "The boys are turning into such real people now. We let them ski together without us for an afternoon, and Jack and I got some time alone. I told him I was thinking about going back to work. And wanted to plan a trip to Egypt. He said we should go for our anniversary and leave the boys with his mom. I think we're going to do it."

"That's so awesome," Emily said, smiling at her sister. "What about work?"

Ari bit her lip. "I applied for a leave replacement this morning. One of the math teachers at the public high school near us is going on maternity leave next month. The job would go through the rest of the year. I don't know if I'll get it, but I'm excited."

Emily threw her arms around Ari. "I'm so excited for you!" she said. "Even if you don't get it, I'm so excited you tried."

Ari hugged her sister back. "Me too," she said. "What about you? How are things with you and Ezra?"

Emily took a sip of her hot chocolate. "We're trying again." She almost hated saying it, as if the words would somehow tempt bad luck.

"Oh, Em. I'm happy for you. For both of you. So the plan would be to have a baby before booking a tour?" Ari said. "And then bring a nanny on the road? Ezra's okay with that?"

Emily thought about the logistics and closed her eyes for a brief moment. She didn't have a plan, just two dreams she was trying to meld into one. There was no guarantee she would get pregnant right now. And there was no guarantee she could book venues, either. That she'd even be able to tour. "I think we're just going to take it all day by day," Emily said. "And if I'm lucky enough to have a baby and a tour, well, we'll figure it out then."

Ari nodded. "I'm planning too far ahead," she acknowledged.

"Maybe a little," Emily said, trying to let go of the anxiety her sister's questions raised.

Ari stopped walking and looked into a store window at a green sleeveless top. It was a cowl neck and seemed like it was made of silk. "How about that shirt?" she asked, pointing.

Emily turned around. "It's my color!" she said. "Nice find. Let's go check it out."

A little while later, Emily was alone in a dressing room, putting on a pair of tight leather pants and the hunter green cowl neck. There was no way to know if she was pregnant yet; still, she was glad the leather pants had a little stretch to the waistband. Just in case. She slipped on a pair of black heels that were in the dressing room, but they didn't look right. She'd figure out shoes later.

"What do you think?" she asked Ari when she stepped out of the dressing room.

"Simple, cool, not trying too hard—and stunning," her sister said. "You look like you're ready to bring down the house."

"I am," Emily said with a smile. "I am."

EMILY WAS SUPPOSED to get her period two days later. But she didn't. She told Ezra, but she refused to talk any more about it. She was too afraid of what might come next.

67

A COUPLE OF weeks after her date in SoHo with Ari, Emily was going over her schedule from Diana. It was D-Day. Or maybe C-Day. The feeling of anticipation had been coursing through her veins since she woke up that morning.

"What should I wear?" Ezra asked, looking at Emily in a pair of boxer briefs and nothing else. He'd told her the night before that he was worried about looking the part, about being cool enough to be a musician's husband. She'd reassured him with a kiss and told him that she'd help him pick his outfit.

She walked over and kissed him again, the scent of his aftershave assaulting her as she did it.

He ran his hands down her body. All she had on was a pair of underwear and a bra. Her period still hadn't come, her breasts felt swollen, but she told him she wasn't going to take a pregnancy test. Not yet. She didn't want to know, to get attached, until she was sure the baby was there—and would stay. Schrödinger's baby, they called it.

"Do we have time?" he said, running his fingers around her nipples, making them stiffen.

A thrill shivered through her body. Emily glanced at the clock on her bedside table. She knew she was supposed to be at the venue in an hour. "If we're fast," she answered.

Emily had barely finished the sentence when Ezra scooped

her up and brought her to their bed. He ran his fingers over the crotch of her underwear, and Emily could feel the silk sticking to her, making her want him even more than she already did.

"Please," she breathed, and he knew what she meant.

He stripped off his underwear as she stripped off hers, and when he slid inside her, she felt the familiar sensation of completion. Her body felt made for this, for him, and he slid even deeper, pressing against whatever it was inside her that changed the pitch of her breathing, made her buck against him. "It's your Skene's gland," Ezra had once told her, but Emily didn't care what it was called or why it felt so good. She just wrapped her legs around him and pulled him in tighter.

The two of them rocked together until Emily felt her back arching and an orgasm rippling through her body. Then Ezra braced his knees on either side of her and brought himself to a climax, too.

He rolled off her, both of them breathing hard.

Emily reached out and grabbed his hand in bed. "Man do I love you, Dr. Gold," she said.

"I love you, too, Dr. Gold," he replied, smiling at her. Then his eyes widened as he saw the clock behind her head. "We've got to get dressed!"

She sat up. "Your dark-wash jeans," she said, answering the question he'd asked ages ago, "and your cranberry sweater. And those suede chukka boots Ari and Jack got you for Hanukkah."

She put on her hunter green cowl neck—Priya had told her it made her hair look fiery—the leather pants, and the shoes she'd finally settled on: the cowboy boots she'd worn to perform in Mexico. She was Rob's inspiration, but in a way, he had been hers, and she wanted to pay homage to that. She did her stage makeup quickly and left her hair loose, in its natural waves.

"Ready?" she said, as she tamed a few flyaways with hair spray and flipped her head over to spray it upside down for extra volume.

"Ready," he said, appearing behind her in the bathroom. "I'm so, so proud of you. Have I mentioned that?"

"Maybe once or twice," Emily said to him smiling, "but I never get tired of hearing it."

68

WHEN EMILY GOT to the green room, Ari and Jack were there, sitting with Priya and Neel, their VIP passes letting them in early. Ezra's parents were on their way.

"I'm so happy for you, Em!" Ari said, when Emily sat down next to her. "I spoke to Dad before. He said to tell you to break a leg. I promised I'd send him a video."

Emily felt her eyes moisten with tears. "Thanks for doing that," she said. She hoped maybe next time she played, he'd come. Maybe before that she'd go out to see him and they could talk, the way she had with Ezra. Maybe their relationship could be repaired, changed, strengthened. In the meantime she had her sister, she had her husband, she had her friends, who loved her. That was more than enough.

Emily took a breath and tried to focus on the moment, to get herself in the right headspace to go on stage. This was it. She was reclaiming herself, taking back a part of her that she'd given up, hopefully starting a brand-new career—one she knew she was meant to pursue. She'd treated music like an addiction, avoided places that would trigger her desire to play, to be on stage. But now she realized that what she'd thought was bad for her was actually something that nourished her soul. Like being addicted to water or air.

Tony walked into the green room—he had a VIP pass from

Rob but had told Emily he'd visit her, too. "No crown?" he asked Emily, touching his own bald scalp.

She shook her head, feeling her waves brush her shoulders. "I grew up," she said. "Thought it was time for my hair to acknowledge that."

Tony laughed. "I guess we all did, huh?" he asked.

"Places in five," a man with a headset said, opening the door.

"Thank you, five," Emily responded.

Ezra's parents slipped in the door, and they, along with Ari, Priya, and Ezra, all gave Emily a hug.

"Go knock 'em dead," Ari whispered. Jack flipped on the big-screen TV in the green room so they could all watch her from there.

Emily smiled, took a deep breath, and walked out on stage, Ezra following her and then waiting in the wings so he could see her perform in person—and so she could see him, too. The audience was dark, but she could feel all thousand of them—quiet, tense, electric. The stage was dark, too, except for a spot focused on a grand piano, set up just for her. Emily felt the adrenaline race through her as she took her first steps out into the darkness. She was where she was meant to be.

She sat down on the piano bench and adjusted the mic. And she began to play. She shared her story through words, through music. And she felt transformed. She felt filled with light and energy and love. She'd written these songs to make sense of her life, to make sense of her feelings. And now she was sharing them with the world. Her heart was open, like Rob's. Like Ezra's.

When she finished her second to last song, the one she'd written for Ezra in Mexico, there was a rush of applause. Emily felt it wash over her, wash through her.

"Thank you for being such a great audience," she said into the mic. "I know you're all excited to see Austin Roberts tonight, but I've got one more song before you do. It's called 'Dark Night of the Soul,' and it's a song that I wrote about something my love and I went through together." The song was powerful as a duet, but here, now, it had to be a solo.

Emily started playing, imagining that the music in this song wasn't for the crowd but for the cells that might be dividing inside her. For Ezra, who was singing along in the wings.

As Emily played, as she sang, as the audience focused their attention on the stage, she remembered how it felt when Ezra's voice had twined with hers. She remembered how they'd forgiven each other's mistakes and let their love grow stronger.

When she got to the final line of the song, she sang the lyrics they used together when the song was a duet—she sang "our" instead of "mine." And when she looked into the wings, Ezra touched his hand to his heart. He'd noticed. After the song ended, Emily echoed the last line of the melody on the piano and then held the damper pedal so that the notes resonated for a moment after she stopped playing.

The audience burst into applause, but instead of looking at them, she looked back at Ezra. A piece of his hair had flopped in front of his glasses, and he was grinning more than she'd seen him in a long time.

Then Rob was standing in the wings, too, his guitar at his side, giving her a V for victory. And she felt it—that victory, the audience's applause and cheers filling her. She'd opened her heart to them, and they'd reflected that love right back at her.

She stood up, thanked the crowd and, smiling and waving,

walked off stage. In the wings, she squeezed Rob's hand before landing in her husband's arms.

"You are incredible," Ezra whispered to her, under the sound of the applause.

And they kissed until the applause faded into nothing.

69

THEY STAYED TO watch Rob perform, and then they all cele-
brated together with pizza and mixed drinks. Emily had been
worried about what would happen between Ezra and Rob when
the two of them actually met, but after they shook each other's
hands, they mostly talked to other people. Though she could see
both of their eyes darting around the room every few minutes to
look for her, to make sure she was okay.

Rob's manager had flown in for the show—Ira, a tall guy with
a shaved head, dressed in black jeans and a button-down. While
everyone else was getting food, Rob and Ira chatted in a corner of
the room. Emily looked over, wondering what it was that they
were talking so intensely about. Then Rob caught her eye and
waved her over.

"I was really impressed tonight," Ira told her.

"Thank you." Emily wiped her mouth to make sure she didn't
have any tomato sauce on her lips. "It was nice of you to come see
Rob's show. I know managers don't do that so often."

"Well," Ira said, "when my hot new artist tells me he's found
another hot new artist, and his tour manager agrees, that's something I've got to check out for myself."

Emily was speechless for a moment. "You came for me?"
she said.

Ira handed her his card. "Let's talk tomorrow," he said. "Rob just assured me it'd be cool if I worked with both of you."

Then he walked away to refill his drink.

"Sonny and Cher," Rob said to her. "Johnny and June Carter Cash." He clinked his empty glass with her club soda, then followed Ira to the makeshift bar.

Emily was stunned.

"What was that about?" Ezra asked as he came up next to her, sliding his hand around her waist.

"Something we need to talk about later," she said as she gave him a kiss on the cheek.

A manager was interested in her!

Emily looked down. What if she was pregnant? She took a deep breath.

She'd figured out so much in the last few months. She knew, with every inch of her soul, that she would figure this out, too. *They* would figure this out—she and Ezra. Because every decision she made wasn't just about her now. It wasn't even just about them. It was about their future, their family. She would remember that. They would choose well. Together.

xxxiii

YOU'RE GOING TO *have a little sister. She's already a trouble-maker, poking her feet into my spine, pushing down against my blad-der. But I try not to complain, because she's here. She's growing. She's big enough that if she was born tomorrow, she'd be okay. I can't tell you how relieved I felt when we hit that milestone. She can survive outside my body in a way that you never could, that the baby after you never could.*

We're not sure what to name her. I never named you, and I'm sorry for it. I'm sorry that whenever I think about what you would be like, I don't have a name to attach to the image. You would be nearly thirteen. Almost in high school. Probably taller than me, or just about. With friends and ideas and passions of your own. Maybe you'd play piano, or guitar, or drums. Or maybe you'd love math like your aunt Ari. Or maybe you wouldn't have made it this far, like Malcolm. I try to keep all the what ifs in play, not just the good ones.

Your father and I have been in touch, between our shows. We've talked a lot about you, about what would've happened if you'd been born, and we both agreed it would've been hard. That neither one of us might have made it to the place we're at now, that we might have given you to a family who would have been able to take better care of you than we could. It's hard to live in the land of what if. And the longer you live, the more what ifs you collect.

I won't lie—touring while pregnant has been rough, but I didn't

318

want to sacrifice one dream for another, so I did it. And sharing my music, feeling that connection with the audience, made every difficulty worth it. I played my last show in Philly yesterday. And now I'm home for a while, at least until your sister is born. And who knows how long after that. Your aunt Ari wants to know the plan, but right now there isn't one. Right now the plan is to wait and see.

DO SOULS GROW *older when they're not on this plane? Do souls even have an age? I imagine my mother always at the age she was when she died, but I always imagine you getting older. Perhaps it's neither one of those things. Perhaps a soul is a soul. Perhaps it exists in the body in a fully formed state, relearning the world around it until it's once again set free. If that's true, I hope you've met your grandmother. I hope you've met your little brother or sister, the one I lost last year. Eden. Or Edward.*

If you were here, with us, on Earth, I'd ask your opinion on what to name your new sister.

YOUR FATHER WROTE *another hit single. It's about you, actually. He sent me the song after he recorded it. It's called "Lost Angel," and from the lyrics it's hard to know exactly what he was writing about. But once he told me, it was easy to see.*

I'm still the theme of his life, he said.

He's still not the theme of mine.

But I'm hoping that my theme is changing. That instead of looking back and seeing only loss, what I'll see instead is love.

I loved him, I love the baby I'm carrying and the ones I lost. I love Ezra. I love my parents, my friends, my sister, music.

My life has always been filled with love. I just didn't know where to look for it.

It's taken me thirty-four years to figure it out.

I'm glad I did.

In your father's song for you, he sings about a lost angel watching over those he loves. If he's right, if that's true, please watch over your sister. Please keep her safe.

I'm sorry I wasn't able to do that for you.

But I'll remember you forever.

I'll keep your memory safe.

In my heart, you'll never be lost.

acknowledgments

I STARTED WRITING this book a few months before my husband, Andrew, and I got engaged, and continued working on it through most of our first year of marriage. Loving him and being with him made me think so much about the transformation that happens when two people decide to unite their lives. I feel so lucky to have found Andrew and to have grown with him over the last years, creating a life in which two became one but also remain two. I'm so grateful for his support, his excitement about my books, and—most of all—his love.

During the time I wrote this, I had so many readers who graciously and generously offered their thoughts and feedback and made this book so much better than it was originally. My deepest gratitude goes to my writing group—Marianna Baer, Anna Godbersen, Anne Heltzel, Marie Rutkoski, and Eliot Schrefer—and to Talia Benamy, Jessica Carp, Gillian Engberg, Sarah Fogelman, Suzanne Foger, Kim Grant, and Cheryl Klein, all dear friends (one's also a dear sister) who shared their ideas and experiences and asked astute questions that made me think more deeply about my characters. Thank you, too, to the various experts who offered their thoughts and answered my hours of questions about therapy, music, and medicine: Carrie Bashoff, Greta Hanson, Lock McKelvey, Elizabeth Salick, and Ira Sweetwine. I so appreciate the help—and loved learning more about all of these fields.

This book never would have happened without my dream agent/editor duo. Thank you to Miriam Altshuler, whose excitement for these initial pages gave me the confidence I needed to continue, and who is not just an agent but a partner, a champion, and a friend. And to Tara Singh Carlson, whose intelligence, thoughtfulness, and thoroughness are awe-inspiring, and who I am so grateful I get to work with. I can't imagine creating books without both of you incredible women. Thank you, too, to Reiko Davis at DeFiore and Company, and to the phenomenal folks at Putnam and Penguin Random House who design, copyedit, market, publicize, license, and publish all my books so beautifully: Ivan Held, Christine Ball, Sally Kim, Helen Richard, Ashley Di Dio, Leigh Butler, Tom Dussel, Kate Boggs, Alexis Welby, Ashley Hewlett, Katie McKee, Ashley Clay, Brennin Cummings, Nishtha Patel, Kelly Gildea, Katie Punia, Vi-An Nguyen, Sanny Chiu, Anthony Ramondo, Monica Cordova, Ben Lee, Claire Sullivan, Andrea St. Aubin, and Maija Baldauf. And thank you to the folks at Penguin Young Readers—especially the team at Philomel Books—for being such an understanding and supportive cheering squad while I juggled everything.

I also want to thank my ever-growing family whose love and support buoy me: My mom, Beth Santopolo; my nearly-stepdad, David Turret; my sisters, Alison May and Suzanne Foger; my grandparents Beverly Franklin and Larry Franklin; my nearly-stepbrothers and their families; my in-laws Dan, Flavia, and Becky Claster; and all of my nieces, nephews, brothers-in-law, aunts, uncles, and cousins. And, of course, my dad, who has been gone for five years but will always be in my heart and my mind.

acknowledgments

I would be remiss if I didn't thank all the music teachers in my life, particularly Robyn Chase, Nick Lieto, Jim Dragovich, and Eric Williams, who made me fall in love with making music. I'm not even close to as talented as Emily, but I treasure all my time singing in the show choir and concert chorale, playing flute and piccolo in the band, and learning my favorite songs on the piano. You all gave me a remarkable gift.

Finally, thank you to the baby who was the size of a poppy seed the week I finished writing this book, and who continues to grow as this book goes through production. You've already changed the way I think, the way I act, and the way I feel about everything. I hope your dad and I make the right choices for all three of us as we travel on our journey together.